2002

WI

D0114289

That's True of
EVERYBODY

Other Books by Mark Winegardner

FICTION
Crooked River Burning
The Veracruz Blues

NONFICTION
Prophet of the Sandlots
Elvis Presley Boulevard

AS EDITOR
We Are What We Ate
The 26th Man

That's True of
EVERYBODY

Stories

Mark Winegardner

HARCOURT, INC.
New York   San Diego   London

Requests for permission to make copies of any part of the work should
be mailed to the following address: Permissions Department,
Harcourt, Inc., 6277 Sea Harbor Drive, Orlando, Florida 32887-6777.

www.HarcourtBooks.com

Library of Congress Cataloging-in-Publication Data
Winegardner, Mark, 1961–
That's true of everybody: stories/Mark Winegardner.—1st ed.
p. cm.
ISBN 0-15-100864-7
1. Middle West—Social life and customs—Fiction. I. Title.
PS3573.I528 T48 2002
813'.54—dc21   2001006199

Text set in New Baskerville
Designed by Cathy Riggs

Printed in the United States of America

First edition
A C E G I K J H F D B

Contents

These stories have been published, sometimes in somewhat different versions, in the following magazines: *American Short Fiction, The Barcelona Review, DoubleTake, The Greensboro Review, North Coast, Northeast Corridor, The Oxford American, Passages North, Playboy, Ploughshares, Story Quarterly, TriQuarterly,* and *Witness.*

That's True of
EVERYBODY

Thirty-Year-Old Women
Do Not Always Come Home

Bowling wasn't what it used to be and neither was Harry Kreevich. Once, the pro bowling tour got good ratings, tape-delayed, Saturdays on network television; back then, Harry's place, Cuyahoga Lanes, hosted important events. The great Nelson Burton Jr. once bowled a 300 game there. Harry considered him a personal friend. But Burton retired. So did the great Earl Anthony. There were no more giants in the sport. Tour events moved to newer facilities. As bowling's TV ratings dwindled, so did Harry. His wife Anna, whom Harry had loved until the end but who had been, in Harry's opinion, frigid, bought a book about masturbation called *Women: Selfloving,* and left him. His older daughter Debra, the painter, moved to New York and married a creep. His younger daughter Jane spent ten years in college and finished with an unfinished Ph.D. in English and no discernible skills, so Harry invited her home and groomed her to take over the alley. To his surprise, Jane turned out to be a frugal, careful manager. Theft went down. Profits rose. Harry began to date. No one special, but it was a start. Things started looking up. Then the new lane girl disappeared.

She had reminded Harry of Debra, though not in the looks or personality departments. The lane girl was a big midwesterner with a husky voice and white, American teeth, plus long thick legs and a stunning amount of blond hair, styled in a way that screamed *Parmatown Mall!* Debra, like her mother, was dark, thin, smart, and pretty, with a lone shock of white hair that arrived, overnight, in her late twenties. But both Debra and the lane girl had the pout. When Harry told the lane girl she was hired but, sorry, he had a policy against pay advances, *boom!* Debra's pout. Lower lip barely stuck out, eyes blinking only twice. Harry gave her the money (she said she needed it for the deposit on an apartment) on the condition that she please not mention it to Jane. For two weeks, Harry had the lane girl of his dreams: smiling, quick, graceful with the drunks. Anything went wrong with an order, she flashed the customers the pout, and *boom!* all was well. She hit it off with Ray, the bartender, who was black and seemed honest but was hard to get to know. (Ray had been there a year; about all Harry knew was that he was pursuing a teaching degree at a pricey Catholic school on the east side.) The new lane girl made enough tips on just two league nights to pay Harry back. But on the day of her first payday, she didn't show up.

At first, Harry just thought she was late. Who misses work on payday? An hour passed. A senior citizens group from Rocky River began to arrive. "We're about to be buttslammed, Dad," said Jane. She'd pressed herself into service at the main counter. "Where's the new girl, what's-her-face?"

"Karen," said Ray, overhearing. "She has a name. Karen." He sat in front of the bar. He was reading a library book by someone with an Asian name. The dining lounge was empty.

"Can someone call Karen?" she said. "Dad?"

Harry went to his office. The number on the lane girl's employment application was in Cleveland Heights. The phone had been disconnected. No further information, a voice said, about this number. "Any minute, probably," Harry told Jane, "she will be here."

Cuyahoga Lanes was filling up with old people, tottering in, lugging their own shoes and balls. Last of an era. The average American home, Harry had read in a trade magazine, no longer contained a bowling ball.

Harry decided to wait the tables himself. The seniors didn't order much. When they did, he was often forced to say sorry, no no-salt, no-fat chips, but he'll look into it. No veggie burgers. No soy milk. Sorry.

The seniors went home sharply at nine. For the next two hours, the alley was dead except in lane eight, where three young men in goatees and polo shirts were getting noisily drunk. Ray asked Jane if she'd talked to Karen. "Yesterday at work," she said. "But we didn't really *talk* talk."

"Does anyone know where she lives?" Harry asked.

"God knows," said Ray. "But I don't." He sang: "'That's the difference between God and me.'"

Jane found this very funny. Harry didn't know the song.

"What do we know about her?" Harry asked. "Boyfriends and whatnot. What," he said, looking at Jane, "do the women know?"

"Oh, Daddy," Jane said. "You're so cute."

Mrs. Urancek, the ancient Slovenian cook, couldn't even remember Karen's name. Harry called his other lane girl, a married young redhead named Maureen. A baby wailed in the background. "Sorry, Mr. K," Maureen said. "She and I never said more'n hi and bye."

Jane and Ray told screw-in-a-lightbulb jokes for a half hour. Then she said he could go home.

At eleven, Harry ushered out the college boys, making sure they returned their shoes. The janitors arrived, a fiftyish Mexican couple. The only conversation Jacinto and Luisa remembered having with Karen concerned Elvis. She felt many of Elvis's movies were underrated. Luisa agreed; Jacinto disagreed. "All crap," he said. "Every one." Luisa elbowed him, and he chuckled. "Our first date," Jacinto said, "it was *Girl Happy*."

Jane closed out the register, and Jacinto let Harry and Jane out the locked side door. As they crossed the parking lot, Jane waved the canvas bank-deposit bag in the summer moonlight. "Maybe you're right, Dad," Jane said. "Maybe something's wrong."

"Probably it's nothing," said Harry. "Don't worry."

TWO DAYS LATER, Harry flew to New York to see Debra. She had an opening in what she called a small, influential gallery, in a warehouse in TriBeCa. "Brace yourself, Dad," Debra had said on the phone. "My new work is a real leap from my old work."

"What am I, a philistine?" he said. "Artists are supposed to make leaps."

"Mom was shocked."

"Your mother isn't me." He was hurt Anna had seen the paintings first. Harry was a Sunday painter. He painted scenes on old saws, scenes of old farm women, wagons, scythes, frolicsome boys and girls in fields of grain: images of his childhood in Croatia. His family had emigrated in 1947, when Harry was eight. Things had been bad in Croatia then, but now! He could only imagine. He wouldn't have the heart to go back. He painted the pictures in his mind. He knew it wasn't really art, like what Debra did. Debra had training, the best schools. She'd been written up in *New Art Examiner*. She'd won a grant from the United States government. Still, Harry was proud that, each June, when he set up a tent at a craft fair, his saws sold briskly.

The gallery was in the basement of the warehouse, and

the opening did not begin until 11 P.M. Beforehand, he, Debra, and her husband-the-creep had dinner upstairs, in a restaurant owned by three famous actors Harry had never heard of. Today there were so many new stars. Too many.

"When was your mother here?" Harry asked. The pointlessly huge tables forced diners almost to shout.

"Last month," said the creep. He did that, answered for her.

"She and Jack were en route to Paris," Debra said. Jack was the new husband. "A layover."

"Paris," Harry said. "Huh."

The creep, Eric, a record executive, told a tiresome story about Parisian rock music. He was tall, with a high voice, and had never, in Harry's opinion, taken Debra seriously as a painter. In their apartment, Eric had a home office and a fitness room. Debra was forced to share studio space in a part of Brooklyn where she'd been mugged twice.

Dinner was served before Harry had an opening. "So," he said, "what's shocking about your work?"

"You'll see," said Eric. "Man, will you see."

"Maybe my daughter would like to answer."

"I'm right here, Daddy," she said. "No need to call me 'my daughter' with me right here."

Harry nodded, in concession.

"A year ago," Debra said, "when I got the NEA, I made a list of the things I liked about my work and all the things I didn't."

"Good idea," said Harry. Harry was a list-maker.

"What I liked was the light and the space," she said. "I didn't like how austere my work was. How serious."

"Not too serious, I never thought." She had been doing odd still lifes—bowls of fruit and cheap toys, with dozens of TV sets in the background. Harry loved them. "But to grow is important."

"Well, I'm doing nudes now."

"So?" said Harry. His stomach lurched. "There is a long tradition, nudes."

"Mom was shocked."

"Enough already with your mother."

The check came while Debra was in the bathroom. The waiter left it near Eric, who looked away, as if forgiving a rudeness. The table was so large, Harry could not reach for it. "Here," Harry said, pointing. "Let me."

Eric frowned. "This?" He picked it up and looked at the total. "I got it," he said. "When we're in Cleveland, you can get it."

Harry gamely protested. Eric—though he was in the music business, and Cleveland now had the Rock and Roll Hall of Fame (of which Harry was proud, and kept meaning to visit)—was the sort of man who bragged about never having set foot in Cleveland.

Debra took them downstairs for an early preview. Two young women were setting out wines and adjusting the lighting.

The nudes were penises.

Close-up, painted in shades of gray. Erect and limp, all races, circumcised and not, dangling from squatting positions, fat men and thin. One penis was so alarmingly small, Harry wondered if it was a freak. The paint was thick, purposefully cracked.

"People you know?" Harry said, trying to sound cosmopolitan.

"Models," Debra said. "Plus a few friends. The friends said it helped their self-esteem."

Harry did not want to know how.

"There hasn't been as much done with the penis," she said, "especially by women." She laughed. "Women *painters*."

The laugh put Harry at ease. "Right," he said. To his surprise, he found himself able to study the paintings, with appreciation. It was not what he'd hang at the alley (which featured four of Harry's saws, two of Debra's still lifes, six posters of Cleveland sports figures, and an aerial photo of the city he'd bought at the Cleveland bicentennial celebration). Still, though he didn't have the training to explain what impressed him, his instincts were that this would help Debra make a name for herself. *The penis,* Harry thought, *truly is a sad, slouchy little guy.* "This work is amazing, sweetheart."

"That one's mine," said Eric the creep, pointing.

"Ah," said Harry. The creep pointed to a series of small paintings in which a penis was half inserted into different sorts of fruit, citrus and otherwise. Harry felt sick and must have looked it; when he made eye contact with Debra, there it was: the pout. "A strange thing happened at the alley," Harry blurted. "A lane girl disappeared."

"Disappeared?" said Debra.

"A 'lane girl'?" said Eric, amused.

"She didn't come in to pick up her paycheck. She'd only been there two weeks."

"People disappear all the time," Eric said. "Who knows what kind of bug-out she's having. Believe me, she'll turn up."

"How do you know?" asked Harry. "Did you ever know anyone who disappeared?"

"As a matter of fact," Eric said, "yes. I used to volunteer as a counselor at Jewish Social Services. You'd be surprised how many Jews disappear. How long has she been gone, a day?"

"Three."

"Is she Jewish?" Eric said.

"Why?"

"Curious." Eric shrugged.

"It's illegal to ask that," Harry said.

"She'll come back," Eric said. "It's about love, drugs, or alcohol. Unless it's a psychotic episode."

"A psychotic episode," said Harry. "How comforting."

"I've always loved his accent," Eric said to Debra. "Almost Jewish, but not. Isn't it great?"

"I am right here." Harry did not think he had an accent. "No need to talk like I'm not."

Eric looked at him, blankly. "Well," he said. "Okay."

At eleven, the place was still empty. Five or six people. "New Yorkers," Eric said. "We're always late."

It pained Harry to hope Eric was right about something. On a tilt-top table near the refreshments was a sheet listing the titles and prices. Harry was afraid no one would pay so much for work like this, no matter how accomplished.

Across the gallery were two men (one taking notes), both dressed in loose-fitting suits that Harry supposed cost as much as a nice used Plymouth. They had Debra cornered and were effusively interpreting her own paintings for her. Debra nodded at everything they said. She made eye contact with Harry. Her forced smile widened and turned genuine. Harry felt blessed.

By midnight, Harry was exhausted and ready to go back to his hotel. Suddenly, as if there had arrived out front a bus full of affected undertakers (so much black!), the crowd arrived. The young women who'd set out the wine began to affix red dots to the laminated title cards beside some of the paintings. Did this mean a sale? Harry never saw money change hands.

"The red dot means a sale," Eric stage-whispered to Harry.

"Ah," Harry said. "Thank you."

More dots went up. Harry felt guilty. The artist's father should buy something. He made a lap of the gallery and chose a piece that focused on the model's thigh. Harry thought it might only be on second glance that you'd notice the painting had a penis in it. He slipped a check to the woman pouring wine. She pointed to another woman. "For *Study Number Thirty-seven*," Harry said to that woman. "Ship to the address on the check, please. Mark down the sale as 'Anonymous.'"

Harry sought Debra out. "I'm beat," he said. "I know you have to stay until the bitter end. I'll take a cab and see you in the morning, for breakfast."

Again, the quick pout. Again, he thought of the lane girl.

"Okay, Daddy," she whispered. "It meant so much to have your friendly face here. This is so weird. All these strangers. It's about me, but I feel apart from it, too. Like being a bride."

"You are a beautiful bride," Harry said. "You have made good work. Be proud."

"I am," she said, "now. Coming from you, it means something."

HARRY ARRIVED AT Hopkins Airport late the next night. Jane wasn't there. He called home, got no answer, waited an hour, then took a taxi. His house was dark. Jane's new red Jeep was gone from the carport. Harry headed up the porch steps, sweating in the cool darkness. He flicked on the lights, saw the legal pad on the kitchen table. A ransom note, he was sure, asking for money in exchange for the lane girl and now Jane. Harry had been robbed six times at work. He knew about crime.

He was wrong. It was from Jane. Harry had forgotten to give her his itinerary. She apologized for not being there, but what else could she have done? In a PS, she wrote that she'd be out late and not to worry. He said, "Ha!" He said it very loud.

Harry filled a metal iced-tea tumbler with ice and vodka. He turned on a television set but did not even look at it. He went to his basement workbench and spent two hours painting a saw with a beach scene from Split. It brimmed with safe children and blue water.

In the morning, Jane's bed was undisturbed. She had not come home. She did not always come home. She was thirty. Thirty-year-old women did not always come home. He had to accept that.

Harry went in early to work. When Jane arrived, she came straight to the office and bluntly told him she was moving in with Ray the bartender. They had, apparently overnight, fallen in love, though Jane claimed they had been dating for weeks; how could Harry not know? Harry did not know. Harry had no idea.

"What about the lane girl?" Harry said. "Karen."

"I called information," Jane said, defensively. "No listing. So I called the in-case-of-emergency number on her job application."

Why hadn't Harry thought of that? "And?"

"And nothing," said Jane. "It was long distance. Las Vegas. I kept leaving messages on a machine—maybe six calls total—but nobody ever called back. What can you do? The message on the machine was a hair-metal song. No 'please leave a message' or 'wait for the beep.' Hair metal."

Jane disapproved of this hair metal, which pleased Harry, even though he had not heard the term before and could only imagine what sort of music it codified. "I'm calling the police," he said.

"Daddy," she said. "Please. She's got her story, and one day she'll come get her check and tell us what happened. Either that or she won't. We'll never know, and that's that. Did the beer guy come in?"

"He just left. I paid him cash. We're square."

"Did you get a receipt?" she said. "I can't believe you pay those guys cash."

Harry had read an article in the *Plain Dealer* that said the world would do away with cash by the year 2010, which, Harry was afraid, he would live to see. Harry Kreevich was a man worth about half a million dollars who did not have an ATM card. He liked talking to the tellers.

Ray came into the office now and asked to use the phone. He told Jane he was going to order a new, larger bed from a toll-free number. You could do that now. A bed! Same-day delivery.

"Go ahead," Harry said. "I suppose congratulations are in order."

Ray looked confused for a moment. "Oh, right," he said. "I got you. Thanks, Harry."

"Excuse me one second," Harry said, reaching past Ray, opening his desk drawer, pulling out the beer man's receipt, waving it at Jane. "I am not a fool, you know."

Jane laughed. She was a washed-out version of her sister. Book-smart, more sure of herself. "I know, Daddy. I'm sorry."

They set up shop. Saturday: teen leagues, with one-tenth the kids they had when Jane and Debra were girls. Jane put cash into the register at the counter, Harry into the one at the bar. They made eye contact. "So?" Jane said, hopefully. She used her head to point inefficiently toward Ray.

"So your sister is painting penises." He said it a little loud, and flinched.

"I know," Jane said. "She sends me slides. They're good. Less austere than her old work."

Everyone, it seemed, knew everything that came as news to Harry Kreevich. "I bought one."

"A slide?"

"Please," Harry said. "Pay attention, young girl in love." At this, Jane smiled. She had a pretty smile. She should smile more. "I bought a painting," Harry said. "One of Debra's."

Ray emerged from the office. "Done," he called, to both of them. Done with the office, done ordering their bed. "How 'bout that Tribe, eh, Harry?"

"This may be the year," said Harry. He was not a baseball

fan, but everyone in Cleveland was saying this may be the year. They had been saying this for several years now.

"I can't wait to see it," Jane said. "Debra's painting."

"They're shipping it," he said. "When are you moving?"

"Tonight," she said. "At least get a start on it."

Harry bit his tongue so he wouldn't say anything that would sound old-fashioned. "Tonight," said Harry, pushing the cash register closed, "is as good a night as any. No time like the present."

WHAT TIME WOULD *want* to be like the present, that was what Harry Kreevich wanted to know. Once, he believed in the American Dream. He started as a pin boy at Erieview Lanes in the Slavic Village. He worked his way up until he was made assistant manager. He married Anna, the actual girl next door. They scraped and saved. They took his immigrant father's life insurance policy from the steel mill and paid cash for their own, new alley. It was in the west suburbs. Like true Americans, Harry and Anna Kreevich progressed westward. They ran the alley together, had two lovely daughters, and built a house in Bay Village, four blocks from the lake. Harry was raised to believe American lives were arcs of progress, all trends generally up. That's how it was, until it wasn't. When did *that* happen? By the time he noticed, it had been that way for a while. He felt that way a long time before Anna left. Maybe it was all Ronald Reagan's fault. (Harry, a little drunk, said this to a nice lady realtor he dated a few times. It scared her off. Realtors liked Reagan.)

Harry had modernized, computerized, expanded, made the Brunswick sales rep rich. But the pro bowling tour went elsewhere. Nelson Burton died. Anna was in Paris with her lawyer husband, diddling herself. Harry once asked Anna if he could watch her do that; she was shocked. Now, Harry was reduced to dating tired-looking divorcées he met from the personal ads they placed in the *Plain Dealer.* This was not progress.

Cleveland was booming and, according to what everybody said, no longer a joke to the rest of the world. But if you asked Harry, the rest of the world didn't know crap. The old Cleveland was a great American city, where his father worked hard in a steel mill and people made things. Now it was a place where all that people made was fancy food, public drinking, and play. Ask someone why Cleveland is booming and they will say, "Look at the downtown restaurants and all that neon in the Flats and also the tax-abated playground for millionaires where the Cleveland Indians play." Or they will mention the revived theater district. Or the Rock and Roll Hall of Fame. Food, drink, and, most important of all, play. Harry liked all of these things, and he should talk, making his living off people eating popcorn, drinking beer, and bowling. But this was nothing to build a *city* on. Nothing to build a *society* on.

What were people thinking? Where would all this lead? That's what Harry Kreevich wanted to know. His late-night theories were "nothing" and "nowhere."

Harry, not yet sixty, felt spent. Balding, paunchy, divorced. Told by his doctor to exercise, he took long walks, alone, down dark, well-edged sidewalks. Having Jane around and how lately she'd made things better—*that* had to be temporary. Harry had hired the perfect lane girl, and what happened? She disappeared. Of course.

FOR A WOMAN who'd never had a full-time job for longer than a year, Jane was rich with things. The books! Hundreds of them, alphabetized on white laminated shelves she'd assembled herself. Ray had a truck, and all Jane was taking was what would fit in two trips: her summer clothes, half her

books (many liquor boxes full), and all her rock music com-
pact discs. Except for four of the bookshelves, her furniture
stayed.

"I'm going to take a quick look," Jane said, "for any last-
minute whatevers." They were nearly finished loading up for
the second trip. Ray owned a duplex he was renovating himself, in Tremont. That used to be a rough place. Jane said it
was coming up in the world. Harry hadn't been there in years.

Ray and Harry loaded up Jane's racing bike. The truck
was full. "Why is it," Harry said, "people pick the hottest day
of the year to move?" It was in fact only a run-of-the-mill hot
day. Harry just wanted to say something. He and Ray had
done most of this work without saying more than *your side first*
and *easy*.

"Just say it, Harry," Ray said. "I know you're thinking it."

"Thinking what?" But Harry knew what Ray meant.

"C'mon," said Ray. "I'd be thinking it if I were you."

Harry shrugged. "It's a new millennium, right?"

"Your grandkids would be black. That's how it is, in America. How are you with that?"

"Is she pregnant?"

"No," Ray said.

"I love my daughters," Harry said. "I hope I live long
enough, they will give me grandbabies to spoil." He reached
for a half-finished can of beer he'd set on a shady flagstone.
"Does that answer your question?"

Ray considered this. He finished his beer. He patted
Harry on the back and laughed. "They got others back in
Croatia like you?"

"I don't know," Harry said. "I left when I was ten years old.
I haven't been back since."

Just then, with Ray's arm still around Harry, Jane came
down the porch steps carrying Harry's VCR and one of
Debra's still lifes. She hadn't asked to take these, but Harry

didn't say anything. "My two guys!" she said. "Let me take a picture." But her camera—which Harry gave her last Christmas, his first year of shopping alone for the girls—would not work.

DATING MADE HARRY KREEVICH think of death. Even on first dates, women talked about diet taboos, or brushes with breast cancer, or how their parents were racked with Alzheimer's. Yet Harry resisted dating younger women. It is a slippery slope from the young girlfriend to the foolish accoutrements: red sports car, hairpiece, lifetime membership at a Vic Tanny health club.

He had spoken twice on the phone with this new woman, Beverly, who was in public relations, and they had met once downtown, for coffee. This was how it was done, from those ads. Neutral spots first. If things work out, you make a date. Harry always let the woman pick a place. He wanted them to see he was not the kind of man who had to make all the decisions.

Eat, drink, and maybe someday play. Harry *was* trying to build something with this frivolity, but what, exactly, he didn't have words for. *Companionship* is too sad a word, and wrong. Not *love*, either. *Love* was too simple and too complicated a word for the word Harry did not have.

Beverly lived in Chagrin Falls, so far on the east side, it wasn't Cleveland anymore. She picked a restaurant four blocks from her home, an hour's drive for Harry, plus another half-hour when he got lost. Before he set foot in the place, Harry had decided that dating this woman was pure folly. Inside, the place looked like a hunting lodge designed by someone who disapproved of hunting. Nothing on the menu was less than twenty-two dollars.

For most of the meal, Beverly was charming. She and Harry reminisced like old friends about the baffling miracle of parenthood (Beverly had four sons), the surprising, inevitable ways children turn out. They talked about music that even oldies stations never played and movie stars no one talked about anymore. Stewart Granger. Olivia DeHaviland. Ida Lupino. "All dead, probably," Harry said. He winced. Sure enough, as they finished dinner, Beverly told him one son was dying of AIDS. She began to cry. Other diners stared. *They think we're married,* he thought. *They think I've hurt her.* The waiter, sadistically, kept refilling her coffee. When they finally got out of there, Harry walked her to her car and said he had to get up early the next morning. It was barely dark. They shook hands, and he was back in his car, pointing its hood ornament west.

Harry got onto I-480. He told himself that when the Lee Road exit came up, he might not take it. He'd scribbled the lane girl's old address on one of his own business cards. He'd made sure he had his Cuyahoga County street map. Yet he still thought maybe he wouldn't go. In truth, he'd thought about the lane girl all night, half listening as Beverly wondered whatever happened to Pérez Prado.

He went.

Lee Road, though it served as what Harry would call a main drag, was one of those streets that went from two lanes to one, back to two, then to an ambiguous width that was more than one and less than two: a street created as if no one but people who lived nearby would ever drive it. Harry persevered north, enduring the honking horns of impatient natives, until finally there it was, Sycamore Road. Harry overshot it, turned around, and was almost clipped by a BMW blaring rap music.

The street was a single quarter-mile block. Big trees and nice-enough houses. But even in the waning light, Harry could tell—shabby lawns, sagging porches—that this part of town had gone to rentals. The lane girl's old house was an up-down duplex, an ugly frame house painted a shade of dull blue popular in 1970s bathroom fixtures. The address didn't say up or down, so Harry started with the down. A young black woman answered the door. She was dressed in an untucked security-cop uniform and carrying a sleeping baby.

"Do you know a Karen Borkowski?" Harry whispered.

"We just moved in," the woman said. "Don't know anybody." She excused herself and closed the door.

He could hear the noise of a television from upstairs. He rang the other doorbell, waited, rang it again, and waited a long time before he saw in the stairwell a shirtless white man, built like a football player gone badly to seed and to beer.

"Do you know a Karen Borkowski?" Harry said.

"I know *the* Karen Borkowski," the man said. "Who are you?"

"She works for me. I own a bowling alley." Harry pulled out his card. "She's missed work. I'm concerned."

"And you drove all the way over here?" the man said. "You must be a great boss. Got any openings?"

"No," Harry said. "Unless you want to wait tables."

"Kiddin', chief. I own this house, those two there, plus two more in Shaker. Keeps me as busy as I care to be. Name's Parker." The men shook hands. "Karen lived downstairs. She and my fiancée, Holly. They had a falling-out. Holly moved up with me. I thought Karen went to live with her folks, in Arizona someplace."

"Nevada, I think," Harry said.

"Whatever," said Parker. "Karen's a good egg. I never saw what made Holly and her get on each other's nerves. That's how it is with chicks. Try to figure it out, you'll go nuts. Am I right?"

"Right." It was the only thing to say. "Maybe your fiancée would know where Karen is."

"Sorry, Harry." Of *course* this was the sort of young man who would presume familiarity. "Holly's in the hospital. Broke her leg last night. Stepped in a bucket. If she's got any ideas, I'll have her call you."

"No boyfriends?" Harry persisted. "Or"—he almost said *psychotic episodes*—"problems?"

"Not that I know of," Parker said. "She was a regular girl. But like I said, I'll have Holly call—"

"Have her call me either way."

"—if she knows anything," Parker said. "Look, it's nice of you to worry about your waitress, but I got chow nukin' in the mike."

Food cooking in the microwave, Harry finally figured out, but by then he was alone on the dark porch. He had an odd impulse to leave his Ford parked at the curb and set off on foot, to walk and walk, for days and days, until he got to a place where no one knew him, no one cared where he came from. And so he started walking. Six blocks later, he stopped at a Dairy Mart and bought cigarettes. He had not smoked in twenty years. He crossed the street to Cain Park, where he'd once taken part in a craft show. In the distance, in an outdoor theater, a man with a guitar was giving a concert. "You must be Daddy's little pumpkin," the man sang. *That can't be right,* Harry thought. *I'm hearing what I want to hear.* It's the same in painting, Debra once said. People see what they want to. An artist leaves room for people to believe what the artist would never dream of. Harry's saws meant what Harry meant them to—no more, no less. He sat on a park bench and listened to the music and smoked four cigarettes, then threw the rest in a trash can, walked back to his car, got in, and drove to Bay Village in silence. He was in the garage before he noticed his radio had been meticulously stolen, no dangling wires or broken dash, as if the thief knew he had all the time in the world.

Harry showered and shaved, which nowadays men did in the morning. But Harry, like his father, had a light beard and was a nighttime shaver. *Where are you, Karen Borkowski,* he thought as lay himself down to sleep, *and what is the meaning of this?*

In the mystery novels Anna read, many of which were still strewn about the house, Harry would become an amateur sleuth. He would solve the crime; solving the crime would solve much else. So much else! But this was not one of those improbable, exciting books. There may or may not have been a crime. Harry might never know what happened. He would not discover in his ordinary self an extraordinary gift for sleuthing. He would solve nothing. Accepting that, Harry realized, was its own, small solution.

He got out of bed, filled his largest aluminum tumbler full of vodka and iced tea and went downstairs. He spread out his painting things and a great old barn saw he'd found at a junk store way out in Elyria. He stared at his supplies. He felt like painting, but he did not know what to paint. He finished his drink, made another, stronger one, then came back downstairs and got to work before he could catch himself thinking. He found himself painting women. All dressed in white robes. One was his daughter Jane and one was his daughter Debra and one was the Virgin Mary and one was his mother, who was a store clerk and a saint, too, and had died ten years ago from diabetes-triggered complications. Harry did not like to think of that. He did them all fast. There was so much space, on that long saw, for more figures. He stopped. He was sweating, more than he had when he was helping Jane move. He was drenched. He looked at what he had done. Terrible. They were terrible. All four women looked exactly alike. None looked like herself. To Harry's relief, none looked like the lane girl. They all looked like a cartoon character, a famous one. Harry couldn't think of her name.

He took out the turpentine and wiped the saw clean.

With this, Harry Kreevich went upstairs and fell asleep, alone in a king-sized bed, alone in a big dark house, surrounded by the cast-off belongings of his lost wife and two lost daughters—that and the drone and glow of the bedroom television set. He slept the sleep of the dead. When he woke up, he was stark naked, which was not the way he usually slept. Stranger yet, the clean, turpentine-smelling saw was in his bed, though he did not remember bringing it with him. For no reason he could think of, it comforted him. He ran his hand along the saw's smooth surface. The television was still on. It was Sunday morning. Protestants were singing a hymn Harry didn't know. *I should go to Mass,* he thought, which he hadn't done since Christmas. He ran his index finger along the teeth of the saw, daring himself to cut himself. His plump fingers pillowed out and whitened from the pressure.

Harry did not cut himself. He broke out laughing. Someone watching this might have mistaken it for crying. But there was no one to watch, about which Harry was awake enough to be glad. So Harry Kreevich's opinion is the one that counts. Call it laughter.

A WEEK LATER, Harry and Ray were behind the bar together, and the dining lounge was busy, who knew why, when the top story on the TV news reported that a body of a young woman had washed up on the shore of Lake Erie, near a popular seafood restaurant. Whenever TV people have footage of paramedics pulling a dead white girl out of a scenic place, they will make it a big story.

"Jesus," Harry said. "Oh, no."

"Easy," said Ray. "It could be anybody."

That was hardly a comforting thought.

They called for Jane. By the time she got there, the news had progressed to the gruesome ends of other lives. Still it was

Jane who took control, who called the TV station and also the cops for details.

It was not the lane girl. (Harry felt both relieved and disappointed.) The dead girl was a college kid whose boyfriend had been arrested last year for beating her with a Thermos. The boyfriend shot her and threw her in the lake. He proclaimed his innocence. "I don't believe you," Harry angrily said to the TV above the bar.

Six days later, the boyfriend confessed.

"Good call, Harry," Ray said.

"Thank you." Harry was beginning to really like this Ray. He was truly happy when Jane and Ray got engaged. He was even happier, a few months later, when they were married, and he gave Jane away, and at the reception, Debra and Eric announced that they were going to have a baby. After the grandbaby was born—a girl, Sara Jane—Eric turned out to be a patient, talented father. Even Eric was something Harry was getting used to.

Parker's fiancée never called. And since Harry did not get Parker's number and was unwilling to drive back to Cleveland Heights, that was that. Off and on, Harry tried the number in Las Vegas. Always the answering machine, with its caterwauling hair metal. Harry left messages. No one ever called back.

Harry looked for the lane girl's face in shopping malls and crowded places like the Rock and Roll Hall of Fame, which he eventually visited (hair metal, he learned, had been big in the 1980s), but he never saw her. He gradually forgot what she looked like. He stopped calling the number in Las Vegas. He threw away her paycheck. But for the rest of his life, when he picked up a telephone and heard a click, he would wonder if that had been her.

As for Debra's painting, *Study #37*: When it arrived, Harry took it to a frame store in Parmatown Mall, where a nice young man suggested different frames and mats and had the good manners not to say anything untoward. Harry picked it up a week later. He hung it on his family room wall. When different women came over, it proved to be quite the conversation piece. "What I like about it," Harry would say, "is the light and the space and also how it is not austere."

Someday, he was sure, a woman would hear him say that, and hear how he said it. Someday, someone would hear what it was Harry Kreevich was really trying to say.

Ace of Hearts

In May of 1947, when I was a girl of fourteen, my mother again left us, as my dad and I had predicted and hoped. We were living in a cottage on a fallow farm near College View, Indiana, where I was finishing the ninth grade, my eleventh different school since kindergarten. While my dad and I watched from the porch of the main house, sipping lemonade (his spiked), she flung wig boxes, hatboxes, jewelry boxes, suitcases, electric fans, and a basswood console radio into a blue '39 Chevy. Although the radio was his, won in a card game the night he limped home from the war, and the car was a loaner from the dealership where he worked, my dad did nothing to stop her. Meanwhile, our landlord, a haunted young doctor named Frank Gold, stood in the hayloft of his barn, dressed in a coat and tie, shooting at rats with a gun he'd taken from a dead Nazi. It was a warm evening. Finally my mother got in the car. As she backed out of the drive, I smiled and waved.

My dad looped his arm around me, and I felt the curve of his bicep against my neck. He smelled of Skin Bracer. "Now what'll we bitch about, Tess?"

We laughed. In the barn, Frank's wife Constance Monroe, a history professor at Crenshaw Teachers College, the first married woman I knew who'd kept her name, yelled at him to stop firing that damn gun right this damn minute. I pointed. "Them."

My dad nodded. "They'll do." But his attention stayed fixed on Constance Monroe in a way that seemed to have little to do with annoyance.

"How broke are we?" I said. My mother always cleaned us out.

"I had a good week. Four Buicks and an Olds. We'll be okay."

"With you managing our money?" I said. "Ha."

"Think you could do better?" he said.

Frank climbed down, exchanged words with his wife, climbed back up, and continued pumping bullets into the rotten barn siding. Constance, a broad-shouldered and striking woman, tried to pull the barn door closed, gave up, and strode back toward the house.

"*Anyone* could do better," I said. Especially me, who could solve for *x* faster than my algebra teacher.

"True," my father admitted. He refilled our lemonade glasses and dropped his wallet on my lap. "So take it. Pay the bills. Give me pin money. What's left when your mom gets back, you can keep."

I studied his brown wallet as if it held answers to life, asking about the rent (twenty-five dollars a month), his paycheck ("thirty to sixty a week, after Uncle's cut"), hoping this would show him I could really do it, in case he was kidding. Inside the wallet, he had nine dollars, his driver's license, my third-grade school photo (I was fat), two playing cards (a joker and the ace of hearts), and several scraps of paper: phone numbers. Leads, I guessed. Prospects. "If you mean it," I said, "you got a deal."

"Deal," he said. We clinked glasses. Perhaps to balance my mother's gift for lies and hyperbole, my dad told the truth, and exaggerated only when he sold cars or gambled. *I'm rich,* I thought: $180 a month, subtract $25 for rent, $35 for food and electric, $50 for my dad to blow. That left $70 a month. If she was gone until Labor Day, I'd have two hundred bucks, easy.

Just then Constance Monroe threw open the front screen door. "Tess. Mitch." She pointed to the whiskey bottle on the porch rail. "May I?"

My dad shrugged. "All yours."

She had a belt, took the bottle from her lips and did not gasp. She might as well have been drinking tea. "Thank you."

"Don't thank me," my dad said. "It really *is* yours. I took it off your sideboard."

She frowned. "That's the kind of tenant I have, a thief?"

"A borrower." He held her stare. "A poor working man who means well," he said, "and whose woman done gone."

Darkness had fallen; the only light came from inside the house. They kept looking at one another, Constance leaning on a porch spindle, my dad swinging. In the barn, Frank whooped that he'd nailed one. The thudding of the bullets stopped. Finally Constance broke the silence. "Men," she said.

My dad grinned. "Women," he said.

They both broke out laughing.

"I'm going to bed," I said, "if anyone cares."

No one seemed to.

I pulled the Murphy bed from the cottage wall and sat in my mother's old pajamas with a tablet of paper left over from ninth-grade English, thinking what to buy. *School clothes,* I wrote. *Nice dresses. Books. A bicycle.* I didn't want makeup or jewelry, didn't know enough of the world of girls to know what clothes were trendy, a phase I went through a decade later, teaching social studies in Red Oak, Iowa, buying rock-and-roll records and falling in love with my husband, a rakish crop duster. Back then, I was an only child who'd moved around too much to have girlfriends or girl vanity. I remember thinking at the time: *What do I* need*?* I couldn't say. I turned off the light and tried to go to sleep, which I also couldn't do. I got up, walked to the tiny rolltop desk at the window, where my mother had tried to fashion a studio set off from the room with a yellow dressing blind, which she'd knocked to the floor but not taken. I set it back up, then searched the desk drawers and cubbyholes, all empty save a snapshot of my dad in uniform, clowning around on the hood of a Jeep. I ran my hands over the peeling shellac of the desk's surface. I resolved to refinish that desk, to make that corner of the room my own.

My dad came in hours later. I pretended to be asleep. He had just enough whiskey on his breath to smell loamy. He kissed my forehead, whispered, "I'm sorry"—for what, I didn't know—then went to bed himself, his room still a shambles from my mother's departure.

MY MOTHER WAS a waifish, neurasthenic woman who'd gotten pregnant, dropped out of Northwestern, and been disowned by her father, a taciturn Standard Oil executive. This crushed her, which I saw, in childhood, as pathetic. Thirty years later, when my dad and I were feuding about his lack of regard for his health and about my hazy idea of my long-dead mother as a Wronged Woman, I understood. Too late, like most real-life epiphanies.

She had a history of leaving, never for any reason I could see. Sometimes she packed her every belonging, other times she just vanished, including once with the radio on, dinner in the oven, and a copy of the *New Yorker* open on the kitchen table. She never said where she was going, and, the rules of the game established, we never asked. A few weeks later, we'd get a letter telling us where she was, but these often bore postmarks from elsewhere. A few months after that, she'd return, and things went back the way they were: two edgy, smoking adults, keeping their distance, sneaking bewildered glances at each other—and, occasionally, me. They were astonished to be parents, a condition that unnerved my mother and amused my dad.

I was six months old the first time she left—on her first anniversary, a characteristically theatrical gesture. She later told me she was hoping to punish my dad into appreciating her. Instead, he solicited advice in diapering and burping from a neighbor named Eve (this was not an innocent relationship) and took me with him to work, stashing me in an empty back office at a Crosley dealership in Evansville, where I was doted upon by secretaries, customers, and my dad. He was a man who excelled at what interested him: football, drinking, gambling, womanizing, sales, and now fatherhood. At first, he had no intention of using me as an aphrodisiac, but being a single father in 1934, he admitted years later, drew lovers to him as if summoned from their homes by a high thrum only women could hear.

According to my mother's journals, she returned from her first leave-taking (she'd been with a sister in Chagrin Falls) and "life returned to 'normal.'" If my parents discussed or argued about my mother's departures and reappearances, I never heard it. They would not discuss it with me; life just moved ahead. Of course, no child understands the mechanics of his parents' marriage, or fully wants to.

I SPENT MOST of my fourteenth summer in line at the water department, the phone company, the power company, and the bank, paying bills and suffering the hard, disdainful glares of ruby-haired clerks—an ordeal for a chunky girl in the depths of teenagery. As I ran my errands, I'd pass by the soda fountain at Hook's, its booths full of majorettes and basketball boys, and I imagined that they, too, were talking about me (childish; they didn't care enough about me to interrupt their tribal rites). The only places I felt unexamined were the carport behind our cottage, where I was inexpertly stripping my mother's desk, and at the public library, where I hid in far corners and read about presidents, painters, alienated young men, plucky girl detectives, talking house-pets, and France. Everywhere else, I was aware of stares and whispers. College View was a small town, especially once classes ended at Crenshaw. Even though we were professional transients living outside of town, everyone knew our business, and disapproved.

They knew, that is, that my mother had left and my dad and I had not; that I was depositing twenty dollars a week, in my name, at Wabash Valley Savings, while my dad made about that much a week at poker (they evidently didn't yet know he cheated); and that we were living with that shell-shocked Jew doctor from Philadelphia and his freethinking malcontent of a wife. Constance, I learned from a teller, lobbied, during the war, for the college to admit Negroes ("Here!" hissed the teller, "Why *here*?"), a battle she lost—and, with it, any chance she had of fitting in.

"That's the difference between children and adults," said Constance one day in her hopelessly messy office, where I'd meet her to get a ride home. "Children want to fit in. This town is infested with hundreds of small-minded, gigantic, old children."

"So what do adults want?" I asked.

"We don't know," she said. "That's what makes us adults."

Despite myself, I was beginning to like this woman, even though—like the rest of town—I suspected that she and my dad were sleeping together. He had, of course, never been an especially faithful husband (nor my mother a faithful wife), but I did not necessarily know that then.

I'd been surprised to learn that Constance had been married before (to her childhood sweetheart, one of the war's early casualties) and, more so, that she was my dad's age and thus seven years older than Frank, who was the oldest twenty-seven-year-old man alive. Two weeks after my mother left, my dad sold Constance a new black Buick, more car than Frank's tiny practice and Constance's tinier salary could handle, forcing her to teach summer classes in Western civilization at Crenshaw.

Frank kept firing his gun, day after day, until, somewhere around the Fourth of July, he hired an exterminator. After that, he seemed to lose any sense of purpose, moping around the property, always overdressed, and going to bed at sundown. Sometimes I could feel him watching me as I sanded that desk. I'd look up, he'd smile wanly and look away, and I'd rewrap my sandpaper around an old toothbrush and go back to work on the pigeonholes.

When my dad got home from poker, long after dark, Constance would be swinging on that porch. I confess to spying. They'd sit close, smoke and drink, tune her radio to jazz stations from Saint Louis, talk about world affairs, local fools, and war stories. I never saw them kiss. Once, briefly, they held hands.

A MONTH AFTER my mother left, my dad and I received our letter, posted "Falls Church, Va.," and written on the stationery of the Alcazar Hotel in Cleveland, which looked on the letterhead like a Moorish castle. She claimed to be staying with an aunt in Tampa. In her perfect hand, she wrote that she loved us; that she left *because* she loved us; that she'd visited the Statue of Liberty, Dorothy Parker's summer home, and, that day, Rock City; that she was confused, tired, and was taking daily sitz baths. Nothing about if and when she'd be back. Enclosed for me were one dollar and a lock of her auburn hair.

For my dad, a news clipping about a "wronged wife" in Atlanta who'd killed her "philandering husband" in his sleep by crushing his skull with a golf club. On it, my mother, a good golfer, had written *Must not have been the 1-iron; no-body can hit that*. My dad, who did not play golf, nevertheless found this funny. Though I was not the first teenager in the world to conclude that her parents were crazy, I did have more cause than most.

AT THE TIME, I did not see the obvious parallels between Constance and my mother. To me, my mother was a distant person, given to bouts of silence and moodiness. Constance was loud, sane, and direct; to the extent she was moody, it was always the same mood: Go to hell. Which I loved. Obviously, both were smart women chafing at living in a parochial and masculine world. This wasn't easy for a young girl of the 1940s to grasp.

IN 1942, SICK of my mother's complaints about the society life she'd left behind in Cleveland, my dad had enlisted in the Navy. Stationed in San Diego, he served America for three proud years as a member of the base football team. He'd been a starting flanker at Northwestern when he'd dropped out to get married, and those war years, knocking heads with other college and some pro players, must have been for him a grand reclamation of his youth, at least until he got his war wound, a ruined right knee, inflicted by a once-and-future member of the Detroit Lions. Meanwhile, my mother dispatched me to the homes of sundry heartland aunts and cousins while she, I learned later, went to New York, failed miserably as a playwright, and had a boozy affair with a distinguished actor. Had I known this about my mother during her lifetime, things between us might have gone better. But perhaps that's just sentimental.

In the two years from my dad's discharge until my mother's departure in 1947, she did not leave. She had not left me with my dad since I was eight. After a while, she seemed like a grown child who hadn't the wherewithal to get her own place. "She'll go pretty soon," my dad said that winter. We stood in the window of Cox Studebaker in Fort Wayne, where he was sales manager. I was on Christmas break. The sales lot was snowbound and empty. "I can tell."

"Why?" I asked.

"She just will," he said. "The money's running low."

"Is that why she leaves?" I said.

"No." He shrugged. "Sort of." Our eyes met. He was thirty-four, ancient to me, but the winter sunlight hit his face in a way that let me see the strong-jawed, dilettante, golden boy he'd once been. Years later, it hit me: This was how he saw himself.

On New Year's Day, we moved the length of Indiana to College View, to that little cottage with kitchen- and porch-privileges in the main house, escaping debts and bad company in a way you can't do anymore. Today, computers find you. But in those days, you could get small loans from local merchants, blow your money, and, when the dun letters started to come, pull up stakes and move. Which is how my parents had lived their married life up to then.

"BET YOU'RE LOOKING forward to school," said Constance Monroe. We were riding together in her vast Buick the six miles into College View, each in pants outfits, hers blue, mine white.

"Kind of," I said. It was Labor Day. School started tomorrow. I'd bought a closetful of school clothes and still had nearly two hundred dollars. I expected my mother home any day, and once she arrived, we'd move and I'd change schools. I was too familiar with children's cruelty to new kids to look forward to this.

"Mitch tells me you're a straight-A student," Constance persisted.

"We move around so much," I said, "doing well in school is just a thing to do, you know?" *In lieu of having friends,* I thought. I looked out the window, away from her, at the rolling fields of alfalfa. "I can't explain it."

"I understand." Constance put her hand on my knee, a forced, awkward moment. "Being a smart woman, in today's world..." Her voice trailed off in a way she must have meant to be meaningful.

"I know exactly what you mean," I lied.

"There they are," said Constance, honking the Buick's grave horn. Frank and my dad—who'd both had work to do that morning—stood hunched over a rusty grill in Clearwater Park, a grassy cliff overlooking the Wabash River. On a picnic table were a watermelon, four tiny steaks, and unshucked corn—Frank's contributions, no doubt. My dad would have brought the beer and the pop. They were attempting to light the charcoal with gasoline.

"You're both going to die," I said, helping Constance get the Jell-O mold, plates, and silverware out of the car.

"You're right," my dad admitted. "We all will, someday."

"Cute," I said. But the coals seemed to be catching, and, as Constance did battle with her Brownie camera, my dad and Frank shook hands and posed before the grill, like dutiful politicians at a plant opening.

"The lens cap," said Frank, in his soft, even voice.

"What about it," said Constance, taking it off.

As we waited for the coals to ash over, my dad produced a new football, and we all joined in, throwing it around peacefully until Constance—who styled herself as a tomboy but threw as badly as Frank, who threw like a girl—suggested we play keep-away. "Three people against one in the middle," she said.

Frank, who had not so much as loosened his tie, took out a handkerchief and mopped the sweat from his long, hollow-cheeked face. "Looks like rain," he said, which was so.

"How 'bout it, Mitch?" she said.

Back at the picnic table for another beer, my dad just shrugged. This is how I'll always remember him: a beer in one hand, a cigarette in the other, a football between his knees, squinting into the distance and shrugging.

Finally Constance got us to go along. She volunteered to be in the middle first. My dad put out his cigarette, rose to his feet, and threw me a spiral, about twenty yards and right on the money. I caught it. He gave me a wink.

Constance, who ran better than she threw, came loping toward me. I heaved the ball beyond her outstretched arms and back to my dad. It was a good throw. Both he and Frank cheered.

My dad pump-faked toward Constance, once, twice, taunting her to come near, laughing, then tossed another spiral, this time to Frank, who shuffled back and forth, eyes more on his charging wife than the ball. He got drilled square in the forehead. Constance dove, covering the ball with her body, though Frank made no effort to get to it.

"You're in the middle, Frank," she said. "You're it."

"Am I ever," he said, rubbing his head.

"I didn't lead you enough, Frank," said my dad. "Sorry."

"It's not your fault," said Frank. "I don't blame *you.*"

It was then I was certain: Constance and my dad *were* having an affair. Or at least Frank thought so.

As the storm drew near, Frank stood marooned in the middle of a crude right triangle formed by his wife, my dad, and me. My dad made the long throws down the hypotenuse, and I usually caught them. The first couple times I dropped the ball, I scrambled after it, delighted to be beating an adult at anything. But after a few vicious tussles between Frank and Constance, all won by Constance, I started feeling sorry for him. My dad must have felt the same, because he broke the game up to go pee in the woods. When he got back, he went straight to the middle. Constance, though, insisted it was still Frank's turn. My dad rolled his eyes but acquiesced. "We only have a minute," he said, pointing to the coals. "Go deep, Tess," he yelled.

As I did, I vowed to drop the ball and let Frank have it. Then the game would end and we'd all go eat.

My dad waved me back. I kept running, with Frank, bless his sad heart, doggedly pursuing me. Finally, my dad released the ball, a short, wobbly throw. I kept running, leaving easy pickings for Frank. It was perfect.

Next thing I knew, a gunshot rang out and I was writhing on the ground, pain leaping up from my right ankle. I looked down, expecting to see splintered bone and bloody gristle. Instead, it was just my ankle, swelling but in no way shot. I'd stepped on a rock. About ten yards away, in a daze, was Frank, his pistol limp at his side, like an exhausted referee. The football lay on the ground nearby, blasted to shreds.

My dad and Constance ran toward us—confused, it seemed, about whether to attack Frank or aid me. Then Frank snapped out of it and was in fact the first person at my side.

"Get away from her," said my dad.

Frank, his hands already on my ankle, looked up at my dad. "I'll buy you a new ball, okay?"

There was a long pause, broken only by my groaning. Then my dad, an expert at seeing the absurd in a situation, said, "Jesus, Frank, what a duck hunter you'd be," and broke out laughing. Constance followed. It began to rain. And I hated them, hated every adult in Indiana, in the whole world. Every kid, too, for good measure. "What about me!" I shouted. "God damn it."

Everyone laughed more. I have never been good at swearing.

Even Frank smiled. "It's a sprain," he said. "I should take you to the office." He looked at my dad. "On the house."

My dad shook his head. "Call it even for the football."

"We'll take my car," said Constance.

"We need beer, anyhow," my dad said. "C'mon, let's load Tess and all our crap into the Buick."

As they helped me up, I saw a cloud of smoky steam rising from the rain, steady now, that poured onto the grill.

FUNNY HOW PIVOTAL moments in a person's life keep pivoting. In my teens, I saw that summer as a brave, impressive experience. In my twenties, I thought I'd been dragooned into premature adulthood. In my thirties, I came to know my mother and saw things better from her point of view. In my forties, I quit teaching, went to law school, embraced the women's movement, and mythologized my mother into feminist archetype. In my fifties, I learned things about my dad, which changed my view again. Now, a month before my sixtieth birthday, I think all these things are true, and also false. Now I see this as a story about Frank Gold and how he prepared me to look inside the man I married. On the surface, Roy, who is now retired from Pan Am, is like my dad: dashing and able, what was once called a man's man. But that's only his surface. His childhood, which he was once loath to talk about, was a horror. Both his father and, years later, his twin sister committed suicide, and that's not the half of it.

Our marriage has turned out well, at least by the standards of the institution, which we imagine to be more fragile nowadays than it once was. Ha.

I MADE CONSTANCE and my dad stay in the waiting room. I was no child. My dignity had been wounded enough.

I perched on Frank's sticky vinyl examining table, listening to thunder, as he bandaged my elephantine ankle. He had a sure, kind touch, and I wondered why he had not been able to build a practice here, until he glanced at me with that tormented face. And I just blurted out, "Frank, what's wrong with you?"

He didn't even look up from his work. "You mean why did I shoot your dad's ball?"

"No." That was clear enough; I'd have done the same, in his place. "What is it that's . . . well . . . wrong?"

"Wrong how?"

"I'm sorry," I said. "It's just that you're so sad all the time. At least that's how you seem. Quiet. Sad." I felt childish and inarticulate.

Frank finished with my ankle, then scooted his chair back. Recently my dad told me that Frank Gold had been a wisecracking kid, the child of émigré Jews, and something of a boy genius. He graduated from Penn at age twenty, from med school at twenty-four. He and Constance, who'd just finished her Ph.D., drove to Maryland and were married the night before Frank reported to the Army. He'd been sent to a field hospital in Austria, the first stop for emaciated survivors of the concentration camps. He tended to a parade of the walking dead and, in order to cope, something in his heart shut down. He was never the same. When he came home, he and Constance, facing the postwar housing shortage, thought it might help to leave the city and start over in the middle of nowhere.

This, if anything, made things worse. Of course, no one would tell such a story to a kid, just some injured tenant. What he said to me was, "How old are you?"

"Fourteen."

"That's a tough age." He pursed his lips. "I guess they're all tough ages in their way."

"I guess," I said.

"All I can tell you is that I've seen things," Frank said. "Do you understand?"

I claimed to.

He put his hand on my shoulder. He was, when you got close to him, reassuring and gentle. "You miss your mother," he said, "don't you?"

I had not seen this coming and answered quickly with what I thought was the truth. "Not really. She leaves a lot."

"But she'll be back, huh?"

I frowned. "Oh, sure. Of course."

"That's good," he said. "You know, everyone expected things after the war to go back the way they were. But things weren't so great before the war. People are just sentimental. Still, since the war—" He cleared his throat. "Since the war, connections between people—family, friends, everyone— have gotten so fragile." He looked me in the eye. "So it's good your mother is coming back."

I looked into those dark sad eyes, hopped up onto my good leg, threw my arms around him, and he held me while I cried, while I sobbed. He never said *there, there* or *it'll be okay*. He never asked why I was crying, as men seem perversely compelled to do. He just let me cry.

My mother did not come back that summer, that year, or for the rest of my childhood. Although she and my dad lived the rest of their lives apart, they never bothered to get divorced. She did somehow keep track of our ever-changing addresses, and her letters came regularly. I did not see her again until my wedding day, when she showed up, invited but unexpected, in a beaded black dress and tried to act as if nothing had happened. This didn't cause as much of a scene as you'd think, mostly because it was competing with the tantrums and intrigues of Roy's family (this seems funny to me now, though at the time, I was mortified). My dad, who got more laconic year by year until death, greeted her by saying, "There you are," as if he'd lost sight of her moments before in the nave. I got to know her then, in the few years before she died, learned about her melodramatic life of breakdowns and delusions. The journals, plays, and failed novels that I found in storage after her death paint a picture of a brilliant, manic woman. I know her better now than when she lived.

As for my dad, his luck soured about August 1, 1947, when he got into a game with some mobsters from Terre Haute who knew every trick he knew. After Labor Day, he started asking me for a bigger allowance, which was about when he and I first started to drift apart: It's tough for your father to retain his mystique when you're lecturing him about where the money went. Then one night, he was thrown onto the front lawn from a speeding white Cadillac, and the next morning, he asked me, with affected nonchalance, how much I had saved up. I told him. The next day, he withdrew the money, paid off my mother's long-gone Chevy, and took a loan (never repaid) on a junky '36 Ford, in which we left town that very night, my rolltop desk unfinished and abandoned, and didn't stop until we got to London, Ontario.

He and Constance had been having an affair, though he insisted it had not begun until my mother left. He wouldn't admit it at all until after he lost that bad leg entirely, and Roy and I convinced him to move into our guest room. In the six years he lived with us, before his death last fall, my dad and I became friends again, drinking lemonade (both of ours spiked) and swapping secrets declassified by the passage of time.

I do not know what became of Frank Gold and Constance Monroe. My last vivid memory of them is from later that Labor Day. The storm had died. Hoping the town fireworks display—scheduled to be launched from the front lawn of the college—had not been canceled, we drove back to the cliffs of the Wabash. Constance insisted we'd be able to see fine from there. We reassembled the meal and, as we ate, played hearts on the damp wood of the picnic table. Frank won hand after hand, with no one apparently letting him. Everyone, including me, drank beer. We kept telling and retelling the story of the keep-away game, and it kept getting funnier, even to Frank. Finally darkness came, and we heard the fireworks start. We were, it turned out, too far away to see.

Song for a Certain Girl

In August, the summer after her ninth-grade year, the girl—
pudgy, moonfaced, with dull brown hair and new breasts—
met the man who became her first husband. Before that,
she'd been seeing a tall boy she danced with at junior-high
graduation, starting with a concentric-circle wheel dance the
chaperons employed to pull the boys and girls from their snig-
gering packs and make them sway clumsily with one another,
parodies of the men and women you see cracking wise on the
color TV. After the dance, screened from view by a dumpster,
the tall boy kissed the girl. She'd kissed boys before, here and
there, no one special. It was the tall boy's first kiss. He was
afraid he'd be caught and made fun of. He would grow up
and write for TV; she was already grown.

The tall boy was from the west side of their town, the oldest son of unpious Presbyterians who owned a clothing store
and a brick home. The girl was from the east side and Baptist,
with black people as neighbors. In the center was a courthouse and actual train tracks. She thought she loved the tall
boy (she never said so). She wrote songs about him on her
grandmother's guitar, songs she didn't let anyone hear. She'd
never been in his house, met his parents, or been shown off to

his friends. When she came to watch his swimming meets, he didn't talk to her. The day before the tall boy left town for a family vacation, a three-week trip to Disneyland in Anaheim, California, he called her from a rotary phone in his basement and said it was over.

"I won't let you," she said. "You can't break up with me unless I let you, and I won't."

The tall boy stammered that this wasn't how it worked. "Look, if I start going out with someone else . . . ," he said.

"It doesn't matter," said the girl. "I'll forgive you." She had her blue shirttail balled up in the white knuckles of her fist. A song she liked was on the radio, one about a stubborn woman who pushed through betrayal and loss to find true love. "No matter what you say or what you do," she said, "we're still going together, you and me."

The tall boy said no, they were not, and hung up. He and his family left for California in their Pontiac Silhouette minivan. The girl went to the BP station, bought a folding roadmap of America, and found Anaheim, California. She herself had been no farther west than Fort Wayne, Indiana, which was an hour away. She'd been as far east as Cleveland (once, she and her mom took a Greyhound there to see Art, her mom's dad; they ate at a Ruby Tuesday's in a mall; her mom and Art argued, and the girl and her mom took an early bus home; the girl never even saw downtown Cleveland, unless a glimpse of the distant gray spires of the Society Building and Terminal Tower counts). She'd been as far south as Gatlinburg, Tennessee, and Great Smoky Mountains National Park (once). She'd been as far north as the party store just over the Michigan line, where they sell warm canned beer to anybody. She took a ruler and an inkpen and connected those four points on the map. Then she drew some angled lines, shading in the quadrilateral. She refolded the map and hid it under her mattress. By her math, it was 2,448 miles to Anaheim.

Two days later, at Sunday church, she played and sang "Jesus Wants Me for a Sunbeam" on her grandmother's guitar. After the service, in the fellowship hall, a man came up and said she'd moved him. He was a friend of a cousin of her mom's. He drove a white Ford truck with boards in back, and he looked like those pictures in her head of the men women sang about on country-music radio. He lived in an even smaller town, thirteen miles east. He worked in a Chinese-food factory there and had his own apartment, up over some-one's garage. Their first date was a movie with Bruce Willis in it. Afterward, the man took her to a diner with a big revolving coffee cup on the sign, bought her pie, and showed her off to his friends. He said he was going to grow a mustache like the one Bruce Willis had in that movie. His hair already did look a lot like Bruce Willis's toupee, only it wasn't a toupee and needed cut. He smelled like Aqua Velva aftershave. He wore brown Dingo boots.

One night when the girl's mom came home from the din-ner shift at Pizza Hut, the girl lay on the couch, with her top and bra pulled up, her shorts and her underpants tangled at her ankles. The man had his T-shirt off, his oily jeans still on; his fingers were looking for trouble. Her mom cleared her throat. If they agreed to speak with Minister Steve, she said, she would not punish the girl. In the minister's mayonnaise-smelling office, the man was moved by the Holy Spirit, or so he said, and proposed to the girl. She thought this was ridicu-lous, but couldn't say so in front of Minister Steve, who kept looking on, nosy and pleased with himself. She said yes. It gave her a thrill to do a bad thing that Minister Steve, her mom, and all her mom's people would think was good. She could have relations all she wanted and nobody could say any-thing. The next week, before that mustache filled in enough to show in the pictures, they were married. Her ring was a band of pure silver.

The wedding was small and in the little white Baptist church, the only one in the county. Her much older half sister Janelle took the photos, using a succession of disposable cameras. The man's parents were dead; the rest of his people lived in southern Indiana and couldn't afford the trip. No one knew how to get hold of the girl's father. Her mom, citing tradition, refused to give her away. That role was played by the organist's surprised husband, who didn't even have long pants on. Shorts, dark socks. The girl wasn't stupid. She understood how this looked. But she held her head high and walked down the aisle with her eyes on the mural of the crucified Jesus. *Please,* she thought. *Please.*

The reception was held under the deluxe aluminum awning of the cousin's double-wide, in the town's nicest trailer court, which happened to be owned by the tall boy's grandfather. (If you enjoy meanwhiles, picture the tall boy riding It's a Small World, fighting with his little brother, Todd, and not thinking about the girl.) The man had told the girl they'd have their honeymoon in the new Ramada Inn up by the Ohio Turnpike, but as they drove there, he said it was booked. They'd be staying across the road at the Seashell Motel, which was thousands of miles from any sea. The only time she'd ever been in a motel was that trip to Gatlinburg and the Great Smoky Mountains, when she, Janelle, her mom, and Janelle's daddy (Mr. Dixon, who was back in the picture there for a while) all piled into one room with a king-sized bed in a newly remodeled Knight's Inn near Pigeon Forge, Tennessee.

The man parked his truck by their door. He carried in the luggage: hers, an old mint-green piece of hard-sided Samsonite; his, two plastic bags from Kroger's, one with clothes, the other full of sixteen-ounce cans of Bud Light beer. She stood at the threshold, dressed in new beige slacks and a matching knit blouse. She fingered her ring. "Oh, Mr. Man?" she said. "You forget something?"

The man already had the cable TV on, his tie off, his shirt unbuttoned, and was sprawled on the threadbare chenille bedspread, sipping beer and watching the Detroit Tigers play baseball. He moaned and mentioned a bad back that she hadn't known about and painkillers he hadn't told her he was on. But as he begged off, he called her *baby*. She smiled, let herself in, and locked the door behind her.

The place had been built in a time when Formica was dark and plentiful. There was no telephone. The curtains had Southern belles and mansions on them. The air-conditioning was a dripping window unit. Over the bed hung a big framed piece of cardboard with painted seashells glued to it in the shape of an Indian-chief head. The room was clean. The girl dragged her suitcase into the bathroom and put the hook in the eye to lock the door. She faced the mirror. She stared into her own eyes as she took off her clothes, applied perfumes and powders and ointments and decided to leave in the side pouch of the suitcase the diaphragm her mom had insisted she get and that the girl had been humiliated to be fitted for. She was married. God would provide.

She began to cry, though not so loud as to be heard over the sound of the TV and AC. The girl rarely cried. She'd cried the day after her daddy came into her room one night smelling of whiskey and stood silent and still at the foot of her bed for a long time. She felt a menace she could not name or anticipate, though all that happened was he finished his drink and left the empty glass on her dresser and got into that Camaro he was so proud of and left town to take a job with a company that did door-to-door baby photos, or so his letter said. The girl was only six then. When her mother read her that letter, that's when the girl cried. Long sobs that hurt her rib cage. He didn't say where the company was located, and neither the girl nor her mom had heard from him since, during which time the girl found it hard to cry anymore. Even last year when her grandmother died—the woman who cooked for her, watched her after school, and taught her how to play guitar—the girl didn't cry. Even now, in the bathroom at the Seashell Motel, where many women before her had looked into that small mirror and cried, she didn't cry for too awful long. She fixed her makeup, slipped into the pink nightgown her half sister had lent her, unhooked the door, and saw the man asleep on the bed.

"Baby?" she said. "Hey, baby." She turned off the TV set, which woke him up.

"Hey," he said. "I was watching that." Then he caught sight of her and said, "Whoa."

The curtains were open. She didn't have the nerve to close them, because of what that meant, but she didn't want to leave them open, because someone walking by might see.

No time for that. They got naked as babies. The man pinned her to the bedspread, didn't even pull down the covers, and the bristles of his thin mustache scratched her lips. Down there, he was hard, jabbing, grunting from his failure. The girl had thought she knew what to do, but she couldn't move and couldn't find any words. She closed her eyes. She asked Jesus to make this turn out okay, to help her husband thrust himself inside her, fill her with his seed, so she might know the joys of married love.

Abruptly, the man, her husband, threw himself on his back and said an ugly word. He'd gone soft. He cupped his hand around the back of her head, lifted it up and pressed it down his chest and his stomach to where he wanted it. She opened her mouth and received him. He kept his hand planted on the back of her head, fingers twined in her dull hair, and she performed for him their first act of love as man and wife. After, he went to sleep. Darkness fell. With the taste of him still in her mouth she curled up against him, shivering, still atop the bedspread. She kept meaning to get up and close the curtains, but she didn't want to wake him. She did not sleep. At dawn, he awoke, went to the bathroom, came back to bed without brushing his teeth, climbed on her, and they just couldn't. This simple human act, and they couldn't manage to fit themselves together. The girl blamed herself and satisfied her husband again the only way she could think of. Again he fell asleep. Later that morning, he woke up, got dressed, said he'd be right back, and left. She got under the covers. Still she was shivering. He came back with a big jar of Vaseline. He stripped, pulled back the sheets, took a fist-sized dollop of Vaseline, and slathered it over her and inside her. This time when he got on top and poked at her, it worked. She could hardly feel him, for all the Vaseline. Only the weight of this grimacing, wiry man on top of her. This stranger, her husband. She looked up at the water stains on the ceiling, looking for Jesus' face or any sort of sign. Then her husband yelled as if he'd been shot and for some reason pulled himself out of her and wrapped his hand around his own penis, pumping it madly while his seed dribbled out, gray pearls that fell onto the adorable paunch of her stomach.

Outside, there was applause and male and female laughter. Someone *had* seen! Her husband stood up, shouted more ugly words, and yanked closed the curtains. Car doors slammed.

"I love you," the girl whispered. She blinked back tears. For a long time the man was quiet. Finally he said, "Back atcha, baby doll." He got her a wet washcloth so she could clean herself up, got himself a beer, switched on the color TV, to a game show, and sat there shouting out wrong answers.

They barely touched or talked. They didn't even eat until late that afternoon, when they showered and got dressed and walked over to the Ramada Inn.

"I'm so sorry." He reached his hand across the table. "I'm not as . . . ," he said. "I mean, I know you wanted me to teach you, but..." He looked across the restaurant, as if the sneeze guard at the salad bar were the most interesting thing ever.

The girl squeezed her husband's hand. "It's okay," she said. "Everything will be all right."

He did not look at her.

"But can I tell you something?" Finally, he looked at her. She scrunched her nose and, in a whisper, said she didn't like it, that Vaseline. She couldn't wash it completely off. She could still feel it, oozing out of her. "Let's do it naturally." She tried to smile. "We'll learn, together, how to be man and wife, the way God intended."

All the man could do was nod.

When the waitress came, he said they'd both have the all-you-care-to-eat chicken. Afterward, he was shocked at the size of the bill. He was the one who'd ordered four four-dollar Heineken beers. The girl just had water. "Here's the first secret I'm telling you, man to wife," he said, getting up to pay. "They weren't booked up here. It just cost too much." He shrugged. "Hope you understand."

"I do," she said, for the second time in two days. She didn't mean it.

They spent another night and day at the Seashell Motel. The more she got to know him, the more he seemed like a stranger. Nothing got better. He lost more and more patience, drank can after can of Bud Light beer. Her jaw muscles burned with pain. Right before they checked out, he climbed onto her and tried again, and again it didn't work, and he raised his fist and looked like he was going to punch her. He didn't punch her. He stopped himself. He slapped himself on the top of his head, again and again and again.

All she said was, "We're through." She knew from watching talk shows that if he raised the fist once, he'd raise it again, and eventually when he lowered it, it would not be his own head he was hitting. She did not cry.

The man, her husband, begged for mercy. Broke into tears and swore it would never happen again. After more of this than she'd have thought he had in him, she relented. They were charged extra for late checkout, which was all the man could talk about on their drive to his apartment, up over someone's garage. Her mom had packed her things—clothes, AM-FM radio, and the guitar—and left them sitting on the wooden steps to the apartment. Fortunately, it had not rained. Under her breath, the girl praised God for small mercies.

This time the girl did not stand waiting at the threshold. She went inside first. She took out the guitar and rubbed its warm, battered wood and sat on the beer-smelling couch and stared out the window at the main house, where the landlords, she hoped, had nice lives. The phone rang. The man answered. Sure, he said, give him five minutes. He kissed her good-bye with his scratchy mouth closed and left to go meet the boys. She watched his truck disappear around the corner. She tried to write a song, but the words wouldn't happen. Even when she tried singing old songs her grandmother had taught her, the girl kept forgetting the lyrics. She kept thinking of the fist the man, her husband, raised against her. She couldn't sing anything, not even hymns.

BY THE TIME she and the man had failed at love so often they gave up trying and the man had raised his fist once more (though still not hit her) and the girl had canceled her appointment at the doctor's to see what might be wrong with her and had instead packed her things, left her wedding ring on top of the TV, and got a ride to her mom's house from her older half sister, Janelle, and her mom called Minister Steve to see if it was possible to get an annulment, but he said, sorry, once *does* count—by then, the girl had missed the first two months of the tenth grade.

She reenrolled under her new name, was given a locker surrounded by seniors, and found herself in classes with "general" in the title. The tall boy had a locker among the other sophomores and was taking college-prep everything. Once in a while, they'd make eye contact in the hall. He never said anything, but he always smiled and nodded. She smiled back. Seeing him was like opening a dresser drawer and finding a dear, forgotten toy—broken, useless, still there.

She worked hard to catch up. One teacher told her to find a study partner, but her old girlfriends treated her like bad marriage was a virus they could catch from her. Another teacher told her to bear down; high school was a new world, more complicated than junior high. A time when you learn that everything you knew is wrong. She heard this and shook her head. She could teach these teachers some things.

At night, she sat in her mom's house with the kitchen and TV-room TVs both on, gnawing inkpens and staring at the route Magellan took around the world or at story problems starring people with names like Jacinto, LaShawnda, and Emiko. She couldn't keep her mind on it. She kept waiting for the man, her husband, to beg her to come home. To say they needed to talk. To say he was sorry. But he never called, never stopped by. Sometime that fall, according to the girl's mom's cousin, he was a no-show at the Chinese-food factory, his things were gone from his apartment over the garage, and that was all anyone knew. Southern Indiana, the girl guessed, where his people were. She took out that BP road map. How many trips to, say, the package store right over the Michigan line does it take to equal a trip to let's say Evansville, Indiana? She never got story problems like this, ones that seemed worth the trouble. Her attention strayed to the TV. Her favorites were the reality shows: rescues, mysteries, heroes, funny videos. She disliked comedies, all those fake, pretty people in fake, faraway cities like New York, Los Angeles, Seattle, and even Cleveland. Her mom made them watch doctor shows, lawyer shows, and, worst of all, those shows where everyone is in high school forever. Luckily her mom was only home two nights a week.

One day walking home from school, a warm day for early winter, the girl ran into the tall boy coming out of the library. Who knew why, but he said hello, she said hello back, he asked if it'd be okay to walk her home, and she said, sure, why not? They talked about the school basketball team and the tall boy's fastest swimming times and what music he hated on the radio (nearly all of it). When they got to her house, she asked if the tall boy would like to know what had happened to her. He said he thought he sort of knew. Her new name gave it away.

"Well, I'm getting it annulled," she said, which was still a possibility. Her mom was arguing that man's law is not God's law and that once didn't have to count, that the girl should go to court and forget about that once. "It's different from divorced. It's like it never happened, the marriage."

At that word, *marriage,* the tall boy flinched.

But he followed her into her house. They drank Kroger's brand cola and talked about small things. When he thought he needed to get home for dinner, he stopped at the door and turned around. She was right behind him. They kissed. She watched him run home. When she saw him actually jump up in the air and kick up his heels, she laughed.

They started seeing each other again, more on the sly than ever. They'd meet at her house, under the crumbling bleachers at Park Stadium, and in groves of pine trees on the edge of town. Sometimes he wrote papers for her or did her math, careful to do C work—though, really, who'd have suspected? No one from the tall boy's life seemed to know the girl existed. Plus, by now, the schoolwork the girl did on her own had improved. But the secret kissing and groping became a habit.

What did they do? Not *it*. The boy wasn't even pushing for it. They ground their clothed bodies together. The tall boy slipped his clammy hands under the girl's ill-fitting bras. At most, he put his finger inside her and, with rank ineptitude, tried to pleasure her; she would let him know, sometimes, that this was sinful. She reached inside his jeans and grabbed him through his underwear and made him come. (He was four-teen; a strong breeze could do the same.) Then the tall boy would clean himself up and the girl would talk about Jesus, sin, adultery, hell, fornication, and country music songs sung by thin, pretty women. After that, he'd walk home. She imag-ined him, halfway to that nice brick house where she still had never been, hearing a siren and breaking into a run, thinking she'd called the cops, that the bright future his parents were forcing on him was going to blow up.

He'd once been dumb enough to confess this to her.

As school wound down, the girl got a job at a church camp in the Irish Hills of Michigan, farther north than she'd ever been. That's nice, said the tall boy. He'd be busy, too, what with working in his parents' store and, especially, the summer swim team. Hovering unstated between them was the fact she was still married. So again, they broke it off. This hadn't been a part of their daily lives, after all, just a strange, sweet thing, shiny with guilt, along the edges of what it was to be sopho-mores in a small town in Ohio.

At camp, the girl's job was to serve meals in the dining cabin and to clean up. In exchange, she attended camp for free: Bible study, canoeing, making string-art pictures of Jesus, shooting arrows at hay bales, and sneaking out of the cabin at midnight to smoke cigarettes and drink fortified wine on the beach of a mossy pond and then, the next morning, praying for forgiveness. She told the counselors not to call her *Mrs.,* since her marriage was getting annulled. Word got out, but the idea that a girl in one of those bleak cabins had been married—married!—was hard to believe. When kids asked her, she laughed and said nothing. At the nightly bonfires, she played her old guitar along with the two music majors, from a Bible college in West Virginia, who'd been hired to lead the singing. She was as good as either of them. She wanted to sing her own songs (it's easy to change a song about *loving him* to one about *loving Him*), but she never got the nerve. She sang her songs alone in the woods behind the dining cabin, in the half hour of free time after she finished the lunch dishes. The last week of camp, she and one of the music majors, a red-headed man with a beard, wrote a song about the camp that mixed names of the counselors and campers in with those of Bible characters. When they finished, he leaned toward her and kissed her. She kissed him back, then caught herself, pulled away, and reminded him she was married. He asked for forgiveness. She said he had to ask God for that. When it came time to perform the song in public, the girl played guitar and did not sing.

When she got home, she saw in the paper that the swim team had finished third in their championship meet. The tall boy had won two events. She called him. "Congratulations," she said.

"For what?"

"Your swimming."

"Oh," he said. "That."

His voice was so dead she had to think fast, to save face. "My annulment went through," she lied. "Can you come over?"

"What does that mean?" he asked.

She could tell he was thrilled and afraid. "It means," she said, "just what you think it means."

There was a long pause. "I'm not sure I think anything."

He was so dumb! "Just come over, okay?"

"I will," he said, "if I can. My parents need me this week at the store."

He did not come by. The girl wasn't sure if she was surprised or relieved.

She'd already lied and told the boy she was annulled. Was it worse to go before the law of man and—advised by her own mom that once didn't count—say the marriage hadn't been consummated?

One afternoon, a week before Labor Day, before their junior year was to start, the tall boy showed up at the girl's house, riding a fifteen-speed racing bicycle. That was just like him, not to get a mountain bike and be like everyone else. Except the girl herself, who didn't know how to ride a bicycle.

"I was in the neighborhood," he said. "Riding around and stuff."

"I'm sort of busy," she said. She'd been watching a comedy show about a rich man with a butler and three orphans, marveling that anyone, anywhere, had ever found this funny.

The tall boy asked about her summer. She said it was fine. She asked about his. It was fine.

"So," he said. He was still standing astride his bike.

"Want some water?" she said.

He tugged the skin of his throat. "Yeah," he said. "I'm parched."

Parched? That was what it was about this boy. Not just the racing bicycle. No one she knew said *parched.* When he was with her, she let herself think he was a boy who could take her out of their town to a place where people have nice lawns, personal computers, and fragile bicycles, and men don't leave, and everyone has brainy kids who grow up to say *parched.*

The tall boy chugged two glasses of water. They sat on the couch in the TV room and watched a show about crazy people stuck on an island. "A three-hour tour," the boy said. "Why would they have all that luggage for a three-hour tour? Why would they have *any* luggage?"

"Beats me," said the girl. "I've never even been on a boat."

Canoes at the camp, yes. But that wasn't what he was talking about, canoes.

They got back to their old ways. This time when she touched him, it wasn't through his underwear. As he left, he said that his parents and his little brother, Todd, were going away that weekend. "If you want to, like, stop over, that'd be okay."

Saturday morning, the girl got dressed in a yellow bikini that some of the other girls at the camp had said she looked good in. She told herself maybe she'd go for a swim at the public pool, which was on the west side. She pulled tight cut-offs over her bikini bottom and took a towel. It wasn't such a long walk. She went barefoot. It was the end of summer.

The tall boy was in his driveway, shooting baskets. He saw her, put the ball away, closed the garage, showed her into the house, locked the door, took the girl in his arms, and kissed her. She asked what he thought he was doing. "Really, I have no idea," he said. "That's the gospel truth."

Was that blasphemous? Or reverent? "I have no idea, either," she said.

The house was just a house, but it was so up-to-date and *nice*, as if, in preparation for her visit, it had been painted, carpeted, remodeled, and spring-cleaned. "Have you read all these books?" she said. One living-room wall was lined with bookshelves, crammed full. At her house, the lone small bookcase was strewn with Avon decanters and commemorative shot glasses.

"Some," he said. "They're my parents' books."

Before they knew it, they were in each other's arms and their clothes were coming off as if peeled by a divine hand. In times past, the tall boy had glimpsed the girl's nipples and had often had her pants unzipped but not pulled down. The girl had seen the tall boy in a tiny Speedo and had her hand on his penis. This was the first time they'd been naked together.

It was the girl's second naked and aroused man, the boy's first naked and aroused girl, yet they hardly looked anywhere except into each other's eyes. He pulled her gently down onto the rich gray carpeting, so thickly padded it felt nicer than a bed. "What do you think you're doing?" she whispered.

And the tall boy grimly said, "I have no idea."

By then, they knew where this was leading. They rolled around and touched each other. They moved their hands in hapless, fumbling arcs over the curves of their unformed bodies. They kept looking at each other, and it reassured the girl to see fear in the tall boy's eyes. Suddenly, moved by some unseen spirit, the boy rolled the girl onto her back and began to jab himself at her.

"I'm sorry," she said. "I may have a problem."

He was trembling. She told him she'd had problems before, with the man, problems they'd taken days and been unable to solve. The tall boy stopped moving but remained on top of her. Their naked skin pressed lightly together.

"Maybe it's wrong," she said, "for us to do this."

"You mean you never?" he said.

"Once," she said. "Only the once."

He looked lost. He kept starting to say something. They still weren't looking upon their nakedness, just into each other's eyes, and that, probably, was what made the girl reach down and take hold of the boy, inexpertly jabbing herself with his penis. Suddenly he was in. She said, "Oh!" He also said, "Oh!" They looked into each other like the terrified children they were, but now it was too late. She thought to twitch her hips. His eyes were open so wide. Her hips started doing a little more than twitching. The boy was on top, but he was frozen. She slowed down a little, and the boy pulled out and came all over that cute, round stomach.

He rolled over. He had his smooth back to her. The girl looked up at the smooth ceiling. Everything in his world was smooth. He got up and got her a warm washcloth and gently cleaned her. "I'm sorry," he said.

"It's okay," she said.

"No," he said. "I'm really, really sorry."

This time, she didn't say it was okay. They got dressed. She wished she'd worn a T-shirt over her bikini top. She found the bath towel she'd brought from home and draped it around her neck.

"I'm sorry," the boy whispered.

She realized that because she hadn't said it was okay, he was starting to wonder if he was going to get in trouble. Saying it was okay would make him feel better. She felt womanly not to say it. She got up to leave. The tall boy followed, begging her to tell him what was wrong. She told herself she wasn't going to say anything.

"Please," the boy said. "I don't know why, what I'm feeling but..." He asked her to sit down, on a bench in the mudroom. She looked out the window, counted to ten, to make him sweat, then sat.

The tall boy kneeled. "I don't know who to tell," he said. "I don't know who to talk to." He told a story about his best friend Jason Hartsock, a boy from the swim team and the college-prep classes, whose mother, the tall boy said, was dying of cancer.

The girl hardly knew Jason Hartsock. She did not know that his mother was dying of anything. It was a cheap plea for sympathy. She wanted to go home.

But the boy went on and on about the homemade bread Mrs. Hartsock used to make and give to her friends, and about how great it made the Hartsocks' house smell, and how his mother and Mrs. Hartsock talked endlessly on the phone or, together, over endless cups of coffee, and how Jason's big brother Bret had said that if his mother died, he didn't see how he could believe in God anymore.

For some reason, the girl was not shocked. Instead, she let the boy rest his head on her lap. She stroked his hair, and he kept talking about how Jason Hartsock had started going to parties and drinking twenty-plus bottles of Little Kings Cream Ale. When anyone said anything to Jason Hartsock about his mother, he'd change the subject and talk about sports, even golf.

The boy started to cry. The girl kept stroking his hair. Who ever saw a boy so big cry so long?

When he finished, he washed his face, and they stood in the mudroom and gave each other a hug. They kissed good-bye. He said good-bye. She said okay.

The girl stopped at the pool, paid her admission, and set up her towel on the cement sundeck. She took off her shorts. She lay there all afternoon in that yellow bikini. No one talked to her. She was happy about that. She tried to write a song in her head, a song about men. She ought to at least get a song out of all this. But it was hard to write anything without her guitar.

And so she got up and, ignoring the lifeguard's shrill whistle, climbed the steps to the high dive. She had never once done this before. For one thing, the high dive was closed except to the diving team. For another, she could barely swim. But she was good at floating, more so since she'd become a woman. The swimming instructor at camp had said this was natural.

When the girl got to the top, the lifeguard was screaming at her. She walked straight to the end of the board and jumped awkwardly off, closing her eyes and plugging her nose. She crashed into the water. It felt cold and harsh against her sunburned body.

Underwater, she opened her eyes.

Underwater, she asked God to show her the way.

Can You hear me, God, from underwater?

She felt her feet touch the smooth painted bottom of the diving well. A sharp pounding feeling pushed at her ears. She wanted to stay underwater until she saw her sign. Surely God would at least send the angry lifeguard into the pool to save her? Her lungs began to burn. She felt a kind of gulping spasm in her throat. Her body betrayed her: She began to float toward the bright light of the surface.

MINISTER STEVE WAS full of it. Courts disapprove of a person under the age of consent avoiding a consummated marriage, but the general rule is to grant an annulment as a matter of right. Allowable grounds include mental incompetency, intoxication, impotence, venereal disease, non-consummation, bigamy, incest, fraud, duress, lack of mutual consent, or that the underage spouse feels he or she made a mistake. Once the girl walked into the legal-aid office, things fell smoothly in place.

The girl was married once more before she finished high school. She had the baby, went to summer school, and graduated with her class. She is still married. She lives in the small town. Four kids. At that little Baptist church, on the third Sunday of every month, she sings her own songs.

She never saw her father again (he sells new house trailers at a sales lot in a certain suburb of Las Vegas, Nevada, that will remain nameless) or her first husband either (he died a while ago, off the coast of the Florida panhandle, while trying to save a buddy who'd gotten a little drunk, hooked a tarpon, and fallen overboard). The day the tall boy wept in his parents' mudroom was the last time he and the girl ever spoke. (He is currently writing a pilot for a TV show set in a candy factory in a small town in Ohio; he has not set foot in his hometown since his parents retired to live near his brother Todd, who is the youngest mayor in the history of one particular suburb of

Phoenix, Arizona.) Mrs. Hartsock died a slow, hideous death. Jason Hartsock and the tall boy went to different colleges and lost touch. Bret Hartsock got up in the middle of his mother's funeral, said an ugly word, and stormed out. He no longer believes in God.

Tales of
Academic Lunacy
1991–2001

I

The Visiting Poet

It is 1991. Until now, Murtaugh has lived life amassing the sort of history, carriage, and mystique that makes blooming, disaffected women imagine themselves in bed with him. This is no easy job. At its expense, checkbooks go unbalanced and student poems go unread. Upkeep on his rented lodgings goes unkept. Phone calls to his daughters go unmade. Calls from them go unreturned. He does mean well. He loves his daughters and displays their pictures. When Tracy and Annie visit, he pulls out all the stops: movies, theme parks, concerts, ball games, rafting, skiing. He is that best and worst of divorced fathers: Mr. Entertainment.

Perhaps—even after the harassment scandal, even after his younger daughter stood hatless in a spring snowstorm and begged him to grow up—he hasn't changed. This year, he took his usual one-year gig at a small college in a small town, where he stars (even at his age) in the usual lunchtime faculty basketball game and where he has the usual classrooms full of Christinas.

That's who takes poetry workshops at pricey church-run schools. Christinas; transpose the eighth and ninth letters and what irony! Willowy Christinas, dressed in black, with too much makeup or none at all. Vegetarians. Recyclers. Smokers. A Christina without the code would be a mere Shannon or Julie, those wholesome diarists who round out his classes, even the prettiest of whom accept their fates as taxpayers and yard-tending neighbors. Christinas are outside time. They exude uninjured, tragic beauty. They are the hippest young women at the squarest old schools, a plight from which Murtaugh offers brief deliverance.

Responsible people might see Murtaugh's life as a dangerous relic from another era. But that's part of it; Christinas like to shock themselves. He beds two or three of them a year. Sometimes one, rarely four, never five. So far never zero. The Christinas find Murtaugh as tragic as he finds them, although their sense of *tragic* is forged by TV, which they claim never to watch. But in bed, he gets them to sing the theme song to *The Brady Bunch*. Never yet has one failed to know the words. A sad thing, this, but he and the Christina laugh. He rests a hand on the lovely dent below her buttocks. She strokes his chest hair, comments upon it. He goes down on her. When she can take no more, she pulls him up by what's left of his hair, handles on each side of his skull. She condomizes him; he enters her. Afterward, he tells her she has talent.

Murtaugh and the Christina then discuss the frauds they know, both at the college and in the world of art. Murtaugh drops names of writers and actresses he's met, drunk with, beaten, and fucked. The Christina summarizes her sexual history. They fall asleep.

The scandal disrupted all this. Exhibit A: he's been here two months. He's had the chance to bed a Christina, an unusually busty one named Emma, with gray eyes and a knack for villanelles. She had her hand on his crotch, and he let the moment pass.

So maybe Murtaugh *has* changed. But into what? If he could answer that, he'd have changed a long time ago.

LAST YEAR, MURTAUGH'S gig was at a huge research institution out in one of those rectangular states, a place where people get lost, the last place you'd expect people to be in your business.

Her name was Jill and she was no Christina. She was half Cherokee, half Irish, and six feet tall, two inches taller than Murtaugh. They met after a reading by an old confederate of Murtaugh's who, like most of that circle, had quit booze, achieved tenure, and married a plain-looking lawyer.

Jill wore go-go boots and earth tones, which should have tipped off her true identity. Academics rarely dress like grown-ups. It's like the old joke: why do dogs lick their genitals? Because they can. Same deal with academics. Few could hold down real-world jobs, fewer yet could dress the part. People in academia comport themselves as they do simply because they can.

Or *could*, then.

But Murtaugh mistook Jill for a student, which she looked young enough to be. She turned out to be a newly tenured thirty-two-year-old associate professor of music. He didn't learn this until after they'd slept together. Murtaugh had her pegged as a closet poet. In fact, she hadn't attempted a poem since fifth grade. It took him weeks to find out she'd grown up in the Ozarks and SAT'd her way into Harvard, where, presumably, she affected that Brahmin accent. He read her superficially, as quick to pigeonhole as the lit-crit colleagues he reviled.

Jill could play the hell out of the piano—classical, honky-tonk, anything—which she did their first night at his place, a sublet from a dean on leave, the usual farmhouse with a baby grand. Murtaugh had never seen a tall nude woman at the piano. She lit a candle and played, her long hair sweat-damp and mussed, back straight, breasts cast into relief by the flickering light, her deft fingers a metaphor for Jill herself.

The next day, Murtaugh wrote a poem about her fingers. He showed it to Jill. She found it sexist. Three weeks later, it was accepted by a national magazine. He started writing a series of poems about her body. Magazines snapped them up. He wrote a poem about her heart, based upon an incident in which he and Jill snuck into the med school and did it on an examining table, in a room ringed by chest X rays. *Playboy* paid Murtaugh five hundred dollars for it.

After Christmas break, he invited Jill to move in with him. She accepted. He continued to bed the occasional off-campus Christina. For a while, a good time was had by all.

THIS YEAR, MURTAUGH also has the usual forlorn Ricks. Here's their Ur-poem: A *sensitif* looks into a hot red car, past an unworthy jock, to the jock's stunning, captive girlfriend. The last lines concern walking into the wind on a rainy day. Rare is the Christina who falls for that. The best a Rick can hope for is a one-nighter, and it'll be the Rick who gets used and dumped. Ricks should find a nice Pam or Lisa from over in the business wing; get married and underemployed; have kids; purchase a minivan, a house, and a family pass to the zoo; grow miserable; get a paunch and a divorce; lose everything; and get on with it. Even then, they won't be able to bed Christinas. They'll be fat, bitter, and desperate. Three strikes; grab some bench.

Ominously, one of this semester's Ricks has talent. Worse, he's thick-skinned, athletic, and—in that corn-fed, midwestern way—confident. One day, the Rick (whose name is John

Kilgore) catches Murtaugh after class, and they work interminably on a passably adept poem. They seem at last to be done, but the Rick won't leave.

"I don't know," the Rick says, stammering. "It's like, I don't know how to say it, to ask this, to ask you what I, like, need to." He looks at his shoes. Scuffed black penny-loafers. Kid'll go far. "But, well, Dr. Murtaugh, have you—"

"Mister," Murtaugh says. "I'm not a doctor." Murtaugh hates being called doctor. He is a master of fine arts with four well-received books. That, he intones, is what entitles him to be a professor. He does in fact have a Ph.D., but even when he applies for these visiting gigs (he is more often invited, as was the case here), he conceals this residue from his past.

"Whatever," says the Rick. "What I'm trying to ask is if you were ever married." He points. "No ring. But I wondered."

Murtaugh frowns. "Why do you want to know?"

The Rick says he's engaged and scared he can't earn a living as a writer. Maybe law school? Or is that a sellout? His fiancée said she'd give him the time and space he needs, but... blah, blah, blah. The Rick gets up. "Sorry. Forget it." He grabs his motorcycle jacket and backpack and leaves, closing the door purposefully behind him.

Murtaugh sizes up the closed door, knocked woozy by the horse hooves of one of God's heavy-handed ironies, the sort of coincidence even poets dare not contrive. It goes like this: once upon a time, Murtaugh, too, was an earnest young man with literary urges and a fiancée, a redhead who is now a buyer for a chain of discount bookstores that do not stock poetry. At the time, he and the woman were in the hormonal bliss that the young mistake for love. Yet Murtaugh took seriously the job of artist and feared how marriage would change him. So, suffused with the zealotry of a good student, the pretense of an overpraised boy, and the panic of a prospective groom, Murtaugh had asked the young professor of his undergraduate fiction workshop the same thing, more or less, that the Rick just inflicted upon Murtaugh.

Looking back, the professor was a cliché of academia: aging golden boy who never published anything beyond his one book of early promise. "You poor bastard," he'd said, leaning back in his squeaky chair, chuckling, twisting his wedding band. "The old life-versus-art question."

Murtaugh, choosing art over love, broke off the engagement. Then, alone, he lost his nerve, became a hobby writer, went to a top-drawer grad school, and got a Ph.D. His dissertation was so tediously clever that he's forgotten what it was about.

MURTAUGH IS SUCH an ugly name that he threw his hands up and ceded his daughters' christenings to his wives. (Murtaugh so rarely uses his own first and middle names that he wouldn't respond to them; his byline involves initials.) The wives, in his opinion, chose good names and raised the girls to be the canny, street-smart beauties you'd expect from girls whose mothers were burned by having once been reckless enough to marry Murtaugh.

His older daughter, Tracy, is seventeen and lost to him. She saw too much: broken plates, ruined holidays, bad arguments in the dark. Murtaugh thought he loved Tracy's mother. They were grad students together, had hoped to get tenure together. Except that she never published word one. Murtaugh, on the other hand, carved his dissertation into six chunks and published them all. It was too easy. Murtaugh started having affairs, which, in memory if not in truth, was tied to his decision to become a poet.

Murtaugh and Tracy's mother took jobs at different schools: he in Boston, she in Cleveland—a commuter marriage. While Tracy's mother volunteered for committees, kept office hours, graded papers, and tried to raise a child more or less alone, Murtaugh neglected the job he'd been hired to do and started writing poems, partly because they were short, partly because he'd started a novel he couldn't finish (he still has it, filed under "Buick Title"). A year later, he snuck off to get an M.F.A. at Columbia. He wrote countless poems on the train; by the time he finished his thesis, every poem in it had been accepted for publication somewhere. The last nail in the marital coffin was a vacation at her parents' lake cottage in Michigan. Murtaugh stashed his teaching assistant (this was his last year in that Boston job) at a motel two towns away. Tracy's mother found out. Tracy witnessed her mother's attempt to drown her father underneath an aluminum dock, which can't be a good thing to see.

When Tracy came to visit last year, she took a quick liking to Jill, who gave Tracy piano lessons and taught her to drive. After the harassment charges hit, Jill called Tracy to explain. Tracy congratulated her. "I'm with *her,* Daddy," Tracy said. "She *had* to tell. I mean, that's dis*gust*ing. At my last school, they fired the band director for that."

Murtaugh started to point out that he had slept with young women who are of age. Then he remembered he was speaking to his daughter, a girl one year from being lawful prey for men like her father. He stopped explaining and tried to apologize.

Apology: he had, with Tracy, gone to that well too many times. She hung up.

His daughter Annie is fourteen and another story. Murtaugh was in one place for the first three years of her life, a time in which he changed diapers, mowed grass, and gave pony rides. That marriage ended well, brought about not by infidelity (Karen never knew) but the strains of their divergent careers. You'd think no one could wind up in two commuter marriages in a lifetime, but a human life tends to be an exercise in what you wouldn't think possible. It was, he and Karen agreed, nobody's fault.

Karen was and is smart (Phi Beta Kappa, sixteenth in her med-school class at Duke, and now a surgeon in Phoenix) and athletic (varsity swimmer in college, triathlete now) and too wonderful for words (patron of the arts, gourmet cook, careful gardener, terrific mother). This wonderfulness was the problem. Men think women like Karen are overcompensating, repressing, or in some way inferior to their beer-swilling selves. Maybe someday men will catch up. Studies suggest not.

When Karen reproduced, did she ever. Annie is Karen only more so, which makes Murtaugh fear for her. At fourteen, she is gorgeous in a coltish way that boys her age are— thank God—too thick to see. She's read *Anna Karenina* and can discuss it more sensitively than any undergraduate Murtaugh has ever had. Taught.

MURTAUGH, THE OLDEST man on the court, takes the ball at the top of the key, holds it in front of him, taunting the taller, younger, history prof assigned to guard him. Murtaugh isn't fast, but at this level, competing against the bitter, myopic white people who staff schools like this, it's enough to be quick. He head feints one way and goes the other, slicing across the lane, past the two other defenders, and in for a layup. "Game," he says.

"I hate myself," says the history professor.

"My bad," says the dean of humanities, a blond priest named Frank. "Should've helped on D." He's thirty-five, too young to be a Frank, too young to be a dean, too hunky to be a priest. He's clearly being groomed for bigger things; priests capable of making it in the real world blast through the ranks. "Good take."

Murtaugh accepts Frank's casual side-five. "Thanks."

"No one with a shot like that," Frank says, "should be on a one-year contract."

Murtaugh laughs—not that this is funny, just that he figures that's how Frank means it, as a joke.

Murtaugh spreads the scoring around. But whenever a game gets tight, he cans one from outside. His team cannot lose.

Afterward, he and Frank hit the weight room and wind up on adjacent treadmills. "Seriously," Frank says. "We need more people with national visibility." Frank is going twice as fast and is half as winded as Murtaugh. "How does full professor sound? With tenure? We can talk money in my office."

Murtaugh shrugs, using his windedness to dodge this bullet.

Frank steps off and admires himself in the mirrored wall. "I know," he whispers, "about the incident with the woman." He mops his brow with a red towel. "Come see me. We'll talk."

LAST YEAR, ON a humid March afternoon, Murtaugh lay sprawled and sated on his living-room floor, alongside a Christina. Her name, as fate would have it, was Christina. She had a fiancé and wouldn't do the actual act, not even oral sex. They'd kissed and dry humped and masturbated each other, then, at her suggestion, taken turns masturbating themselves while the other held on. This was a new one on Murtaugh. He'd found it surprisingly sexy. The Christina's orgasm was a bucking and wondrous thing.

Murtaugh hadn't expected Jill for hours. "Hello," was all she said at first. She stood for a while in the doorway to the kitchen. The Christina covered herself with an afghan. "Have we been introduced? I'm Jill." She shook the young woman's hand. "I live here."

"I'm Christina." She was ash white. "Hi."

Murtaugh rose, hands fig-leafed over his genitals. He nearly claimed this wasn't what it looked like. Instead he took the offensive. "You and I are through, Jill. I found someone else."

He felt like a small, mean animal.

Jill went to pack a suitcase. On her way out, she paused to say a civil good-bye. Dressed now, the Christina sat shivering in a wing chair, her head in her hands. Jill pointed at her. "I know you. You were in my music-ap survey. And I've seen you at readings." She turned to Murtaugh and smiled. "You're through," she said, and left.

FICTION TEACHES YOU that people change. History, experience, and poetry all teach you this is a lie. Murtaugh, who'd fancied himself a novelist, who'd published stories in fine places, grew to be exclusively a poet, reversing the usual pattern.

This did not go uncommented upon. He was working that year at a Lutheran college in Minnesota. A colleague, a married woman named Barbara, sold her first novel for $55,000. Half drunk at someone's retirement party, Barbara announced that she would never write another poem. "The money's on the right margin, Murtaugh."

"But the truth," he said, "is on the left." He stood ramrod straight, a parody of rectitude.

"Fine," she said. "Go left, young man."

Barbara and Murtaugh had an affair. They met at rustic inns, where they spent Barbara's money on sex toys and the repair of antique canopied beds. They went skydiving and had the needy sex couples have after tempting death together.

Are there male Christinas? Murtaugh doubts it, not hetero. Too bad; name an earnest young man who wouldn't benefit from a fling with an older, smarter woman. Women would have fun in Murtaugh's usual position. They'd handle it better. Murtaugh would encourage women to try, but who'd want to bed a Rick?

Speaking of Ricks: John Kilgore got a poem accepted, in a journal that paid him. Murtaugh was ten years older than the kid before he published a poem in as good a place. He'd encouraged the kid to submit, mostly to get rid of him, and now the Rick is awash in gratitude. To celebrate, he throws a party, which Murtaugh is begged to attend.

The Rick lives in a townie neighborhood, in a ramshackle group house. Murtaugh arrives just late enough. Many, many pretty young women are drinking and dancing. A motorcycle is parked in the living room. The Rick rushes to the door to take Murtaugh's leather duster and Brooklyn Dodgers cap. Murtaugh keeps them on, claiming he can't stay. But the costume is part of the persona.

He spots two women he presumes he can have, a Christina from his Tuesday workshop and some psych-major Kimberly whom he's never seen before. She eyes him but good. That he and the Kimberly eventually leave together, can you call that change?

JILL HAD DISCOUNTED the rumors about Murtaugh and students until she'd seen a smoking gun. After that, she hunted down leads like a good scholar, finding all three Christinas he'd bedded that year. One he'd been with only twice. She was unstable, and Murtaugh tried not to sleep with anyone crazier than he was. The woman had subsequently convinced herself she'd slept with Murtaugh to raise her grade. That was all Jill needed.

The truth was, Murtaugh slept with the Christinas because they were going to get As, not the other way around. But he gave the committee what it wanted: the facts, not the truth.

Yes, he had slept with the women in question. No, it had not affected anyone's grade. Yes, he knew he had shown poor judgment. "But with all due respect," he said, as decorously as he was able, "could someone show me what policy or law I violated?"

He had them dead to rights. The policy was a morass of committee-encoded double-talk that could mean anything but in fact meant nothing. Had the school possessed the guts to adopt a direct policy (say: *amorous activity between faculty members and enrolled students is unethical; unethical faculty members will be fired*), they'd have had him. But no institution in academia is that direct. In those days, before the humorless aging hippies who run these places fully implemented their agenda of rigid leftist sanctimony, rarely was anyone in Murtaugh's position in real danger of getting in real danger.

LAST YEAR, ANNIE came to visit him during her Easter break, as she always does. He had not told her about the harassment thing; he was using her as an escape from all that.

He picked her up at the town's four-terminal airport, and they embarked on the usual fusillade of fun: college baseball, the Cowboy Hall of Fame, a rib burn-off, a rock concert by a band Murtaugh's age in an arena 215 miles away. On the drive back from that, Annie stared out the window of his old station wagon, a T-shirt and souvenir program in her lap. "I want to know," she said after a hundred miles of empty chatting, "who you are."

The rain had turned to spring snow.

Murtaugh pretended to be confused by the question.

"I come all the way out here," she said, "and all I get is a tour guide. What's next? The zoo?"

Lucky guess. "I don't get to see you that much, honey. I want us to have fun together, sweetie."

"I want you to be a dad," Annie said. She turned in her seat to face him, a lawyer pleading her case. "Why don't we ever rake leaves or go grocery shopping, or, like, wallpaper the half bath?"

"It's not my house. I can't very well wallpaper the half bath in somebody else's house."

Annie swore at him and went into the kind of adolescent funk Tracy used to affect. They rode the rest of the way home in silence, through wet snow that piled up before you knew it. Murtaugh wondered if class would be canceled. It was—for only the third time in the school's history.

In the morning, Murtaugh made pancakes. If domestic was what Annie wanted, that's what she'd get. She still wasn't talking. She sat at the oak dinette, hunched over Murtaugh's copy of *Death in Venice,* handling her silverware with the efficiency of a surgeon's daughter. "Why don't you get a newspaper?" she said.

"They don't deliver the *Times.* And the local rag's a rag."

"I need a sports section. Spring training." Another flash of Karen, who is a walking encyclopedia of baseball.

Murtaugh drove Annie to the Safeway at the edge of town and handed her fifty cents. She rolled her eyes. "I got it." She returned with copies of *USA Today* and the local daily.

They were the only car on the road. The snow kept coming down in flakes the size of dimes. He let her out by the front steps and parked the car in the barn. For a long time, he sat listening to the ticking of cooling metal and the rustle of barn sparrows. Annie was right; he'd gotten into the habit of being a certain way, so much so that he couldn't think how to turn things around. But if he lost her, what then? How low can you go?

As he walked to the house, he saw her. She'd just come outside, without a hat or a coat, a section of the local paper held before her like a torch to ward off beasts. She was crying.

"I can't believe you," she said, as menacing as a thirteen-year-old can be. "I cannot fucking believe you."

He stopped in his tracks. He nearly told her to watch her mouth, as if he were the one with the upper hand. But he knew what had happened, what she'd read.

"I don't know you," Annie said. Snow had already covered her head. From where Murtaugh stood, it looked like the news had shocked her hair white. "I don't want to know you. It's like you're this person, this terrible person, who doesn't believe the rules apply to you. Jesus, Murtaugh, would you please, please, *please* just grow the fuck up?"

JILL HAD GOADED the unstable Christina into going to the school paper, which had, thus prompted, done a series of articles on sexual harassment, in which they named names. Other papers, and TV stations, picked it up. In the middle of all that, when Murtaugh feared he might never live things down, might never escape from himself, he'd been invited to this sad little school back east. It felt, at first, like a pardon from the governor. And he was off.

Once, Murtaugh would have argued that people never truly change. Perhaps it's just wishful thinking, but now he'd argue otherwise. This, ipso facto, represents change, doesn't it? Maybe Murtaugh has been too long in academia, home of the split hair.

If change is possible, Murtaugh is certain it's not linear. He's had moments this year of progress and regress. He's tried mending fences. Tracy was warmer to his overtures than he'd expected. He calls her every Wednesday night, and he's only forgotten twice all year. She goes to a third-rate non-resident coed prep school and thinks she might major in accountancy. Seventeen years old and that's what she says: "accountancy."

Annie went back to Phoenix and did not speak to him for months. He'd call and she'd hang up. He asked Karen for advice. "Give it time," Karen said. "She's as angry as they come, right now, and part of it might be her age." He heard a sad smile in Karen's voice. "But most of it's just you."

Murtaugh gave up on the telephone and began mailing her a letter every Monday. He vowed to keep it up whether she ever replied: for the rest of his life, if need be. After a few weeks, he stopped getting around to it. In November, Annie sent him a birthday card. "I wouldn't have minded it if you'd have begged a little more," she'd written. "But I'm ready to be your daughter again. This must mean I'm even crazier than you are, since I doubt you'll ever really be ready to be my dad." The letter included six lines from a Stevie Smith poem.

FRANK CLOSES HIS office door, presses a slip of paper into Murtaugh's palm and motions for him to sit. On the paper is a number, half again what Murtaugh now earns. "Have a Frangelico," the dean says. Two cordials are already poured. It's noon. "It's a new thing I've started doing when I have visitors."

"I'll pass." Murtaugh points to his tennis clothes in demurral. He has a court date with Annie, who is in town and waiting outside. "I warn you," he says. "I'm on leave all the time. I don't serve on committees. I don't counsel students. I don't fill out self-evaluations. I don't respect authority. And if you're not careful, I might take you up on your hastily tendered offer."

Frank laughs. "Writers," he says. "You creative writers." Priests go on retreats to learn fake badinage. He downs his drink and picks up the other glass. "Between men now: this sexual harassment madness these days is really something, isn't it?"

What do you say to that? Murtaugh nods. "Something."

"Women can say anything at all. People find scandal inherently believable. What defense do you have?"

"None," Murtaugh says. He has become the world's foremost authority on delivering the right answer.

"This used to be an all-boys college. Once, half the faculty were Jesuits. Now, five percent. I often feel I was born too late." He walks to the window, dreamy as an old dog. "I'd have been more at home in another era," Frank says. "The nineteen forties, let's say. Don't you decry the demise of men's hats?"

Murtaugh smiles. This is the first time he has heard anyone say the word *decry*. Despite himself, he does like Frank.

Frank picks up the faculty newsletter ("C.V. Guide"), in which Murtaugh mentioned his collection, *Nude Pianist: New and Selected Poems,* coming out from Knopf. "We don't get people publishing like this. That must change. You can help pave the way."

"Ah," Murtaugh says.

"I've seen everything. The newspaper accounts of everything." He turns and sighs, exasperated. "I know how women can be."

Murtaugh is so close to laughter that he bites his cheek. But because Annie's on his mind, the mention of the newspapers stings.

"I don't want to know if those allegations are true," Frank says. "I don't want to know anything you don't want to tell me. Except this. This and only this." He refills his glass, to the brim. "Why on God's green earth have you moved around so much?"

Murtaugh is caught short. This should have been a question he had been asked before, a question he had asked of himself, but it's neither. Moving around is who he is, a force of his nature. His circumstances have allowed it, and when they haven't, he's altered his circumstances. At first, he affects a bad-boy grin. Then he lets it fade, dropping the role and telling the truth: "I don't know."

He accepts the offer of tenure.

MURTAUGH BOUNDS DOWN the steps of the administration building, past a rusting brown sculpture of Saint Joseph.

Annie will be happy to hear this news, he's sure of that.

When he catches sight of her, she's sitting on the tailgate of his beat-up old station wagon, dressed in a blue Phoenix Firebirds hat and a plain black T-shirt. She's smoking a cigarette. Beside her, holding what is undoubtedly a stack of some new poems Murtaugh will have to read, is John Kilgore, also smoking. His motorcycle is parked beside the wagon. Annie and Kilgore each have their legs crossed toward the other's. She is holding his helmet, rubbing it, and they're laughing. Murtaugh stays in stride, making his way toward his daughter, moving through the sunlight as if it were water, overcoming the urge to run—to her or away, he's not sure which impulse is stronger.

II

The Untenured Lecturer

There once was an earnest man who, in his late thirties, had a heart attack, remarried, bought a high-end personal computer, left his job as a statehouse reporter, and, despite a lack of talent, was admitted to a creative-writing program at a big concrete university in one of the rectangular states, where he wrote the longest master's thesis in school history. He'd been a good statehouse reporter. The man's name was Phil Workman; his thesis was a 773-page autobiographical novel called *Legal Adulthood*. No one on his committee read beyond page nineteen.

The tenured professors of literature loved Phil Workman. He reminded them of themselves when they were his age, though some of them were much younger than he was. The writing professors liked Phil Workman personally—he was nothing if not likable—but his lack of talent made them embarrassed to talk to him. They rarely returned his phone calls. Their comments on his stories always contained the phrase *this has potential,* which everyone knows no one ever means.

But the professors of literature controlled the hiring of part-time faculty, so when Workman received his terminal degree, they hired him to teach four sections of freshman

composition each semester, beginning that fall and continu-
ing for the rest of his life. Seventy-one people had applied for
this punishing job, including another recent graduate of the
writing program, Hayley Roarke, who'd already sold a story to
a national magazine. The tenured professors of literature
found out how much Roarke was paid for that story—a story
read by more people than would ever read all of their opaque
fraudulent books and articles put together—and behind her
back began calling her Jane Grisham. Everyone knows that
money ruins artists.

Workman felt bad for Roarke, whom he considered a
friend. He took her to lunch, paid, tried to console her. She
thanked him, said she felt better, wondered if not getting this
job might somehow be for the best. Of course it was: she was
hired the following year to teach two creative-writing classes
per semester at a much better school for far more money.
Tenure-track job. Workman wrote her a note of sincere congratulations. A year later, her first novel came out, to choruses
of praise. Workman read it and thought it glib. He didn't tell
this to anyone for fear it would make him look small.

Workman's second wife Amanda read all his work and
encouraged him without fail. "It's good," she'd say. "The characters seem so . . . real." She knew this was what he wanted
to hear—a blessing, since it was all she could think to say.
Amanda, once a cardiac nurse (they'd met after Workman's
coronary), now worked at a plague hospice in the nearest city
big enough to have one. She'd taken only one literature class
in college, taught by a bearded foreigner of inscrutable accent, who told the class one could not prove *War and Peace* is
in any way a "better" text than the menu in the faculty dining
room. Amanda had never been in the faculty dining room,
though she knew this wasn't the point. The man wiggled his
fingers in the air when he said "better." He did the same
when he said "real." When she spoke of the realism in her

husband's stories, she kept her hands at her sides, balled into fists.

For a year after they'd married and moved to the college town, Amanda couldn't find a job, even at the health center. Finally she faced facts; she'd have to commute. A week later, she was hired at the hospice, which wasn't as depressing as people seemed to think, nowhere near as depressing as those department parties to which Phil kept dragging her (even after she had her own friends at work, with whom they almost never did things as a couple). At the hospice, she saw people at their best: noble, honest, caring, and sensitive—qualities in short supply at those parties.

Which, to be fair, were not all alike. The professors of literature *gave* parties, featuring wine, fancy finger-foods, odd references to Frenchmen Amanda never heard of, chitchat about "films," and mean-spirited gossip about department members not in attendance. At these, Phil Workman would be warmly drawn into any conversation he came near, as if he were a favorite performing child. In contrast, the writers *threw* parties, featuring beer, loud off-color jokes, male visiting writers preying upon starstruck lovelies of both genders, chitchat about "movies," and mean-spirited gossip about department members not in attendance. At these, the Workmans tended to get quarantined in some corner with a gloomy teaching assistant and someone's stray wife.

At both types of party, these professors—people who aren't asked to dress like grown-ups, arrive at work promptly, or labor during the summer—bitched endlessly about their jobs. Amanda's wasted, rheumy-eyed patients used less vehemence to complain about the injustice of their disease.

EXCEPT FOR ONE untenured poet—a poseur, though not a bad poet, who wrote in bars, museums, or, she claimed, across the nude backs of her lovers—all the writers at the university wrote at home. Workman used to write at home, too, but he kept finding himself paying bills, doing laundry, or painting the trim of his rented house. He certainly couldn't write in his office at school, which he shared with adjunct instructors—a parade of exhausted mothers and fey young men with goatees. So he got a studio: a small windowless room with a toilet, no sink, and no phone, above a package store, six blocks from campus. He began to write there, laboring on his new novel, *Amicable Divorce,* which was based on his first marriage. He wore a red chamois shirt as he wrote, for luck.

More often than not, though, his time in the studio was spent grading freshman themes. He was a rigorous grader, the last man alive who believed that *C* meant average. He typed his comments, which were often as long as the papers themselves. His students, in their evaluations, often wrote that *Mr. Workman was the best prof I've had so far* but that they wouldn't recommend his course *because its* [sic] *hard, unless your* [sic] *really motivated.*

One fall, four years into this pattern, he had enrolled in his 8 A.M. class a young woman of indeterminate age named Clio Takamira, who dressed in leggings and men's flannel shirts, had long black hair and an unnerving way of holding eye contact too long. She'd been working for the university for years (as a bookstore clerk and aerobics teacher) before beginning to take classes part-time. Her first paper broke Workman's heart. He'd assigned them to write about either a time they hadn't wanted to cry but had, or a time they had wanted to cry but couldn't. Clio's essay took place last Christmas break, organized around three sexual liaisons: with her clumsy boyfriend, a student from one of her classes who'd then blurted a marriage proposal and scared her into dumping him; with her heretofore platonic lesbian friend Ulysses, a tryst on New Year's Eve that Workman found innocent and poetically rendered; and with her deaf stepbrother Lyle, the day before he left to join the Navy, as they gave in to a lust that had stirred in each of them, repressed, since they'd met six years earlier. The paper ended with Clio letting Lyle come in her mouth—something, he signed, no girl had ever let him do. She swallowed, he smoothed her hair, their eyes met, and she gave him the sign for *I love you*, then signed, *but we can't do this anymore.* It was a moment more tender than Phil Workman would have imagined possible. It was the best student paper he had ever read. It made *him* cry.

He gave her a C. In the days of the plague, a C had become what an F used to be.

Workman had never before given a student a low grade on an A paper because he stood humbled before her talent, though he would not have put it quite that way. To him, it was just a strange whim. His comment, scrawled in red ink on the last page, was "This has potential. See me."

For two days, until that class convened again, Workman was haunted by what he'd done. He sat around watching talk shows and was short to Amanda. She asked if something was wrong. He said no. She feared he was angry because she couldn't become pregnant, which had recently been confirmed. He said that wasn't it. She was afraid he knew about the affair (her first) that, for reasons she could not explain, she'd discreetly begun to have with a famous visiting poet named Murtaugh, whom she'd met at a writers' party. She, of course, couldn't ask. Workman, in fact, had no suspicions at all. "Well," she guessed, "are you going through a bad time with the novel?"

"No," he lied. "The novel's going fine."

In truth, the novel was literally marooned on an island (Hilton Head, where he and his ex-wife vacationed). It was going so badly, and his chances of selling *Legal Adulthood* seemed so remote, that Workman began wondering about that which so many people, behind his back, were certain: maybe he didn't have what it took to write fiction. But this was not the source of his woe.

Monday morning, the day he was to hand back the papers, Phil Workman almost changed the grade. But he'd written the C in pen and couldn't think how to transform it into another letter, how he'd explain the scribble or white-out. So he stuck to his guns. Clio Takamira, however, cut class that day. Wednesday, too.

Friday morning, she was there. She came up after class, with a note from the health center that confirmed she'd had the flu. She asked if he had her paper. He did. He gave it to her, his every muscle tensed. She flipped to the page with the grade, started walking away, then glanced back at him. She returned to the lectern, where he was packing his things, smiling like she knew something. He could smell her shampoo: Helicon, the same kind his ex used. The room filled up with the members of an interpersonal communications class—whatever that is.

"I thought," she said, "that maybe I fucked up."

Workman, that rare writer who did not swear in class, winced.

"That I failed to follow instruction," she said. "I'm no good at that. I mean, I don't even *have* a stepbrother, though I dated a deaf guy once. I guess that's why you want to see me?"

"I don't want to see you," he blurted.

She frowned, looked down at his comment, back at him, shrugged, and walked away.

For the rest of the term, Clio would come to see him during office hours. She sat close, each of them hunched over her rough drafts. Her explanatory paper, "How to Fuck Up Your Life," described how her father quit his job in Silicon Valley and opened a sushi bar in a midwestern city that had never elected an Asian American to public office. Workman—blind to the paper's accidental, oblique commentary on his life—gave it the A it deserved, for which Clio didn't seem grateful or even pleased. Her persuasive paper argued that the university should adopt an ambitious, formal mentoring program; big A. Her critical essay, after a brief unit of poetry, discussed not the assigned poems but a chapbook of vitriolic haikus that Clio's mother, a WASP star-child now living in one of those western cities where hippies go to die, had written in the throes of her divorce from Clio's father. Workman gave it an A-plus, the first of his career, which, hopelessly impaired by lust, he had no idea whether it deserved.

For years, Workman had been inviting classes to his home at the hour of their final, to hand in their term papers. He provided salsa, chips, and soda; if they brought beer, fine, but he, of course, didn't supply his mostly underage students with alcohol. Clio's class, though, he invited to his studio. He iced down cheap, flavorless beer in a trash can and told his students, so packed into the room he could smell their hormones secrete, that he hoped they wouldn't drink unless they were of age. Amazingly, the only ones who did were the boys with bill-backward ball caps and Workman, who kept trying not to look at Clio. An hour later, the papers were collected, the beer and all but three students gone: one boy, a B student who was disk-jockeying the Motown tapes Workman played as he wrote; one girl, a chunky A student with designs on the boy; and Clio Takamira, who suggested they order some pizza—that is, if it was okay with Phil. Everyone looked up. It was the first time she'd ever called him anything but Mr. Workman. "Fine," he said. It was a food his doctor recommended he avoid.

Workman went down to the package store to call for pizza. The pizza came and was eaten. In a windowless room, time passes in fits and starts; Workman was startled to glance at his watch and see it was ten o'clock. Amanda would have expected him two hours ago.

Finally, Clio spilled half a jar of salsa on herself. With rank immodesty, she pulled off her leggings and stood in the middle of Workman's studio in a stained flannel shirt and lace panties. Her legs were dark and magnificent. Wars have been fought over less. "Do you have a towel," she said, "or a hair dryer?"

The boy, repeating himself on the tape player and drunk now, gave Workman a look.

"Sorry," Workman said. Then he remembered he had his gym bag with him. "Oh, wait." As Workman got the damp towel, the other girl saw how this was going and stuck her tongue in the boy's ear.

Moments later, Clio and Workman were alone.

Taking shampoo from his bag, she spot-cleaned the shirt and washed out her leggings in the toilet. "This was a great class."

"Thanks," he said. He sat across the room from her, at his desk. He pulled out the Motown tape and replaced it with Mozart.

"There's something I've been wanting to ask you." She rolled her leggings up in the towel.

"Wait," said Workman, pulse racing. "Not yet." Thinking quickly, he slipped her term paper from the stack. It was about the changing role of women in Japan. He'd seen an early draft of it, which, even at that stage, was good enough to be an A.

"What do you mean, 'not yet'?"

"One second." He affixed an A to her paper, recorded it in his grade book and on the grade sheet he'd hand to the registrar. "There." She was no longer a student in his class. He sat down on the floor beside her. "Ask me."

"Do you think I have what it takes to become a writer?"

That's the question? His heart sank. "Yes," he said. "I do."

She squealed. Actually squealed. "Really?"

He nodded. But he couldn't let it go. He placed a hand on her breast.

She spun toward him, eyes flashing. "Phil!"

He recoiled. "I'm sorry." This was not like him. He stood up and walked across the room. "Oh, God. I'm so sorry."

"I didn't know you felt that way about me." She radiated honesty.

"I didn't know either." He seemed earnest, too.

She rose, graceful as an opening flower. "I'm in your class next semester," she said. "I requested your section."

"I don't know what I was thinking."

"Like hell you don't." She was no child. She drew near.

"You have to decide," he whispered as her face came inches from his, "whether you want to be my student or my lover." His throat was dry. He had not been this frightened since his heart attack. "You can't be both."

She smiled. "I'll drop." She kissed the bejesus out of him. "Recommend another teacher."

Moments later, she had him in her mouth. He came that way, reciprocated, and then, after erection problems that he blamed on having not worn a condom for years and that she handled with grace and leniency, he was inside her. It wasn't until the ninth or tenth thrust that it felt real to him. The condom was from a box he'd bought that day. Premeditation; first-degree adultery. They rolled around all night on the floor of his study, sex so crudely passionate that Workman remembered why people call it humping. Clio Takamira wrapped herself in Workman's red shirt and, near the dawn they could not see, admitted she'd made up everything in that first paper. This only made her more attractive to him.

The next morning, Workman dropped off Clio, still wearing his shirt, two discreet blocks from her apartment. When he got home, Amanda had just left, the bathroom still damp and fragrant. She'd left him a note: *This is the man I married,* it read. *A guy who stays up all night writing, like you used to. "Amicable" will be the book that makes you. Keep it up. Love, A.*

It cut right through him; he vowed to end things with Clio.

GIVE AMANDA THE benefit of the doubt for that disingenuous note: she was as guilt-ridden as her husband.

At the very moment Phil had been received into Clio Takamira's mouth, Amanda was emerging from a hotel shower in the city where she worked, having taken the afternoon off to fuck a colleague of her husband's. Through a crack in the door, she saw Murtaugh, spread-eagled on the badly stained bed, staring at his reflection in the sliding glass door to the balcony. He was such a good lover that, between orgasms, you felt creepy, thinking about all the women he'd been with to get that way.

And it hit her: this was a man whose success her husband would cut off a limb to obtain. She fucked the man Workman thought he wanted to be. Was that *why* she'd fucked him? She'd ascribed it, variously, to loneliness, to the pressures of her job, to turning forty, or to the basic human need for reckless adventure. But now she feared it was that other thing. Worse, her husband, whose work could not find a publisher, was a much better *person* than this National Book Award–winning lout whose ejaculate she'd just washed from her hair.

From the bathroom phone, she called home. Phil wasn't there. She assumed that he was at the studio, writing. When bedeviled by the fear of getting caught, one does not imagine the shoe on the other foot. So to speak. Earlier, Amanda had left a lame message on the machine about working late, and now she added another, this one complaining about a nurse who'd called in sick. She made a kissing noise into the receiver, got ready as fast as she could, and told Murtaugh it was over. He sat up, furrowed his brow, but, with unctuous sensitivity, said he understood.

From a gas station on her way home, Amanda left another message, another weak lie proffered in a voice pinched with shame. She got home near midnight, ecstatic he wasn't there, that he hadn't played those messages, all of which sounded like they came from a woman who was fucking someone she shouldn't be. She erased the messages, reset the machine, took another shower, and went to bed.

DAYS LATER, IN the neutral turf of the nearly abandoned student union, Workman made a clean break of it with Clio. She looked down at the dull Formica tabletop and said she understood. She said she had underestimated the guilt she'd feel sleeping with a married man. She accepted his recommendation for another comp teacher, along with his advice that she take a creative-writing class (Fate, that perverse bastard, will summon her to Murtaugh's poetry workshop). As they parted, Workman turned to watch those perfect legs walk out of his life, and it occurred to him that she still had his lucky shirt, and that there would be no easy way to ask for it back.

THEN A STRANGE and terrible thing happened. On a snowy New Year's Day, Phil Workman woke up, cooked a pancake breakfast for Amanda, made ardent love to her, then ate lunch, went to the studio to work on his novel, and instead wrote a wonderful story.

It was about a sad, beautiful woman named Chloe Nakamura, who enrolls in an acting class taught by the burned-out

unnamed narrator. The other students are themselves so man-
ifestly clueless that none seem to notice that she is a natural.
She is that student who comes along once in a teacher's career, the one to whom you'll always compare all the others.

And he wrecks it. He fucks her.

After that, everything's poisoned. Chloe doesn't know,
and now can't ever know, if any of the encouraging things he
told her were true. Even the narrator wonders. He traded the
chance to change both of their miserable lives, for a few capable fucks.

But there's a twist. Chloe steals the red taffeta dress the
acting teacher wore during an off-off-Broadway show in which
he'd received decent notices, wears it to a movie audition, and
wins the role of the repressed lead's slutty wisecracking friend.
Delirious, she rushes to break the news to the narrator and on
a whim, still in his dress, proposes marriage. He hears himself
accept. They drop everything in their lives and get married in
Las Vegas, on the way out to Hollywood, both on a wild, im-
pulsive, exhilarating ride neither knows whether to trust. The
story ends on the set of the movie, with Chloe wowing everybody, and the narrator standing in the wings, alone: unsure
how he got there or what he feels, sure only *that* he feels.

Plot summary cannot do the story justice. For once, Workman's sentences were not curiously dead in the middle. For
once, Workman's rhythms rose and fell like music. For once,
Workman's symbols and metaphors just sort of happened.

He titled it "Midlife Crisis." Even if a blind squirrel finds
the odd acorn, the nut still won't bestow vision.

Somewhere during the writing process, Workman's watch
stopped. When he finished, he imagined it was the next morning. He hit PRINT and went down to the package store, which,
oddly, was locked. Outside it was dark. Two feet of snow had
fallen. It seemed like the end of the world. But it was just the

middle of the next night. He had been writing for forty hours straight.

That spring, Hayley Roarke, on tour for her second book, a collection of stories, returned to campus to give a reading. Workman picked her up at the airport; they shook hands warmly. He'd already read the book, which he liked, and he told her so. In Workman's presence, Hayley felt disconcerted by her success. She changed the subject to ask about old friends and, as a courtesy, his work. He began talking about his novel, then mentioned the strange, uncharacteristic story that had come out of nowhere. She asked to read it. On Hayley's way back to the airport, Workman gave her a copy of the story, which she read on the plane. To her surprise and relief, she loved it. She sent it to the editor at the big magazine that now published most of her stories. *He* loved it, bought it for a princely sum, deleted the last paragraph, and changed the title to "Taffeta."

On the strength of that story, Workman got an agent, a woman whose phone manner included vowels so cartoonishly elongated that he pictured her as the human incarnation of an old house cat. She asked to see *Legal Adulthood.* Her young assistant, an underemployed Ivy Leaguer, became the only person other than Amanda ever to read it. "It's a well-made old-fashioned novel," said the agent, who hadn't so much as touched the thing. It took Workman a while to realize this wasn't a compliment. But, ever eager to please, he accepted this verdict.

That summer, he abandoned *Amicable Divorce* and, in the quiet of his study, wrote three new stories, leaden variations on "Taffeta," which the assistant dutifully sent out to commercial magazines, where they were tersely rejected.

When the issue of the magazine that contained "Taffeta" finally hit the newsstands, Amanda put together a party, which was poorly attended. The tenured professors of literature grew cold to Workman. The writers—who admired the story but seemed to see it as a fluke—were as nice and distant as ever. His students read other sorts of magazines. In no time at all, a new issue of the magazine hit the stands, and the world kept spinning. To a starving man, a single bite is worse than nothing.

MEANWHILE, THOUGH NEITHER Phil nor Amanda had the least suspicion of the other's indiscretion, they—like so many couples after debasing stints of adultery—fell in love all over again, an actual courtship, full of flowers, candlelight dinners, and inventive guilt-free lovemaking. They became reacquainted, engaged anew in each other's bodies, habits, lives, and dreams.

The year after "Taffeta," one of the writing professors sold a baseball novel to the film production company of an actor who'd won a mantelful of statuettes playing louts who contract diseases or suffer crippling injuries and are thereby redeemed. In the novel, the hero suffers from herpes and tendinitis; in the film script, this was changed to cancer and, relying on the magic of digital photography, a severed arm. But the writer had received enough money to laugh at these changes and to resign his teaching job, which Workman decided to apply for.

He prepared his curriculum vitae—sodden with committee work and conferences attended—and sought letters of recommendation. Having been so long at the same school, Workman was forced to ask the writing professors to write letters to themselves on his behalf—and, worse, to ask the professors of literature to send letters to their nemeses. He was so likable, no one had the nerve to refuse, but his superficially positive letters were, in the context of the fulsome prose of several hundred such letters, encoded with negatives. *Diligent,* for example, which means *untalented; drone-like. Mature,* which means *dull. He is a dedicated teacher,* which means *I've never seen him teach, but he seems to spend a lot of time grading papers.* Worst of all, *earnest,* which means *earnest.*

Hayley Roarke had applied for the job, too. Where Workman was called diligent, she was *vastly talented.* In place of *mature,* she was *wise beyond her years. In the classroom, she is passionate, inspiring, and sensitive—a born teacher,* which means *she may be an easy grader, but students love her, recommend her, and flock to her classes.* No one called her earnest.

After he submitted his application, Workman began to wonder if it was what he really wanted. "You need to get out of that place, I think," said Amanda, though she wondered if that was just her own baggage she was trying to leave behind. She was cutting his hair, something each of them found sexy. "Maybe apply to other schools," she said. "Or go back to journalism."

Workman flinched, causing her to jab him with the scissors.

"Sorry," she said. "But what's wrong with journalism?"

"Nothing's wrong with it," he said. "It's just that fiction ..."

But he could not finish that sentence.

"You're the sort of person," she said, "who values only the things that don't come easily."

"That's true of everybody," he said.

"The opposite," she said, "is true of everybody."

He, of course, did not get the job, though he was sincerely pleased his friend Hayley, hired at the associate level, was back in town. He had, after Amanda's suggestion, applied for what few other jobs there were and actually got an offer, from a small, barely accredited college in a faraway harbor town. Workman accepted. Then, the week he and Amanda were going to fly to that town to look for a house, the president of the university, an effete pederast whose own vita included

more coauthors than pages published, read "Taffeta," pro-
fessed to be horrified by its sexual content, and ordered the
department to hire someone else. "It's for the best," Amanda
said, consoling her husband. "Who'd want to teach at a place
like that?"

"Me," Workman said. But he knew she was right.

That fall, every Wednesday, a day he did not teach, Phil
Workman drove to the city along with Amanda, just to spend
some extra time with her. He worked in a small back office,
coming out every once in a while to watch Amanda work. After
a while, he started talking to those victims of the plague, learning about their lives, listening to their fears, marveling at their
unnerving acceptance of fate. That heart attack he'd survived
had given him the reprieve none of these people would get.
One day, on the drive over, he came up with an idea for an oral
history of sorts, a book where these plague victims told stories
about the lives they would lead, the truncated dreams they
would reassemble, if a miraculous cure were suddenly found.

Amanda, as she heard him describe this, felt a warmth
spread over her, and she began to cry.

Weeks later, he sent a proposal for the book to his agent,
who sold it immediately, for more money than Workman
could have made in ten years of teaching. He quit his job. He
and Amanda moved to the city, where they bought a house on
a hill and began to look into adopting a child.

IN THE AGE of the plague, tales no longer end happily ever
after. Where happy endings once frolicked, now we see ironies,
post-ironies, ellipses. If you're lucky and a bit old-fashioned,
maybe a moral victory.

And so it came to pass that, one bright day, two years into
his research on his book, months from its projected comple-
tion, there appeared in the women's ward of the hospice a

frail, far-gone woman of indeterminate age. Workman—who introduced himself to all new patients to see if they'd be willing to participate—did not recognize her until he saw the name on the chart.

"I have it," said Clio Takamira. "I have the plague."

Workman stood dumbly in the light that streamed into her room. What could he say? *I don't have it?* This was true (some time ago he'd had himself tested) but not the thing to say, yet.

"I know why you're here," she said to her old teacher. "They told me about the book." She smiled. "Don't feel uncomfortable, okay?"

He nodded. He wanted to ask her if she'd ever read "Taffeta," but he was struck mute.

"I doubt if you have it," she said. "I know who I got it from, the plague, and it was after."

He nodded again, still thunderstruck.

"Please," she said. "Smile." She got up from her bed, went to her closet, and produced his old red chamois shirt. "Here," she said. "I believe this is yours."

He told her to keep it, please.

"Fine," she said. She shrugged it on over her blouse. "Sit down, okay? And cheer up. Let me tell you my story," she said.

He sat down. The room was spinning. For the first time in years he feared for his bad heart.

"You can give me eternal life. My story," she said, "will be the best one you ever write."

He looked at her. She was smiling, beatific. What Workman thought was *Easy for you to say, you fucking muse bitch.* He considered slapping her. He didn't say what he thought, and he didn't do what he wanted to. He was, finally, the sort of man who didn't want to do what he wanted to do. All he did was nod. All he could say was, "I'll try."

III

Keegan's Load

The rumor was that Keegan had gotten married. If that wasn't improbable enough, the alleged wife was said to be years younger than Keegan and also pretty. We hadn't seen him, or each other, since May. Ours was the sort of forlorn southern college where summer came and everyone scattered. Our composition director jumped on his motorcycle and zig-zagged his way to California, looking up friends and lovers. Our theorist bought a hardscrabble hilltop vineyard. Our medievalist coached his kids' baseball teams. Our closeted-homosexual Romanticist hit Europe. Our fiction writer went to third-tier artists' colonies. Our real poet took banjo lessons, divorced her husband, and finished a book of poems about taking banjo lessons and divorcing her husband. Our African-Americanist had a baby. Our Shakespearean went to Toronto. Those of us motivated by money or self-loathing to teach sum-mer school skulked to and from the classroom with eyes as averted as penitents' and as dead as pedophiles'. Whatever we did that summer, we weren't thinking about Keegan.

When last we'd seen him—at commencement, trembling in white sunlight, reciting an occasional poem he'd written lauding the achievements of a Charlotte shopping-mall developer to whom we were giving an honorary degree—Keegan wasn't so much as dating. He was sixty-six and looked eighty-six, tall and skeletal, with a long white beard and stained polyester clothing he'd go days without changing. He also didn't change his voice: his every utterance was delivered in the Poetry-Reading Voice—stilted, self-conscious, in awe of its own profundity. We disagreed among ourselves about whether he had Alzheimer's or had always been like this. But indisputably Keegan had been unlucky in love. His first two wives had died. He'd politely asked out every unmarried woman at the college—every professor, every secretary, every librarian, all the young women in admissions, even our lesbian security cop. Some of us (out of pity? curiosity? guilt?) went out with him once or twice. But it had been years since he'd had a mildly significant other. Now he had a *wife*?

Yes, a wife. Her name was Bess. The first day of classes, we—at least those of us hip to the role face time played at a college like ours—went to hear the president's convocation speech (when he said "our window of opportunity beckons," we briefly mulled suicide). At the reception, stationed in the middle of the atrium, sipping tepid white wine, nibbling cubes of marbled cheese, were Keegan and the new Mrs. Keegan. She was more than advertised: pretty in a neat, unaggressive way, in her late forties, and black. We tripped over ourselves in guilty liberal solicitousness, pleased as could be to make her acquaintance. Keegan had on a new gray suit. She wore a sequined black dress. He somberly introduced her. We tried not to form a reception line, not to stare. Her head was tilted down, one shoulder dipped as a shield. She was the only spouse there who wasn't employed by the college, the only African American who didn't teach black studies or coach a sport. She was a stranger to us all and overdressed. She called herself "just a housewife" and nodded serenely when we objected to the *just*. They'd met at church, she said. When occasioned, she took her napkin and dabbed dip from Keegan's beard, so fast, it embarrassed no one.

And so Keegan lost his homeless-man aura and showed up freshly scrubbed, Bess in tow, at lectures, readings, dinners, even the grim Friday happy hour in the faculty lounge that most of us thought had been abandoned years ago. They were sighted in trendy coffee houses, places Keegan had never been except to perform his poetry. Alone together, on the periphery of public events, her shy smile broadened to something like laughter, and Keegan, that lugubrious son of a bitch, looked content. We wondered, of course, what was in this for her. It was common knowledge that Keegan, though rumored to be the highest-paid member of our department, had no money. The idea of his naked liver-spotted body quelled conjecture in that regard. The prevailing theory (we are big on theories) was that she had a caretaker complex. "She's a frustrated nurse," our comp director guessed. "My take," said our African-Americanist, "is that during a formative time in her life, she either saw her mother take care of an elderly loved one or did so herself." None of us asked Bess about this directly. We were bigger fans of speculation than fact. Still, we liked her. Everyone said that.

Keegan's three children, from whom he'd been practically estranged, came to visit. We heard that two of the three more or less forgave all.

Ordinarily, when it was Keegan's turn to observe an untenured professor's class, he'd sit in front, remove his shoes, argue with us, then fall asleep. His letter in our file contained a brief fabrication of what went on in class and a rant about our misreading of the assigned text. This term, it was our Romanticist's turn. Keegan sat in back, quiet, attentive, and fully clothed, then wrote a letter saying the class made him go home and reread "Ozymandias." The Romanticist, a deeply good guy, never seriously asserted that perhaps he was just a better teacher than we were.

Our students that term claimed that Dr. Keegan was doing more than going into class, reading the assigned poems, and gesticulating madly. There, he still took off his shoes, but his feet no longer stank. In class and out, he'd been given to Tourettic invocations of the Buddha and the Book of Luke. This abated. He also toned down the portentous pauses in his speaking voice.

Keegan's car, an old boat of a thing, was less frequently parked on the quad.

Some of us began to feel happy for Keegan. Knowing Bess would be there for him, knowing he would not be alone, helped us yearn for his retirement with clear consciences.

Years ago, he'd posted a sign on his door, advertising "Unconditional Rap, w/Dr. Keegan." He was available, it said, every Monday in the department seminar room. Typically, he was in there alone. Long ago, someone (one of us?) scrawled a *C* in front of *rap*. This term, the old sign came down. Bess helped Keegan arrange to bring in speakers: drug counselors, radical priests, weight-lifting motivational speakers, victims of apartheid. Flyers were posted. Attendance swelled to as many as twenty.

A few weeks into the term, Keegan published a new book of poems. His publisher, as had been the case for some time, was a former student who printed the books on a press in his parents' basement. (The books before that came from a vanity press.) Only the goodwill Bess had engendered could explain why the fiction writer and the poet, after years of ignoring Keegan's books, organized both an on-campus reading for him and a book party, complete with a photo scan of the book's ugly cover screened onto a cake. The party was at the poet's retro-kitsch duplex. A reporter from our local daily, a friend of the fiction writer, came to both the reading and the party. He got drunk and went home with one of our students—one of the wholesome large-foreheaded girls seemed honestly to mistake Keegan's incoherence for depth. To be fair, we had many students in this camp. A week later, the reporter did a story on Dr. Keegan that pretended he was not a fraud. It was such a fulsome valedictory, the joke around the college was that we were so sorry to hear Dr. Keegan had died. Keegan lived.

IN THE '60S, Keegan would have been the groovy professor, the one who'd already done everything the students thought belonged to their generation. He was against the war but was drafted and went (Korea, Vietnam: it's all the same to the sort of student we get). He'd come back and spent time in an ashram, a kibbutz, a seminary, and a zendo. He taught high school on an Indian reservation and in New Orleans. He owned a zither. You'd have to think that at some point, drugs were involved. He got his doctorate on the GI bill. He saw Muddy Waters and Miles Davis perform in nightclubs in bad neighborhoods. He brought Allen Ginsberg to our campus.

He married an art-history professor. They fought passionately—the sort of couple everyone expects to get divorced and never does. They had two kids. After a particularly nasty public fight, she left him at a party and drove home into the teeth of a thunderstorm. She wrapped the family wagon around a tree. The kids were raised by her sister in Dallas.

The second wife had been his student, which was common in those days. She had a baby soon after they were married and went to art school at nights. This was thought to be a good marriage. When a hair dryer fell in the tub with her, it was briefly investigated as a murder. The coroner ruled it an accident. We saw it as a suicide, and didn't blame her. Keegan raised his third child himself. She spent her adult life in and out of rehab. We felt sorry for Keegan, for the girl (we didn't know her, but still...). The better angels of our nature just wanted poor Keegan to be happy.

Was Keegan ever a legitimate figure in our profession? When he started out, anyone with a Ph.D. could get a college teaching job. At most schools, publishing was more a hobby of the obsessed than a condition of continued employment. His degree was from a solid place. We always meant to go to the library there and read his dissertation, to see if it was coherent. (Did we fail to do so because we were afraid it might be?) Right after he was first hired (as an Americanist), he published an article on William Dean Howells in a refereed journal that still exists, and placed his dissertation with a publisher that no longer does (our library's copy was stolen; Keegan said he gave all his copies to students). The article was workmanlike and so free of Keeganese (such as his incessant use of *resonance, organic, intrinsic, actualize, orchestration,* and *affirm*) that the department chair and the medievalist practically came to blows over the latter's drunken suggestion it was plagiarized. Not long ago, our Shakespearean found one of Keegan's exams on the copier glass. It was an old ditto master. Our department stopped using ditto machines about when everyone else did. The exam contained twenty true-or-false questions and one essay. Sample T or F: "Faulkner in *As I Lay Dying* gives the fullest resonance of the human situation in opening the reader's heart to the spectrum of the souls of several sons who bear their mother, in their lives, to her grave." The essay question: "Name a writer you read this term who impressed you and explain why."

This, from a four-time winner of our college's highest teaching award.

Who, not incidentally, gave grades that ran the gamut from A to A-minus.

Scotch-taped to Keegan's office walls were yellowed letters from famous poets, sometimes next to snapshots of them along with a younger, just-as-scraggly Keegan. This conveyed a certain gravitas. Until we read the letters. James Dickey thanks Keegan for sending him his book, and says he plans to read it. Howard Nemerov points out that it's customary, when inviting a writer to campus, to offer a stipend *plus* expenses and corrects Keegan's grammar in the poem he'd sent. The postcard from Anne Sexton thanks Keegan for bringing her to our college and says she's never had a beer before a reading in a bar so dark. A poet named Murtaugh avers that "opaque religious poems aren't now much in favor" and, in a PS, says that because of "woman troubles & etc." he is too busy to write on Keegan's behalf for a Guggenheim.

For years, Keegan both advised our undergraduate literary magazine and published his own poems in it. (It was, in fact, the best-known journal ever to accept a Keegan poem.) This continued when the Americanist, who'd in New Orleans been his student, took over as the magazine's adviser. After the college finally hired a real poet, and the younger Americanist, by now the chair of the department, passed the advisership on to her, she instituted a policy excluding the work of the faculty. She'd presumed the students were publishing Keegan in an attempt to suck up to him. Rumor had it Keegan was crushed. She received $650 as the magazine's adviser and was untenured. She reversed the policy. "What the hell," she told us. "If the kids want to publish him, who cares?"

When an ad hoc committee developed our department Web site, the chair, to help us write the content, gave us a file folder of brochures the department had used over the years. In two of them—from the '6os and early '7os, judging by the wide ties and long-gone faculty—Keegan's bio calls him "our bard, who has been nominated for the Nobel Prize." We were stunned that this outrageous lie had been promulgated, believed, that the thought was even *minted*, but there it was. We were pleased to have proof that it wasn't Alzheimer's: Keegan had always been a fraud. We Xeroxed the hell out of that brochure. When we told Keegan stories to colleagues elsewhere, they never accepted this one otherwise.

WE WEREN'T EVEN *allowed* in our tenure cases to use letters solicited from others at the college. That fall, our poet overlooked this rule and included in her binder letters from the medievalist and the fiction writer—letters she'd enlisted two years ago to use in applying for jobs elsewhere, before she divorced her husband and realized she couldn't move (they had kids). She was a good poet but bad with paperwork; she hadn't reread the letters. Both were glowing. Both noted that she was the first person our college had hired to teach poetry writing, after years of ceding such classes to an out-of-field colleague—a delicate situation both said she handled deftly. Though she was more demanding than our students expected, they loved her. Her workshops filled. The fiction writer, who was scheduled to come up for tenure the next year, was cryptic about all this. His letter was the penultimate page of a binder as thick as a truck battery. The medievalist's letter came last. It called Keegan "a hopelessly befuddled hobby poet, who gave everyone As and was beloved thereby."

True as this was, it was a vestige of our sentiments toward Keegan before Bess was around.

The director of composition was the first to sign the binder out. Around midnight, he saw the letters and called the medievalist, who was his best friend. They ran marathons together. The medievalist was aghast. "Just pull it," he said.

"I already thought of that," said the comp director. "But there are two copies of the binder."

The chair, naturally, had the other one. By the time we got to campus the next day, the dean and the president already had copies of the letters. The chair told the medievalist that he was sure to get fired. "I think not," he said. He was newly tenured and happily married to an expensive trial lawyer. "It's impolitic, but I stand by that letter. Look, I never told her she could use the letter for that purpose. Plus, there's a rule against using letters like that."

"You'll get old someday, too," said the chair. "Don't you know that?"

"Fuck you," said the medievalist. "You think that's what this is about? Pull my letter, which you have to do anyway, and this whole thing is done. I'll even apologize to Keegan."

"'*Even*'? First of all, under these circumstances," said the chair, "the letter stays. Second, you're suspended for the rest of the term."

"You can't do that."

The chair shook his head. "Please get out of my office."

The fiction writer, on the other hand, was sincerely mortified. She approached Keegan right before an Unconditional-Rap session featuring an actual swami. Her plan was to pull him aside, apologize, then, in a goodwill gesture, stay for the swami. Also, she was curious. She'd never met a swami. But at the door of the seminar room, Bess stood beside Keegan, beaming, quietly directing people to a classroom that was big enough to seat everyone. Shaking, the fiction writer asked Keegan if there would be a good time for them to talk, and he said right after the speaker finished.

The swami had a thick Appalachian accent. He'd been

trampled in a campus riot up north (when his name had been Luther Suggs), lost his leg, gone to India, and one thing had led to another. There were many questions afterward. The fiction writer stuck it out. Bess saw her waiting and told Keegan she'd be happy to take the swami home. He nodded. She kissed him on the forehead.

On their way to Keegan's office, he and the writer didn't say a word. Once inside, she started talking, a river of words, and Keegan still didn't say anything. In her shame and contrition, she just went on and on. Also, she'd had a few drinks.

"I affirm you," he finally said, and handed her a manuscript. No one knew Keegan had been writing a novel (naïve, we later realized; all of us are theoretically writing a novel). He asked her if she'd read it and show it to her agent.

What could she do? She read it. It was the story of a man who'd gone to Korea, become a sniper, and come home "with his body intact but his soul broken prismatically." He spent time in an ashram, a kibbutz, a seminary, and a zendo, and wound up as a high school history teacher in a city resembling New Orleans. The last paragraph: "His search for meaning brought him here, and it/He manifested itself/Himself in the classroom every day, the man was but a monkey of Jesus, some students would hear him, some would not be ready to hear, but intrinsically he was alive for this, to actualize the resonance of these kids." The novel's title—not explained anywhere in the text—was *Samurai with Breasts*.

Meanwhile, Keegan was excused from the tenure committee's deliberations, though he could still vote. When the poet came to apologize, he told her that no one on this mortal coil could bestow true forgiveness. Nonetheless, he said, this matter would not affect his vote. He stood, put a hand on her shoulder, and said, "I affirm you."

The medievalist wasn't suspended, but the college seized his computer, and reviewed every e-mail he'd sent and every

Web site he'd ever visited. We even heard that a detective was
hired to look for dirt on him. The committee met for a total
of fifty-seven hours over eleven separate meetings. Its deliberations were confidential. The chair said that anyone breech-
ing same would be fired. The college attorney attended five of
these meetings. The poet had come up for tenure with more
published at that point than anyone in department history.
("Poems are short," the chair was rumored to have said. "Anyone can publish poems." The medievalist pointed out that
Keegan never really had. The chair started to answer, and the
college attorney clamped a hand over the man's mouth.) She
was a fine teacher. The medievalist's letter was destroyed more
than once, by persons unknown, and replaced with copies.
The committee used a secret ballot and denied the poet's request for tenure by one vote.

During all this, the fiction writer bought Keegan lunch.
Bess came, too. As they ate, the manuscript sat on a corner of
the table. Bess and Keegan kept glancing at it, but no one said
anything. They talked about Bess's sons—a cop, a jazz gui-
tarist, and a city planner. They talked about Keegan's kids,
too, about whom Bess had more to say than Keegan. She was
compassionate and diplomatic about each child's difficulties,
effusive about their triumphs, workaday and otherwise.

When the check came and the business part of lunch was
inescapable, Bess offered to excuse herself. The writer said
that wasn't necessary, hoping Bess would insist. Bess stayed.
The writer wished she'd had a three-martini lunch. But she
hadn't. She took a deep breath, then began.

She said nothing dishonest. She praised the book's heart.
She praised its authority. She said the book's theological over-
tones and digressions reminded her of late-period Tolstoy.

"Keegan sat there expressionless," she told us. "He reduced this piece of cake he ordered into a pile of crumbs and
didn't eat any of it. Bess looked like some confused and eager

student who just wanted to understand. Keegan, you could tell, was expecting the *but*."

But, she told him, she didn't really think the book was quite working, yet.

"All he said," she told us, "was 'Could you just send it on to your agent and see what he says?'"

She, she told him. Her agent was a woman.

He frowned and then asked if she knew any agents who were men.

"It pissed me off. Looking back," she said, "I guess he thought that was my point, that I was saying the book was wrong for a female audience. But at the time, damn. I just blurted out the truth, that he needed to revise the whole thing, with an eye toward what a stranger might find interesting."

Bess said that *she'd* found the book interesting. She put a hand on Keegan's thigh. She wasn't a stranger, obviously, or a professional in the writing field. But the book had moved her.

Keegan picked up his manuscript, stood, chastely hugged the writer, and left, Bess's hand on his shoulder all the way to his gigantic car.

That same semester, our theorist was up for tenure, too. In six years, he'd published one refereed article and a feature story in an enology magazine. He'd garnered the frankly dreadful student evaluations most theorists do. The committee discussed his case for four minutes. It recommended him unanimously.

WE COULD GET in a car, drive for two hundred miles in any direction, stop a random person on the street, mention where we worked, and be certain the person would say, "Hey, good school." Our campus looked like the set of a college movie from the 1950s, our weather was winningly temperate except in the summer, and our city was your basic southern boom-town. People liked such places. We were expensive enough to be taken seriously by the rich, not so expensive that we couldn't compete with state schools for the rank and file. As in most colleges of this ilk, our faculty was committed to under-graduate teaching and was in varying degrees demoralized. That said, because the job market remained tight and because ours had become the last profession in America that offered a hope of lifetime employment, whenever we went out to hire, we saw brilliant candidates. That spring, we brought three to campus, competing for a Victorianist job. The prohibitive front-runner came first. He had a law degree from an Ivy League school and had been a true-blue Philadelphia lawyer for five years before he chucked it to get a doctorate in Brit lit from a different Ivy League school. His dissertation was on lit-erature and the law and seemed to be on the threshold of being accepted by the press of a third Ivy League school. In his letter, he made a point of mentioning that his wife's family lived near us. We thought we had a shot.

There were thirty students in his sample class. Halfway through, he knew all their names. He listened to them. He ex-pertly balanced discussion and lecture. He was short, a little heavy, self-deprecating, and bald, which kept his intelligence and caged-animal pacing from seeming too much.

At lunch, he always seemed to be talking about us and not him, and yet we came away from lunch having learned quite a lot about him.

By the time we sat down for the department interview, it was in the bag. He was making the intricate nature of his re-search lively and accessible, and we were already so won over that none of us asked one of those long questions that are really speeches about how we're smart and you're not.

When Keegan raised his hand, we were not initially alarmed. He typically asked one innocuous question at these things, late in the game, about the person's teaching philosophy.

"I do not relish. The estimating of another's teaching," he said. "But don't you agree. That your approach to literature. Is too abstract for the students?" He had the Voice going full-bore. "I hear you talking about the law. But. What about the intrinsic themes. And the styles. Of the works?"

The candidate pursed his lips and nodded, as if this were a thorny, worthy question. To our horror, we realized that the events of last semester had squelched the candor from us all. No one, not even the medievalist, had prepped the candidate for Keegan.

"I wouldn't call my approach abstract at all," the candidate said. "Legal issues of rights, ownership, and enfranchisement inform any work you can mention. They have a profound and even concrete effect on the lives of the characters and the life of the culture."

As the candidate cited several specific examples, Keegan started waving his hands slowly. He seemed to be pointing with his middle finger, the way old men sometimes do. We were afraid the candidate might think Keegan was flipping him off. Our African-Americanist reached over, put a hand on one of Keegan's arms. He ignored her.

"Stop," he said to the candidate. "What about the mother. Holding the child. In her arms?"

Apropos of absolutely nothing.

The candidate cocked his round head.

"The mother and the babe," Keegan said. He was still waving his arms. "The Madonna. And the Christ."

Here, several of us were about to say something, anything, but the candidate was too fast.

"Even motherhood," he said, "is a legal concept."

"My intrinsic response to that," Keegan said. He closed his eyes. He raised both hands before his face and extended both middle fingers. He had very long fingers. "Is stick it."

"Ha!" the candidate said, eyes wide, his expression a disconcerting blend of shock, fury, and amusement. He stood. "This interview is *over.*"

He was out the door of the seminar room before Keegan reopened his eyes.

Not even the chair seemed to know what to say to Keegan.

"What's not befuddled about that?" the medievalist said to a few of us, though by now we weren't in the seminar room, either.

"What's not hopeless?" said the Romanticist.

"Word," said the medievalist.

Several of us piled into an SUV with the candidate and issued robust and futile apologies all the way to the airport. On the way back, we stopped at a liquor store. We sat on the Romanticist's dock, in a brackish lake behind his house, and plotted ways we might get Keegan fired. Some of us thought this might be the thing that could bring about Keegan's retirement. We could go to the dean. We could go to the president. Maybe we could even enlist Bess's help. Those who'd been here the longest said it was futile. Our poet, one of our best and our brightest, would soon be out of a job, but Keegan would be here until he died. And he'd probably outlive us all. None of us believed he *would* be fired, of course. Not beloved Dr. Keegan. Still, somehow, he had to go. We were ready to relax our distaste for deus ex machina. Whatever it took, we were for it; even Keegan needed to die.

Keegan lived. But days later, after we had lodged our quixotic complaints with the powers that be, Bess Keegan, forty-eight, died in her sleep. Brain aneurysm. Go figure.

———

THE COLLEGE HAD surrendered its church affiliation decades ago, and our administration was unshy about its desire to tear down the chapel. It was a bastardized Federal-style building, old but not historic, a survivor of various shoddy renovations. The addition of air-conditioning was such a marvel of convoluted ductwork and later-boarded holes that crooked contractors brought their children here to sit on the tailgates of their pickups, sip whatever was in their travel mugs, and savor the view of what was possible when enterprise collides with people who think they know everything. It was the only building on campus that was never locked. We bordered a bad neighborhood. Campus police often chased vagrants out of there. New officers, on their first day of work, were shown Keegan's picture in the faculty directory and told he worked here, was not homeless, and should be left alone unless he asked for help. *Help* involved jump starts, scores of ball games, show times of movies, rolls of toilet paper, and requests to be let into his office to get his keys. Keegan sat alone in that chapel, all hours of the day—reading, writing, praying, sleeping. Our theorist said he saw Keegan grading papers there. Six months ago, Keegan and Bess had been quietly married in that chapel. Now it was the site of Bess's funeral.

At the outset, a stranger might have mistaken the funeral for a wedding. The flowers on the altar were red roses. The families and guests seated themselves as if there were ushers. On the bride's side were about twenty black people. In front were three large and angry-looking young men we presumed to be Bess's sons. The groom's side was packed. Nearly all of us were very very white. In the front row of our section sat Keegan, his three children, and their families. Only a handful of students, but more faculty than ever went to commencement (which was required, technically). Keegan had few real friends, and the excess of our turnout shamed us into conceding our weakness for bathos. Also, we felt guilty about our recent hateful feelings toward him. Bess's death seemed to have been engineered by someone's capricious so-called God to make us take pity on Keegan. We studiously avoided the furious stares of Bess's sons.

At the appropriate time, the priest called upon Keegan to deliver the eulogy.

He stood and shuffled to the pulpit. He mounted its stairs so slowly, the priest, seated on the opposite side of the altar, looked ready to leap up at any moment and steady the old guy. But Keegan made it alone. When he did, he closed his eyes, threw back his shaggy head, and outstretched his arms as if in invitation to be lashed to a cross.

This went on for an awfully long time.

We exchanged glances. We wanted the priest to put a stop to this. We wondered if one of us would have to do it. We wanted to keep from making eye contact with any of the people noisily clearing their throats on the other side of the aisle.

Finally, Keegan let down his weary arms. He pulled a stack of lengthwise folded paper from the inside breast pocket of the same gray suit he'd worn to last fall's convocation. It was the suit, he told us, that Bess bought him for their wedding.

We cringed.

He set the papers down on the Bible and smoothed them.

"I have written a poem," he said, swallowing hard, "for Bess."

This gave us the courage to look across the aisle. People there seemed to relax, slightly.

The poem was more or less what we'd come to expect from Keegan's occasional poems, a blend of the earnestly literal with enough mystical babble to kill an adult horse. It included the names of Bess's sons, which Keegan, eyes closed and head again tilted heavenward, shouted: *"Derek! Alfonso! Tyrone!"* We couldn't keep our eyes off those young men. They didn't move. Behind them, many of the black people wept, but the sons kept it together.

Keegan's pauses between stanzas were so long, we thought, repeatedly, the poem must be over.

When at last he finished, the priest rose.

"Yes, this, too, is for Bess." Keegan nodded, as if he were fulfilling a request. The priest sat.

This poem was included in Keegan's last book. Some of us had heard him read it last semester at his publication reading. Though we couldn't parse its gibberish, it had driven Bess into a fit of giggles. Some of us hadn't known black people could blush. That, as Keegan read his poem, was what we thought of: poor Bess, happy. This got to us. We were not made of stone.

When at last Keegan finished, the priest again rose.

"I would like to honor Bess," Keegan said, "by reading another. Another poem. For Bess."

This time, the priest didn't sit back down. He was also a professor in what was left of our religion department.

This poem was one Keegan wrote years before he met Bess. We'd always understood the "she" in the poem to be the Virgin Mary.

Keegan finished and barreled right into another one. The priest seemed to look at us for counsel, despite which he only moved a couple more steps toward the pulpit.

When Keegan started another, a haiku this time, one of the sons stood. No matter our politics, we were, truth be told, the sort of people afraid of an angry young black man. The son walked toward Keegan. He arrived at the pulpit at about syllable fourteen.

"One final poem," Keegan said. The son and the priest flanked him, each with a foot on the pulpit steps and a hand on his shoulder. "I affirm you all," Keegan said, and soldiered on. When he finished, the priest and the son escorted him down. The young man put his arm around this old man, his stepfather. Keegan's children didn't move. Keegan took a place in the pew beside his stepsons. Our sense that they'd been angry was perhaps culturally biased, and, anyway, an aneurysm was nobody's fault.

As the priest turned to cue the organist, Keegan stood and faced the congregation. "Copies," he said, "of the poems. I have read. In honor. Of Bess. And to grieve her."

Please, God, no! we thought.

"Are available," he said, "in the narthex."

He sat back down.

The stepsons patted him on the back. Keegan's own children crossed the aisle and did the same. They bravely took their places together in that front pew. Keegan began silently to weep. His shoulders shook. Hymns were sung, the priest executed a dull homily, and everyone pretended that nothing unusual had happened.

The poems were free—dittoed and stapled together. Somehow, Keegan had found a ditto machine. There were maybe thirty sets of them stacked on a card table. They went briskly. No one we knew wound up with a copy.

IT WASN'T AS if we didn't reach out to Keegan. We sent cards. We expressed genuine sympathy to his face. We made donations to the United Negro College Fund and to the church where Bess and Keegan had met. Naturally, some of us wondered if *this* might provoke him to retire. He could focus on the grieving process. But the chair told us that when he'd suggested a mere semester off, Keegan had been offended.

For the next few weeks, there was a frenzy of taking Keegan to lunch. He started wearing sweatpants to class but otherwise seemed to be bearing up well. His daughter, we heard, had landed a job at a food co-op and taken an apartment not far away. He got a dog—a greyhound, from the rescue people. He renamed it Martha. Not only was he able in no time to get it to respond to that, but when he'd intone "Martha, Martha, thou art careful and troubled about many things, but only one thing is needful," the dog would roll over, leap to its feet, look to the heavens, and bark.

It would have been sentimental, and perhaps unreasonable, to expect us to like Keegan more because a sad thing had happened to him. Bess's death made the world a worse place, but on the other hand Keegan had known her for less than a year. Soon, our classes, our committees, our futile attempts to hire a Victorianist, our unhealthy obsessions, our families and their attendant crises conspired to push the care and feeding of Keegan from our agendas.

But over Easter weekend, he was returning, on foot with the greyhound, from his daughter's apartment when a once-a-century ice storm hit. He was four miles from home but did not turn back. He made it to within five blocks of his house when the dog bolted. Keegan fell, and the dog dragged him all the way to the mouth of his driveway. He was lucky, his doctor said, only to have broken his arm and ruptured his spleen. The ice must have made the enterprise go more smoothly. Keegan was expected to make a full, uneventful recovery.

Three of us—the teaching load here is three courses a semester—pitched in to cover his classes. The fiction writer took his Modern American Poetry class when the poet refused and the chair said he himself was spread too thin already. When she got to the classroom, only five students were there. She asked if this was Dr. Keegan's class; it was. She asked if they'd heard about Dr. Keegan's accident (it had been in the school paper, along with several of his poems, as if he *had* died); they had. She asked where everyone was (there were thirty-one students enrolled, six over the cap); they said this was more than usual. She took out her book and so did the two students who'd brought theirs. The other three hadn't even brought notebooks. When she began talking about Robert Frost, they looked at her as if she'd falsely accused them of date rape. We're not up to that, they said. We're doing Whitman.

She looked at the syllabus. It said Frost was on tap for today. Whitman was the first writer listed. The syllabus promised to spend two weeks on him. This was week twelve. "I'm not a sub," she said. "I'm the teacher of record from here on out."

They considered her, blankly.

"Okay," she said. "Whitman."

As one, the five students nodded happily.

"The father of modern American poetry."

The one student with a notebook wrote this down.

She turned to Whitman in the anthology. She asked what poem they did last class. No one would look at her. "Fine," she said. "Who can tell me the name of Whitman's great book?"

The students seemed to find their shoes fascinating. Or were fascinated she was wearing hers.

"He worked on it almost forty years? Nine editions in his lifetime? Banned in Boston? Anyone?" Two or three of the students were actually trying, which broke her heart. "*Leaves of...?*"

"Oh, yeah!" shouted a kid in a bill-backward Atlanta Braves cap. "*Leaves of Grass!*"

The other students groaned in embarrassment. They knew that! Just forgot.

"And when was it written?" she said. "What years was he working on it?"

They looked miserable again. The girl with the notebook paged through it. She'd drawn many hearts there.

"What era?" the writer said. "What century?"

The girl brightened. Up shot her hand. "Um, like...," the girl said. "1965?"

"That's right!" the writer said. No one laughed. She had to tell the girl not to write that down.

SUBBING FOR KEEGAN gave us access to his office. That was how our African-Americanist, while looking for something else, came across the letter from the Swedish Academy, which curtly said that section seven of the statutes of the Nobel Foundation forbids nominating yourself for a prize.

Did that make it better? Or worse? *Worse,* we thought.

NEAR THE END of the semester, our poet won an award that many of us had heard of. Her picture appeared in the online version of the *New York Times.* Her tenure case, which had been denied right down the line, was on the desk of the president, who should have made a decision weeks earlier. For once, his pathological procrastination paid off. She received both promotion and tenure.

To celebrate this, the department chair—undoubtedly one of those who'd voted against her—held a reception in the faculty lounge. Our theorist brought several magnums of his own surprisingly drinkable wine. Keegan arrived late, heavily bandaged and using a walker, despite which he'd brought his dog. We mooned over the dog. Our poet pulled out her banjo and played a hilarious medley of '80s hair-metal songs, though she seemed weirdly unamused. *Speech!* someone said. Keegan rose. The poet didn't notice, or pretended not to. She thanked everyone for coming, and for their support, and announced that she'd been hired, with tenure and rank, by a large research university in one of America's rectangular states, a job she'd sought out of desperation and had accepted before her recent unexpected reversals of fortune. We expected her to laugh, or to gloat, but she looked like she might cry.

Keegan sat.

She felt she needed to honor her commitment. She had no choice, she said, but to leave.

The chair rushed over to congratulate her. She was chagrined enough to flinch only slightly when he embraced her. Then he shouted down the buzz she'd kicked up, and said he had an announcement of his own. After years of frustration, he'd finally found a donor—anonymous, as it happened— who was willing to endow a distinguished-chair position. It would be named for Keegan. Keegan would also be the first to occupy it. It came with a raise of some confidential amount and a one-one teaching load.

One-one. Same as that double-barreled bird he'd flipped.

Again, Keegan stood, whereupon the dog, stuffed with cheese we'd fed it, crapped on the rug. Keegan was oblivious. But he also was overcome and could not speak. The turd sat there. A few of us went over to shake Keegan's hand, because what else was there to do? As for the turd, we kept talking as if nothing had happened. No one did anything. Finally, the dog ate it.

Summer came, and again we scattered.

After the year we'd had, many of us—particularly the poet, who spent the summer waging and losing a custody battle, and who moved out West without her children—were moved to yearn for the day when we could urinate powerfully on Keegan's grave. That didn't make us bad people, did it? We'd never have the nerve to do it.

Janda's Sister

Curt Janssen and I go back to when the high school basket-ball coach shot off the tip of his wife's nose, painted his privates blue, and strode naked through the town square of Tullard, Ohio, waving his revolver and singing selections from Disney movies, songs first sung by bears, dogs, and monkeys. The coach knew all the words. The bars had just closed, and my mother bore witness to the event. The coach, she told me, had a thin, lovely tenor that you didn't expect to hear float-ing from the mouth of a fat, gun-wielding lunatic with blue testicles.

The escapade led directly to Tullard High's only state championship and, indirectly, to hooking me up with Curt Janssen. The other things that brought Curt and me together were my fraternal twin Janda and the shoes I won for calling the radio station and identifying the voice of Billy Graham. All that plus hormones. But let me finish the part about the coach.

The assistant coach, a guidance counselor by day, had been sleeping with the coach's wife, which everyone in town knew before the coach did. After the coach got sent to the state hospital, the assistant dedicated the season to his old boss. He also accused Curt Janssen, the starting point guard, of smoking dope and kicked him off the team. Inspired by the loss of the coach and the rah-rah bullying of the new coach, the team banded together, played its heart out, and won the state championship.

I hate sports stories bad.

As for Curt Janssen, I didn't think he knew I was alive (I was a sophomore; he was a senior), until he invited me to join his intramural basketball team. I was shooting baskets after school, in my new shoes, alone in the dim lights of the auxiliary gym.

"It's not coed," I told him.

"Is now." Curt had curly hair and glassy eyes. I suspected he'd been framed, that his eyes were naturally glassy. This was naive; he bought dope by the kilo. "If they stop us, we'll sue."

Why not? I dribbled to the top of the key and let the ball fly. Nothing but net. I said yes.

He told me where to buy my uniform and he handed me a schedule. "Nice shoes," he said.

They were black high-tops with bright gold stripes. I'd replaced the white laces with black ones. "I won them," I said. "Off of WFCY." WFCY promoted itself as the first solar-powered radio station in Ohio. Like that was a reason to listen.

"For doing what?" said Curt Janssen.

The truth: whenever Billy Graham specials came on, Daddy tuned in, filling up his red vinyl chair, drinking beer, shouting amen. You couldn't tell if he was into it or mocking it, but he got more animated with those specials than he ever did with his family. Daddy, a borderline giant, was a graveyard-shift chemist at the candy factory. He was so quiet that it's hard to imagine him now as the lay minister of a church out in Oregon, though I guess that proves the Billy Graham stuff sunk in. It sunk in with me, too, enough to identify his voice and win a pair of shoes from Spradler's Sports Spot. But I needed something better than that to tell Curt Janssen, so I said: "They asked who was the only person to play with the Beatles and the Stones. I called in." I pointed to the shoes. "Voila."

"Eric Clapton?"

"Billy Preston," I said.

Curt Janssen nodded. "Think you're a tomboy, don't you?"

"Far from it." I was lying.

He began to walk out of the gym, but he stopped in the doorway. "Isn't Janda Daxbury your sister?"

"We're twins." Fraternal twins; we don't even look like sisters. I'm tall, black-haired, conceited, lazy, and big boobed. Janda is short, ethereal, political, dogged, and blond. I'm better looking, though not everybody seems to think so.

"Janda's a nice girl," Curt said. "Not long for Tullard, though. Damn, those shoes are nice."

So I broke the gender line at the Tullard High intramural basketball league. Not that this is any big deal. I'm just letting you know. Our game plan was rigid: *pass the ball to Curt.* We lost only once, in the title game, when he was hopelessly stoned. My strength was setting picks. No one wants to slam into a big girl, so they'd just stop dead, which does the job.

Curt Janssen and I became friends, via which he began to date Janda, although he couldn't even date a sophomore without laying the groundwork. He'd come over and hang out with me, eating pretzels and watching martial-arts movies, while Janda invented reasons to come into the family room— misplaced purse, misplaced comb, misplaced homework. Some guys are so slow. I know they fear rejection, but it's pathetic to waste all that time once the signs are there. Janda liked sex and Janda liked smoking dope and Janda liked Curt. If he'd have read the crap in her diary, he'd have just jumped her, which I would have respected more.

Curt finally asked her to the prom, a month in advance. Then they did the usual small-town thing: cruising in his car (a plum-red Mitsubishi Galant), making lap upon joyless lap around the town square, parking at McDonald's, sipping canned beer in the parking lot, and, finally, driving out onto a county road and fucking.

Janda got pregnant on prom night. They'd broken into a house trailer at a dealership on the edge of town. Curt only brought two rubbers; they did it three times, once atop the plastic-covered mattresses in each of the trailer's bedrooms.

When my mother found out, she laughed. Janda had come to her in tears. I'd agreed to stand by for moral support. My mother had finished the dishes and was on her way out to the bars. We stopped her as she opened the door to the station wagon. She got in and just sat there, her face blank at first, listening to the whole story. She chewed on her straight colorless hair, and she looked old. The seventeen-year locusts were out that year, buzzing and whirring and dying all over the sidewalks. The locusts were a year older than Janda and me. It was that part of summer where you first notice the days are getting shorter.

When Janda finished, my mother slammed the car door. Then she rolled down the window and laughed. "Where did you guys think *you* came from? The stork? You know, I got pregnant from two different men. I been meaning to tell you."

Janda and I looked at each other. Our mother popped a stick of gum in her mouth.

"Just kidding," she said. "Ha-ha." She wasn't laughing anymore, or even smiling. "May *you* have twins, too." She started the car, turned on the radio, and closed her eyes, listening to some delicate twangy music involving a young girl in El Paso. Then she put the car in gear and sped away.

JANDA HAD THE baby, but by then Curt Janssen was long gone and so was I. She named the baby Abby Marie, after me. I guess that's sweet. Most people are more sentimental than I am.

Curt's parents had owned the third-most-prosperous dry cleaners in a town that could support only two. Curt wanted to go to Defiance College, but Janssen's Cleaners-with-Martinizing went belly-up a week after he graduated.

"What do you think," he asked me, "should I join the army?"

We were playing miniature golf, the only ones on the course. A month later, the place was sold to developers, and now, I hear, it's a Jiffy Lube. Curt had just taken a four on the dinosaur hole; he was plain rattled.

"Not the army," I said. "The air force."

"Hey, ma-a-a-an." He inhaled from an invisible joint. "I'm *high* on the air force. Although I heard they're mostly gay. The air force."

"So then you'll fit in perfectly."

I didn't know if Curt knew Janda was pregnant. She'd been working up the nerve to tell him; now it was *her* turn to be slow.

"If I ring the bell in the clown's mouth," Curt said, "then the air force it is."

He drilled the shot. The bell made a sound like a measuring cup dropped on a linoleum floor.

"What's the air force fight song?" he said. He turned in his club and gave me the free-game card he'd won.

"'The Wild Blue Yonder.'" I still thought he was kidding.

"Off we go," he said.

The next day, Curt drove his Galant to the recruitment office in Toledo and joined. The day after that, Janda told him
about the baby. Timing is everything.

Two days later, Daddy moved into room four at the Town-
line Motel. This had been a long time coming. The candy
company was opening a new plant in Oregon, and Daddy had
begged to go. Once he got the news, even though the transfer
wouldn't take effect for a month, he moved out. He came
home after his shift, packed, and went. He left a note. My
mother tore it up and ate it.

The day before Curt Janssen left for boot camp, he took
Janda and me to Cedar Point, this big amusement park up on
Lake Erie. Because of the baby, Janda was afraid to ride anything, though she did wait for us. My favorite was a roller
coaster called the Blue Streak. It was blue and wooden, and
when it dropped down hills and then jerked back up, my body
became weightless, outside of time and senses except for the
padded bar that pressed against my hollow-boned teenaged
hips. Curt, heavier, stayed in his seat. But we both screamed
together, and I felt uneasy to think that this guy might soon be
flying jets for America.

When we walked away from the Blue Streak, bandy-legged
and hungry, Janda came up to us with a one-gallon plastic
bucket of caramel corn. "Share?" she said. Janda: ever the
socialist.

I saw Curt look at the sunlight on her blond hair. I saw
him run his eyes down her body: the perfect little boobs, the
for-now flat stomach, the pink legs that barely needed
shaving.

We stayed at Cedar Point until dark. We watched the fireworks display, and on the way home, Curt and Janda sat in the
front seat. "I need to ask you a favor, Abby," Curt said, glancing in the rearview mirror.

"Like I need *her*," Janda said. She wasn't looking at anyone, and I knew not to take this personally. "A woman can choose," she said. "This choice I'm making is a choice. I'm not caving in to anything. I know where I could get an abortion. I know how much it would cost, and I have enough money to pay for it myself. But I refuse to live a life in which I take the path of least resistance. I'm having this baby because it's what I want to do, irrespective of my family or even you, Curt."

"We've been through all that," Curt said. "Ninety-nine million times. Abby, would you just look out for Janda? For me?"

"Don't patronize me," Janda said. This being *the* cardinal sin. "I already have a mother."

"You can count on me, Curt," I said. But I said that just to get Janda's goat. At the time, I was caught up in the way summer felt inside my body—loamy, humid, friendly. I didn't feel committed to do anything.

So Curt left. Janda still wasn't showing, and she still did have a mother, sort of. A few weeks later, sick of that little town, I asked if I could move to Oregon with Daddy. My mother told me to suit myself. As I pulled away in Daddy's car, Janda watched, her forehead pressed against the screen door, her hair swept back, her hand on her stomach, smoothing the folds in a sundress she'd stolen from my mother's closet.

DADDY AND I MOVED into a ten-year-old, half-vacant apartment building in a cookie-cutter development on the edge of a nothing town in central Oregon. I spent the last days of summer at the pool, reading fuck-and-brag autobiographies that I stole from the public library. I took the books back when I finished; I just liked the challenge of sneaking away with them.

Back in Tullard, my mother took up with the coach's wife, the one with the shot-off nose. According to Janda, the coach's wife dumped the new coach, sold her house, and moved into ours—into my old bedroom! People in Tullard spread the rumor that my mother and the coach's wife had gone lesbo. False; they were drinking buddies. Men with the same bond, living like slobs in separate bedrooms under the same roof, would be considered rakish bachelors. Janda swore revenge on the town for this, and she got it.

The school had a rule against pregnant students—unenforced for years, but still on the books. When the new basketball coach, in his role as guidance counselor, suggested that she might be more comfortable staying home until after the baby was born, Janda socked him in the jaw. He told her she was suspended for a month. She said she'd see about that. She stormed out of the office and left the guy bleeding on his desk blotter.

At some point, the new coach must have grasped the impossibility of making people believe he'd been coldcocked by a tiny pregnant honor student (*I* found it perfectly in character, but I'm her sister). The fact that his former lover (a woman whose maiming he'd indirectly caused) was believed to be romantically involved with Janda's mother didn't help him any. Which is when he happened upon that rule. That, officially, is why he suspended her—for the entire balance of her pregnancy.

Janda refused to sign up for correspondence courses, even when the school offered to pay. The new coach rethought his position and offered to drop the suspension, but by then Janda had gotten in touch with the ACLU office in Detroit. Her lawyer said Janda would return to school only if the school dropped that rule and issued a public apology. The school board, with predictable stupidity (this is Tullard, Ohio, we're talking about), dug in its heels. The lawsuit attracted media attention. It even got on CNN. There was a long shot of Janda and her lawyers, standing in front of my old school. In the background, you could see my mother and the half-nosed coach's wife, each dressed in green, and a banner proclaiming Tullard High as last year's state basketball champs.

The ACLU won, of course. For damages inflicted upon her reputation and education, Janda received a certified check from the Tullard Board of Education in the amount of $200,002. The extra two bucks came at Janda's insistence, God knows why. Before she cashed the check, she had it photocopied. She had one copy dry-mounted and framed. She sent me another, along with little Abby Marie's birth announcement and a picture of the shriveled and gorgeous creature, minutes old, lying in the glass toaster they use to warm up newborns. Her eyes are wide open, fixed on the camera, and old: the gray eyes of a resigned adult. She looks just like me, and, like I said, she's gorgeous.

THAT NEXT CHRISTMAS, Curt Janssen showed up—in uniform—at our apartment in Oregon. Unannounced. I was shocked to see him with so little hair; I was shocked to see him period. What could he be thinking? I asked. Why didn't he go back to Tullard?

He shrugged. "I can fly anywhere I want, free," Curt said. "I wanted to come here. I could still go there. I got four days leave. Are you going to let me come in? I have beer."

I slammed the door in his face.

I'd always wanted to do that.

Then I put my ear to the door and listened. I couldn't hear anything. He wasn't moving. I waited a hopeless few minutes and opened the door.

"Want me to leave?" He'd lost the glassy look in his eyes.

"Yes," I said. "Do. Leave."

He stayed, of course.

Christmas morning, we all got up, had coffee, turned on

the TV, sat cross-legged around the thirty-six-inch tree I'd put on an end table, and unwrapped the boxes of candy Daddy had gotten free from the plant. He also got me the top ten CDs in the country; he'd gone to a store, looked at the chart on the wall, and tracked down all ten titles. Why he did this, I don't know, and, as usual, the top ten at that time was full of all kinds of crap. Still, it was sweet. Daddy had wrapped each disc individually.

I gave Daddy a sweater and a bottle of Polo Sport. I gave Curt Janssen a framed photo of his baby. Curt gave Daddy a San Diego Padres cap, and he gave me a cheap gold bracelet. When I opened it, I told him I couldn't possibly. He told me he couldn't return it.

Daddy showered and, wearing a coat and tie and his new cap, went in to work to pick up some overtime.

Curt and I lay sprawled on a futon, the only seat in the room, smoking dope and watching cartoons. He'd become a bit less slow, and (though I'd repressed it) I had always wanted him, anyway, which sped things up. I can't say it was the right thing to do, though its wrongness may have been the appeal. Janda and my namesake were a continent away, while Curt Janssen and I lay there, high and young and vibrating with ill-harnessed hormones. That's the best defense I can mount without lying.

He didn't have a rubber. We did it for a little while, but I made him pull out, and we did the reciprocal rocks-off tango.

On TV, a football game came on. The game was in Indiana: near home. Snow fell behind the parka-clad announcers.

Curt pulled me close. We still had most of our clothes on. "Looks cold back there," he said.

"We can't do this anymore," I said.

"You're right," he said. He bent down and put my foot in his mouth. I slapped him on his bristly head.

He looked up at me, then at the TV. He was as dreamy and bewildered as an old collie. "I mean," he said, "it *really* looks cold." He frowned. "Y'know? Cold as cold can be."

We did do it a couple more times, and the sex got better, as it will, but by the time he left, we'd sworn each other off. We agreed that this never happened. And Curt Janssen agreed to go back to Tullard for the rest of his Christmas furlough.

Now GET A load of this: when Curt Janssen got there, he and Janda went sledding and to a movie, and he proposed.

Proposed! Men. I swear. Janda said no, bless her.

A year later, Curt Janssen got an assignment as a jet mechanic in Pensacola. He came to Janda's high school graduation and proposed again. Janda agreed, on two conditions: that she could find a college to go to down there and that nobody's parents come to the wedding.

She became Janda Daxbury-Janssen, a freshman at the University of West Florida (I'd never heard of it, either), living in a house on the base. Neither Daddy nor my mother had her address, although I found out later that the ex-coach's half-nosed ex-wife sent a blender and a Pick-Me-Up bouquet to General Delivery, Pensacola, Florida, USA.

My mother then took up with the lunatic ex-coach, who'd been acquitted and, during his stay at the laughing academy, supposedly cured. The coach, whose name, I swear to God, is Ed Macaroni, took a job selling real estate, as all burned-out teachers do, and apparently became the better man for it. His ex-wife took an apartment in town, but according to my mother, everyone remained friends. During my junior year at Oregon State, my mother began sending me letters: chatty notes from a mysterious old friend I'd never actually met. She was working as a secretary at the hospital. Ed Macaroni made partner at Buckeye Brothers Realty, whereupon he asked her to marry him. She and Ed had taken up golf. She couldn't spell worth a damn.

My mother's three last names became Ames Daxbury Macaroni, like some store brand you'd have to be on food stamps to buy.

AT OREGON STATE, I set an unofficial school record for changing majors, ten in six years. Forestry, phys ed, psych, Russian, architecture, finance, English; I can't name them all, but I know there were ten. I'm only counting education once, though I declared it twice. I wound up in recreation, which, like so much of life, now seems both appropriate and inevitable.

Daddy came to my graduation, which I could no longer avoid. He was driving a brand-new Korean car. Watching him get out of it was like watching time-lapse photography of a night-blooming plant.

"Be still my heart," I said, showing him into my apartment. My first thought was that Janda was coming, too. But I knew better. As far as I knew, she was finishing her first year of law school at Florida State. Even with starting out at a compass-point school, with a baby to raise and a sweet boy of a husband to endure, Janda finished her B.A. faster than me. She'd taken her lawsuit money and bought a small house in Tallahassee. Curt kept an apartment on the base and drove over when he could. Janda wrote me that she'd taken a boarder, a black woman she described as "one of Florida's better undiscovered poets."

"Who's speaking at this graduation of yours?" Daddy asked.

I shrugged. I was packed up and hadn't intended to go.

"Good," Daddy said. "I hate graduations. Listen, let's get some food and take a road trip."

I motioned at my belongings, packed into Xerox boxes in my living room. "I need to do something with my stuff. Plus, I'm supposed to start next week with parks and rec in Portland"—wishful thinking, though I did have a second interview coming up.

"That's good," he said, looking past me out my kitchen window. "Listen. That car out there: it's yours. I thought we could drive it together somewhere. Your choice."

"Florida." I was learning not to be surprised by him; Daddy had become the world-champion giver of awkward gifts.

"Works for me. I was afraid you'd say Tullard."

I stored my things in the garage of a grad student I'd been seeing, and Daddy and I took off. We drove all night. I chewed three whole packs of Black Jack gum. Daddy tried to get some sleep in the passenger seat, tilting it all the way back, flopping around inside that little car, accompanied by the hiss of the road and a border radio station I'd pulled in from Nuevo Laredo. Near dawn, we stopped for gas. He found a pay phone. "Listen," he said when he was done, giving me a twenty for the gas. "I'm not up to this. What could I have been thinking? Drop me off in Denver, would you? I reserved a flight home. You go on to Florida, though. Enjoy your car."

I looked at him. "Are you my real father?" I didn't have any doubts; I just wanted to see if I could push his buttons, which no one but Billy Graham and Billy Graham Jr. seemed able to do.

"Have you been talking with your mother?" he said, frowning.

"She says you're not."

"I'm another person than I was when I was young, and I don't want to get into that kind of argument anymore." But he said this in a way that made me believe he had been precisely the same kind of person every day of his life.

"Never mind," I said. "Daddy, what was this all about?"

He shook his head. "God bless you," he said, outstretching his arms in a helpless, churchy way. He stood as tall as he could, which was rare for him. "I've failed you," he said. "But you did turn out pretty."

I sped off, intending to make him find his own damned way back to Oregon. But I took the next exit and went back, drove him to Denver, and dropped him off. We hugged each other in the airport, and—walking away, waving to me without actually turning around—Daddy boarded his plane.

I drove on to Tallahassee, which is a very long trip that I cannot with a clear conscience recommend.

CURT AND JANDA'S house was one of those little brick Florida things and for sale. As I drove up, Curt was shooting hoops in the drive.

"Hey," he said, unsurprised, as if I lived two blocks away and visited daily. He wore glasses now, the John Lennon kind. "It's you."

"Been me all my life," I said. "I tried to call."

"Phone's disconnected." Curt sank a long lovely jumper. He was tanned and had clearly been lifting weights. His gray tank top said "University of West Florida." He'd developed a bald spot the size of a sand dollar. "Want a beer?"

I did, but he didn't have any. I asked where Janda was. She was gone. She'd taken Abby and transferred to the University of North Carolina, apparently because of a complicated gender-related controversy concerning the Florida State law school faculty, something Curt struggled to explain as we went to get beer at Publix. On the way back, he told me about his life, which was a long, familiar story that, if you're with me so far, you could tell as well as Curt did, and it wouldn't even take you the whole return trip from the store. They'd been children. They had a child. Janda had money; he felt threatened by that. Curt was in the air force; she'd become a pacifist. He'd had poorly concealed affairs. Her, too, but with Janda, you sort of presume that if she hadn't wanted to be caught, she wouldn't have been. Janda's much smarter than Curt, and that's a gap few marriages, over time, endure.

Curt Janssen and I sat on the front steps of his house. He still didn't invite me in. "So," he said. "Here we are."

"Here we are."

"A long way from Tullard, Ohio," he said. He put his empty beer bottle back in its cardboard holder. He offered me another one, but I was ahead of him, as always. "When you drove up, I thought you were the realtor," he said. "She's supposed to have a buyer, the realtor is." He pronounced the word *real-a-tor*. It put me in mind of Ed Macaroni, and I told Curt what I knew of things back home.

Curt Janssen shook his head. "You couldn't pay me enough to go back there," he said.

"No one's offering," I said.

He clinked beer bottles with me. "Good point," he said. "I'm going to miss her." Florida was darkening now. Though Tallahassee isn't what you think of when you think of Florida. Curt and Janda's house had an actual live oak in the yard. "Abby, I mean."

"You mean what?"

"The other Abby. I'm going to miss her," he said. "Your niece. "

"Oh," I said. "You're nice, too."

"Ha-ha," he said. "You jerk."

We played a game of horse; I got hot and won. I had *h-o* when I iced him. "Maybe I should go on to Chapel Hill?"

"May be," said Curt Janssen.

The realtor drove up then, in a Lexus, with a tall and haggard young couple from Boston, newly hired professors at FSU.

While Curt and I waited, we played another game. This time he killed me, *horse* to nothing. The last couple shots I could hardly see, but darkness meant nothing to Curt. He must have been playing a lot of hoops at night.

The realtor stuck her head out the door. "Mr. Janssen," she said. "The Steinbergs have some questions for you."

"Coming," he said, as if he were answering his mother. He turned to me. "It should have been *us*," he said, slow to the bitterest of bitter ends, and you don't come upon any end so bitter as the first hour after a hot Florida dusk. "Shouldn't it have been us?" He walked toward the house, backward, as if he were being pulled there against his will. "I'm right, aren't I?"

He asked this, though, like it was a real question, one to which he actually wanted an answer.

"Wait right there," he said, and disappeared inside. The aluminum screen door swayed shut of its own spring-loaded accord.

"Wrong," I said, although there was no one to hear me. I picked up the ball from the ruined patch of flowers where it lay. I set my feet and lofted a shot into the darkness. The ball missed everything: an air ball, bounding out to the uncurbed street. I watched it roll, considering whether to make it best two out of three.

I ran out in the road after the ball, got it, dribbled up the drive, pulled up for a ten-footer, and missed again. A brick. The rebound was a line drive right back at me.

I stood in the dark, breathing hard, rubbing my hands over the ball. *What the hell,* I thought.

Best of five.

Best of seven.

Whatever it takes.

Last Love Song at
the Valentine

In 1949, my grandfather Grover Monroe took the tiny farm he'd inherited from his uncle, tore down the house, graded the field and covered it with gravel. Then he put up a concession stand, a box office, and a huge red heart-shaped marquee. He topped off the marquee with pink neon trim, rows of hundred-watt bulbs, and two spotlights that—a half hour to showtime—would send swiveling rays of light into the sky, Hollywood style. Behind where the screen would be, Big Grover dug a pond and stocked it with bluegills. He built everything but the screen himself, with no assistance from anyone but Dad, who was eighteen then and little more than warm-body help. The screen came from a company in Loma Linda, California, arriving on a flatbed truck along with a crew of four Mexicans in a panel truck. They finished the job in six hours and then sat with Big Grover on cinder blocks, drinking Stroh's beer until darkness fell.

For a time, the Valentine Theatre was the most successful drive-in in the state of Ohio. Every Friday and Saturday night that old bean field would be covered with huge cars full of nuclear families and libidinous teenagers. People showed up no matter what the movie was about. The Valentine was, for a generation, both event and ritual.

Big Grover would sit in the box office, wearing a pith helmet, greeting customers by name. Dad became the projectionist. To run the concession stand, Big Grover, a widower, hired a grade-school teacher named Frieda Porath. Soon, because she could run a tight cash register and, more so, because she and Big Grover fell in love, she quit teaching, got married, and became to everyone in town Big Frieda, although she was just a little blond-headed woman.

For years, Big Grover was a dog for detail. During the winter, he'd fly to a convention in California, where he'd go to screenings and sample boxed candies, then stay up all night in his hotel room, choosing the movies for next summer. In 1963, he took Big Frieda, who'd never been farther west than Des Moines. When she saw the Pacific Ocean, she stood in the sand with her mouth open until the tide rose above her ankles, during which time she resolved to move to California. While Big Grover went to the convention, Big Frieda put a contract on a Pasadena bungalow.

"Big Grover's moving to California," my father told me. I was nine years old and floating on a raft in the middle of the bluegill pond. Dad was on the bank, pants rolled up, fishing with a bamboo pole. He wore a clip-on tie.

"He told me," I said. "Will we visit them in the winters?"

"I don't see why not."

"Good."

"Your mother and I are excited about this. We'll be running the Valentine from now on."

"I know," I said. The way Big Grover had put it to me was this: running the business had become like keeping the training wheels on my Schwinn Spyder. You need it at first, but when a thing becomes too easy, it's a crutch, not a support.

Dad pulled out a bluegill and slipped it into a wire basket.

"I hope, son," he said, "that someday this cycle will, you know, repeat." He blushed. "Y'know? One of those someday-son-all-this-will-be-yours things?"

I lay back on the raft and looked at the sky. I couldn't imagine the Valentine without Big Grover. He let me sit with him in the ticket booth, taking money and listening to country music on a radio he kept under the counter. During the day, he and I played catch, with me using the rise beside the speaker stands for a mound and Big Grover crouching down and flashing me two fingers for a curve. He taught me how to swim in the pond, how to whistle with my fingers in my mouth, how to play poker. Dad, meanwhile, would be mowing the grass or reading self-help books.

"So, Jay." My father packed up his fishing gear. "Do you have anything to say? About, you know, all this?"

The Valentine was under a major east-west flight corridor, and the silver fangs of a passing jet grew longer above me. When you are nine years old, travel is something others decide for you, but if I had said anything to my father, it would have been this: *You are a man with a jar full of maggots, fishing for potted bluegills. I am a jet plane. I am a rocket. The moon has my name on it.* But I kept quiet, watching the smoke in the sky.

MY MOTHER MURIEL was once a tall smart girl with low self-esteem and the goal of becoming a nurse. She grew up in Michigan, where her father was a foreman at a lumberyard. When a log crushed his knee, he took his disability money and bought a lake cottage near where the Valentine was then being built. On the theater's opening night, she and a neighbor named Penny Kilgore double-dated with the Yates twins. Penny was known as easy and would years later become locally famous as one of Dean Martin's Golddiggers. Barry Yates had Penny's bra undone by the end of the Chilly Willy cartoon.

During the dancing-popcorn commercial, when Larry Yates tried to keep pace with his brother, my mother slapped his face and took a walk. The feature had begun.

She bought a Grape Crush with no ice, then stood outside the concession stand, listening to the whirring and clicking from the projection room, wondering whether to call someone for a ride or just walk home.

My father emerged from the darkness. "Do you like John Wayne? I do. Or westerns? Do you like westerns?"

"Not really." Muriel blushed. The projectionist had sat next to her in study hall.

"My dad built this place. A family business," Lin Monroe said. "Have you worn glasses long?"

"Since I was nine."

"Me, too. Eight, actually."

They maintained that level of small talk all night, each so enraptured that Dad missed the change to the next reel, which Mom said she didn't notice until the night was rocked by a cacophony of car horns. At the end of the summer, Dad gave her his class ring and his school band jacket, and Mom wrote the nursing school in Cleveland to decline their offer of admission. On Christmas Eve, he put a mute in his cornet and snuck onto the dock of the lake cottage where she lived. Snow fell, and in the yellow glow of the boathouse light, he played "Good King Wenceslas." They were engaged in January and married in June.

At Big Grover's insistence, the wedding took place under the buzzing pink neon of the Valentine marquee. The stone lot was big enough to provide parking for everyone in town— all of whom were invited—with enough space left over for six barbecue grills and five banquet tables from the Benevolent and Protective Order of the Elks, to which Big Grover belonged. Big Grover told me he was dismayed no one ever asked to be the *second* couple married there. "Should have been a natural," he said. "Who wouldn't want to begin a life together underneath a big electric heart?"

Once, driving me to the eye doctor, Mom saw a mile marker with DETROIT on it and started to cry. I asked her what was wrong. "Nothing," she said. On the way back, she told me that she never expected her life to turn out this way. "I wanted to be a nurse," she said. "An old maid. Living in a big apartment building in a city like Detroit." Then she took me for ice cream and, right before I ordered, made me swear not to tell my father what she'd said. I asked why she'd said anything in the first place. She just pulled a five out of her purse and nodded toward the waiting clerk. I swore.

WHEN BIG GROVER and Big Frieda moved to Pasadena, Mom, who'd been taking business courses down at Ohio State, began to keep the Valentine's books. She worked at home and rarely came to the theater itself. In a pinch, she'd take tickets, though she was too shy to greet customers by name or wear a pith helmet. Dad struggled through two years with a ragtag collection of high school kids, ruined farmers, and odd-job careerists. For me, the place lost its sense of wonder, and I stayed away, inventing baseball practices, sneaking into the adult wing of the public library. For the first time, the Valentine lost money.

Big Grover came home for Thanksgiving, 1965. He and my parents went down in the basement while Big Frieda and I played with Legos and watched the Macy's Parade. They'd come up, muttering like strikeout victims, to use the bathroom or to grab more coffee—or, in Big Grover's case, more Stroh's. During the Detroit Lions game, I heard Mom and Big Grover yelling. Just before the Cowboys game, Dad asked Big Frieda to start the turkey. When it was ready, the three of them came upstairs together, though no one spoke. We sat down to dinner at midnight, and Big Grover asked me to tell him all about the football games. That took me a long time, and it seemed to break the tension; Mom kissed Dad on the cheek, and Big Grover tried to loop his long arms around his whole family. We ate dessert in the living room, a taboo broken. Spirits were high. I fell asleep with half a piece of rhubarb pie in my lap.

BIG GROVER HAD agreed to the hiring of two new full-time employees, but it was Dad's idea to have those people be a husband-and-wife caretaker team who'd live in a trailer behind the bluegill pond. Every day that spring, Dad would pick me up after school, and we'd go shopping for house trailers. We must have gone to every house-trailer dealership in central Ohio. The trailers seemed like vast metal clubhouses, filled with blond plywood, plastic-covered mattresses, plaster lamps with duck-dappled shades, and framed prints of cowboys.

"What do you think of this one?" Dad said, climbing the wobbly iron steps to a fifty-by-ten New Moon.

"I liked the Detroiter better." We'd seen it at a dealership near Lake Erie, Wahoo Larry's Trailer Sales, which was surrounded by a fake log fence that made it look like a fort. The sales office was called "The Tradin' Post," and our salesman, a cigar-smoking guy named Howard, wore cowboy boots and gave me a coonskin cap. "The Detroiter had bay windows and swag lights, and I think the price was real good, Dad."

But Dad liked the New Moon. It had a white Naugahyde couch and tiny windows that made the inside dark and creepy, a green crescent moon painted on the side, and absolutely no pictures of cowboys. The weedy little salesman threw in a set of steps, then, in a whisper, said that Detroiters had done poorly in tornado tests. Dad pursed his lips and ran a finger across the Naugahyde. The salesman produced a fountain pen. Dad signed the contract, right on the white couch.

We drove home in silence, until I worked up enough courage to say, "Big Grover would have bought the Detroiter."

My father pulled the car onto the shoulder. "Get out."

I figured we were going for a walk and a long father-son talking-to, so I got out of the car without fear. Then it occurred to me that he might be planning to spank me, although he had rarely done so. Through the car window, I saw Dad's face, knotted in anger, eyes straight ahead. My stomach grew ice-hot. He didn't get out. I stood in the ditch, trembling. Finally, Dad put the car in gear and drove away.

His taillights disappeared over a hill. The sun had set; it was getting cold. I ran into the muddy furrows of a cornfield. When I got to the middle, I sat down and cried, though I was in the seventh grade and knew it was unmanly. I decided to wait until dark, then hitch a ride with a trucker and go join the circus. I'd read a book about a kid who'd done that. He learned to tame tigers, and he made friends with clowns and freaks. This cheered me up, especially when I realized how wrecked my parents would be. But by the time I got back to the road, Dad was leaning against the side of his blue Ford.

"What were you doing out there?"

"I'm telling Mom about this."

"She won't care. She'd have done the same thing."

"You're a mean bastard, Dad." I'd stopped about ten feet short of him. I tensed up and prepared to run.

"Maybe I am. If that's true, son, I'm sorry."

It was dark. I was shivering.

"You need to learn something," he said. "I'm your father."

"No kidding."

"And you have to let me be your father, and not my father."

I had no idea what he was talking about. I didn't think Big Grover was my father; I didn't even *wish* he was. I only knew that he was my friend, and I wanted him to come home.

Dad opened my door for me. On the way home, he talked about how Big Grover never gave him the freedom to make his own mistakes, and he'll be damned if his own son is going to deny him that now, blah, blah, blah. I tried to tune him out by reciting the Cleveland Indians roster in my head. It didn't work. I had to nod and listen. I never told anyone about being left alongside Route 63 that night, but I vowed to get even.

THE HOUSE TRAILER arrived a week later. Dad hired two longhaired Canadians to live and work there: Harmon and Nina Garceau. Harmon drove a Jeep. The day before the Valentine opened for the season, they replaced the white Naugahyde couch with a futon. I sailed the raft into the middle of the bluegill pond and decided the moon on the side of the trailer was kind of cool. Dad took the couch home and stuck it in our basement.

Harmon Garceau could fix anything. He used to be a golf pro and was about six four, with a thin red ponytail that hung halfway down his back. He and Nina climbed glaciers, and their trailer was filled with pitons and ropes and hiking boots, which Nina resoled herself. Harmon mowed the lawn with an old Toro that he worked on every day, propping it up on cinder blocks, taking the engine apart, sharpening the blade, soaking pieces of flanged and threaded metal in a coffee can full of Valvoline. He taught me how to swing the weed whip like a golf club, and when I mastered that, he began taking me to a driving range each Monday morning. He made me learn to swing with my eyes closed. "Bad pros teach you to keep your eye on the ball," he said. "Good pros teach you to keep your eye within the ball." He would blindfold himself with a T-shirt and drive the ball 280 yards.

"My neighbor Mrs. Kammeyer says that you guys are hippies." The Kammeyers had been to our house for dinner the night before. That was the first time I'd heard the term.

Harmon took the T-shirt from his head. "Yippies?"

"Hippies."

"Oh." He lined up five balls on the rug in front of him, pulled out a five iron, restored the blindfold, and hit each ball two hundred yards and straight. "Tell Mrs. Kammeyer that if I was an American, I'd've voted for Goldwater." He took off the T-shirt and tossed the club to me. "And tell her I'm in favor of returning Quebec to France or any other place that'd have those crazy frogs. That is, if Mrs. Kammeyer knows where Quebec is." He smiled, then blindfolded me. "Or where France is, eh?"

Nina was thin and pale and didn't need or wear a bra. She spoke in a thick Canadian accent and had a brother who played hockey for the Boston Bruins. She took over the concession stand, and she got pretty good at it. She added granola, honey yogurt, and lemon curd to the menu, but no one bought them. Before Dad worked up the nerve to tell her to ix-nay the nuts and berries, Nina herself gave it up. "What do I care," she told me, "if people want their teeth to rot out"—*oot*—"and fill up their intestines with undigested meat?"

"I don't know," I said. "What *do* you care?"

"Exactly."

After that, Nina sold the sweetest, most dire concessions you could imagine, using calligraphy skills she'd learned from her mother to make graceful signs that pushed snow cones, cotton candy, and southern-fried pizza burgers. The rabble ate them up.

While Dad stayed in the projection room, Mom and Harmon took turns in the ticket booth. Harmon preferred to be in there alone. Mom, though, would let me play cashier while she studied. In 1968, the Valentine was the only drive-in theater in Ohio to be allowed to show *Gone with the Wind,* which was rereleased that year. We broke all records for the three weeks it played, and all during the run, I took tickets. Mom sat beside me, studying for a final in marketing, and tucking bundles of fives into the bank bag. "When I get done with this degree," she'd say. She wore cat-eye glasses then. She took them off and looked me in the eye, one firm hand on my shoulder. She smiled. "You just wait."

SHE GRADUATED summa cum laude in December 1970. Big Grover and Big Frieda flew in for graduation, and I sat beside them at the ceremony. Dad walked down near the stage to take pictures.

"How *are* things, Jay?" Big Grover asked me after the commencement address, given by an executive from General Motors.

"I don't know. I shot an eighty-six in a tournament up in Toledo."

"That's not what I mean." He was about sixty, though he looked younger: tanned, edgy, a guy with things to prove. "You did know Lin and Muriel offered to buy the Valentine from me?"

That was the first I'd heard of it.

"If Lin wants to be in charge of something, I'm letting him do it before the notion passes." The summa cum laudes paraded across the front of the stage. Mom waved at Dad, and flashbulbs popped. "I'm selling the Valentine, Jay, and buying a piece of a minor league ball club in Bakersfield. This is the most initiative your dad ever showed, paying for a thing he'd inherit in twenty years."

"C'mon," I said. "You'll live longer than that."

We drove home and had a party in our backyard. Dad hung a string of plastic-owl patio lights across the back of the house. Big Frieda cooked up a tub of potato salad, Dad barbecued, and we ate a big bakery cake: a three-tiered angelfood wonder. On top, a doll in cap and gown clutched a small black diploma. At dusk, Big Grover and I took our gloves and went to a softball field. He asked to see my curveball. I threw a few dozen balls, out of the strike zone and without much break. Then we walked across town to the Valentine Drive-In Theater, where the marquee read CLOSED FOR THE SEASON. The lightbulbs had been unscrewed, and the trailer was empty. Harmon and Nina were climbing a glacier in Manitoba. The pond was frozen. Big Grover asked if my dad had told me about sex. All Dad had said was not to do it with anyone I wasn't prepared to marry, but I told Big Grover I knew the basics. We smoked cigarillos together, then he gave me a package of condoms, and we walked home in the dark.

MOM AND DAD borrowed enough money to buy the business and make the expansions Mom proposed in her senior marketing project (for which she'd received a B, back when that was a good grade). That spring, twenty-two years after Big Grover graded the beanfield, construction resumed at the Valentine. They put in a playground near the pond. Then they solved the speaker problem—a problem of both low fidelity and (because people ripped speakers from their posts and drove off) larceny—by purchasing a system that allowed people to tune in the sound track on their AM radios. They bought four acres from the adjoining farm and put in several more rows and a miniature golf course. This way, Mom had written, the Valentine could make money in the daytime, too.

To oversee construction, Harmon Garceau came back early from glacier climbing. For some reason no one would talk about, Nina stayed with her sister in Vancouver. Dad shopped for miniature-golf hazards from a stack of magazines he kept in the projection room. When the hazards came, he supervised their installation at the far edge of the new property. He spent his days out there, alone, gluing down green carpet and assembling motorized dogs.

Mom hired Mrs. Kammeyer to run the concession stand, and once school finished, I worked full-time, too. For a few weeks, attendance compared well with the heady figures of the '50s. Mom stayed home, in a basement office near the white Naugahyde couch, reconciling bank deposits and compiling a five-year plan. She never seemed more self-assured.

Mom and Dad planned a fireworks display for the Fourth of July. They booked *The Green Berets* and hired a company from Delaware to stage the fireworks. Mom let me write the newspaper ads. I billed it as "Valentine Red, White Hot, True Blue, and *Green Berets*." It sounded good at the time.

Nina Garceau came back July 1, Dominion Day in Canada. Her hair was shorter than Dad's. She'd gained about twenty pounds and her face was puffy. Her first day back, she brought Harmon a sack lunch, which he ate while he mowed, and then she invited me to eat with her in the trailer.

"Have you ever been to Vancouver?" she asked. She served me grilled cheese, tomato soup, and Fritos. "It's almost beautiful there." She talked slower now.

We chatted about the improvements to the Valentine. I wanted to ask why she'd stayed in Vancouver, but I couldn't. Nina took away my clean plate and empty bowl, then sat next to me and brushed my cheek with the palm of her hand. "Today's my thirtieth birthday," she said. "Do you know what that means?"

"No," I said. I was seventeen and was struggling to figure out what *that* meant.

Nina ran her hands through my hair, then stood up. She

took off her halter top and stood in front of me, naked and unshy. She stretched, which made her breasts look even smaller. "Neither do I," she said, and she walked into the bathroom. I heard the shower begin to run, and I left.

Since that previous December, I'd really wanted to use those condoms. It was sad, I thought, to have a full pack. I had no experience with this sort of thing, but I thought it over and I concluded that I was pretty sure Nina wanted to have sex with me.

I had watched Harmon and Nina together; I was sure something had changed. They'd always seemed outgoing and happy, yet now they hardly spoke. They hardly looked at each other. Nina spent her days either in the trailer or on the swing set.

The place was packed on the Fourth. Harmon took tickets, and for a while, I helped. He told me I should be proud of those ads I'd written. I thanked him. Harmon was my best friend, and here I was, receiving a compliment from him while toying with the idea of losing my virginity with his wife. I knew it was wrong, but it would be years before right and wrong played a part in choosing my sex partners. Still, it made me nervous to talk to Harmon while I had an erection for Nina, so I told him I had to help Dad close the golf course.

When I got there, the lights were off and Dad was putting away the vacuum. I helped him store the putters. On our way to the projection room, I told him I thought the expansions turned out great, but I wanted him to know I wasn't ever going to take over the business.

"I know," he said. He did not look at me. I can rarely remember a moment when my father looked me in the eye, though I often tried to connect with him. "You're going to college next year, and we'll never see you again. I give you my blessings."

I had approached my father with the idea of getting some

kind of advice. Instead, we talked about all the John Wayne movies that had shown at the Valentine, and I was in bed with Nina Garceau well before the fireworks began.

HARMON AND NINA left at the end of the season and gave no forwarding address. I had made love with Nina twelve times that summer; I had used up the whole pack and was proud. She didn't move much, but she held me so tight she left red welts along my ribs. We said almost nothing. When we'd finish, I would be suffused with the urge to flee. And I was able to do that, because Nina would always roll over and go to sleep, and because there was a back door to the New Moon. Before I could summon up the wherewithal to buy more condoms, our affair was over.

One Monday in late August, Harmon and I were golfing. His mechanics had gone to hell; he didn't even break a hundred. "The nineteen eighties are coming, Jay," he told me, riding back to the Valentine in his Jeep. "I can't be a handyman in a drive-in theater during the nineteen eighties. I read in a magazine that by then, you're going to be able play movies on a computer in your home. The industrial revolution is about to kick in again, in a whole other way."

Harmon was nervous. I'd never seen Harmon nervous before. My gut tightened. He knew.

"I'm going to law school this fall, buddy," he said. "I'm not saying where. Nina's going back to let's just say Vancouver."

He pulled the Jeep in behind the house trailer. The crescent moon was flaking off. "Stay within the ball, buddy," he said. "If you catch my drift."

THE LAST MOVIE shown at the Valentine Drive-In Theater was *Flashdance*. I had moved to Arizona, and I hadn't the stomach to go watch the place die. By the time the Valentine closed, drive-ins had died out everywhere, so I have to tip my hat to Mom and Dad. Their loan payments were out of control, people bought VCRs and stayed home, and the only customers were drunks and teenagers—yet, still, they kept the place open until 1983.

When it closed, Mom found a job in Columbus, but Dad hardly looked. He wrote to the companies that had supplied him with putt-putt hazards, asking if they needed anyone, but most of the letters were returned, addressee unknown. None of the indoor theaters nearby needed projectionists, he said, though I suspect he never applied. Mom tried to get Dad to move to Columbus. He wouldn't, and that strain was the one that proved permanent.

Mom got remarried last year, and he's a nice guy, as dentists go. "You can't tell about things," she told me at the wedding. "I wanted to be a nurse, and now here I am, an M.B.A. marrying a D.D.S." She laughed. I told her I was happy for her.

The last time I was home was two years ago, for Big Grover's funeral. His will decreed that half his ashes be buried beneath home plate at the ballpark in Lodi, the other, beneath the marquee at the Valentine. A judge ruled this request was that of an unbalanced mind—which shows you what judges know—and Big Grover was buried instead in his hometown cemetery, in a plot next to his first wife, which he'd bought when she died, in 1940, and then forgotten about.

I cried at the funeral. I had not cried since that long-ago afternoon in the muddy cornfield, but now I sobbed. Still, I had enough sense, when no one was looking, to slip a new baseball and a can of Stroh's into the casket.

Dad skipped the funeral. I thought I had enough time to go find him before my plane left. We had things to talk about. I presumed he was at the Valentine; the house had been sold as part of the divorce, and Dad still lived in that old New Moon.

The first thing I saw was the tattered screen. The neon was gone from the marquee. The wooden heart had faded to the color of Pepto-Bismol. In place of the spotlights was a portable yellow sign, which read FLEA MARKET TO AY/M NI GOLF OP N.

The bluegill pond had dried up, and grass had grown as high as the old speaker posts. The concession stand was boarded up. Dad had mowed around the putt-putt course and along one side of the drive-in, where dented vans were parked behind a row of card tables piled with broken appliances and pictures of Elvis.

While I tried to figure out what to say to my father, I opened the trunk, took my putter and a golf ball out of the bag, and went to play. I parred the loop-the-loop and the dogleg.

"Mind if I join you?" Dad held a cheap putter in one hand, a green ball in the other. We played two holes in silence. I bogeyed them; Dad aced both. We talked about current events. The weather. I told him Ann and my kids and my job and whatever else he asked about were all doing fine. About anything that mattered, anything I'd driven there to resolve, I was speechless.

We played a few more holes, and I asked about the flea market business.

"They're supposed to pay me twenty percent of what they take in. It's on the honor system." For some reason, his voice cracked. He stopped playing, and he tried to speak, but the words didn't come. His eyes were on that tattered old screen. Finally, he said, "I make out okay."

I wanted to ask him why he hadn't come to the funeral. I wanted to tell him how angry that made me. I wanted to get even with him, for that day he left me on the side of the road, for everything. I could have done it. He was mine for the taking, vulnerable, ready to be the victim of revenge.

And all I did was tap him on his shoulder and tell my father that it was his turn.

We finished the course together. He beat me by two strokes, and I was somehow happy for that. He walked me to the car, stiffly placing his arm around me. We looked at each other, tried to come up with something to say, then shook hands.

I opened the car door. "Do you still play the cornet?"

He smiled. "The cornet? God. I forgot I ever played."

"Do you still have it?"

He laughed. "I have no idea. I stored most of the things from the house over in the concession stand there."

Dad found the keys to the padlocked door, and we went through his old things together. It took a long time, and I missed my plane. Finally, I found the cornet, right under the sno-cone machine. I blew the dust off the case, opened it, and put the mouthpiece in the horn, the mute in the bell. My father held the cornet in trembling hands, tried a scale to warm up, then played "Good King Wenceslas." He missed four or five notes. His tone was thin. I knew this was pathetic, and probably so did he, and he played, anyway, and I didn't say anything. It was good to hear. We looked each other in the eye, which is a weirdly intimate thing to do with a man blowing inexpertly into a brass instrument. By any objective standard, he must have sounded terrible.

Travelers Advisory

R C.'s going in early—to work overtime, he claims. Under the blue halo of the security light, Caroline Day sits on the trailer's black iron steps, cold, coltish, shivering, draped in the gray sweatshirt she stole last year, along with *The Portable Tolstoy,* from the college bookstore of the college she dropped out of. She presumes R. C. is actually going to do some business for Bang Plouck. He has the television on, loud and probably unwatched, keeping him company as he rushes around to get ready. The sound of a real-estate infomercial bleeds through the trailer's walls. She is surrounded by dark pine woods and an iced-over pond. Her blond hair hangs sweat-damp on her shoulders.

When the alarm went off, R. C. and Caroline had taken time to make love. Now R. C.'s running late. He slams the door of her rusty Saturn and tosses his black lunch box on the seat beside him. He rolls down the window. "Hope to God you get that job," he says, shaking his head. He rolls up the window and roars off down the gravel drive.

She considers calling to him, asking him to stop. She'd learned yesterday that her father had died. She could tell R. C. she needs the car to go to the funeral. Instead, she watches the taillights disappear into the woods. She goes in and looks at the clock. She has hours and hours until her interview. About then, her father will be buried in a veterans' cemetery up in Woodbridge, Virginia.

She snaps off the TV, puts on the radio, and finds the only station where they aren't talking about Jesus. Two DJs are trying to be funny. Each time one attempts a joke, the other toots a bicycle horn. She endures this, waiting for the weather. There's a travelers advisory on.

She'd like to play some music, but her CD player is broken. The only CDs she owns are a boxed set of early Sarah Vaughan and a two-disc Emmylou Harris anthology. These have been played so much that she used to worry the laser beam would eat through to the other side. She'd bought the player and the discs with graduation money that came before people found out she wasn't graduating. *Had* she graduated, there'd have been a windfall. Her father retired at colonel's pay and took a job with a defense contractor; his friends and associates have bucks. Her gifts would have been written off, somehow.

Caroline turns off the radio and pours a cup of coffee. She's sore from the lovemaking, and she sits down gingerly in a vinyl easy chair. Her wrists are sore, too, though R. C. used only silk scarves to tie her up. She doesn't like handcuffs. He respects that.

She rereads the letter from her brother. The little pud used stationery from the car sales office where he's the parts manager; she doesn't rate a card. *Not that you'll care,* he wrote, *but Dad finally kicked. Don't blame yourself. Don't give yourself that much credit. Still, you didn't do his heart any good. I would have called. What sort of people don't have a phone? Anyhow, the funeral is Tuesday. By the time you get this, it'll probably be too late.*

Today is Tuesday.

Her father was a tank commander in Vietnam, among

other commands and places, and she was an army brat who'd hardly known him. She'd basically raised her brother after Mom split. When her father retired, he bought a white house in the suburbs, became one with his lawn, and got elected to city council. He showed less concern for her than he did for a routine rezoning.

Caroline's last vivid memory of her father is the day before she'd started college. He carried her things up four flights of stairs; his face was red. His chest heaved. She brought him a glass of water. "Good thinking," her father said, mopping his brow. He stood up. He and Caroline faced each other for what seemed like a long time. Finally, they shook hands. "Don't screw up," he said, as if issuing an order. He straightened his lapels and opened the doors and headed down the fire stairs.

A light snow now begins to fall.

She looks at the pile of dirty dishes in the sink.

She'd have called someone then, if they'd had a phone. Maybe she'd have even driven to Woodbridge then, if R. C. hadn't needed her car. He'd wrecked his months ago and had used the insurance money to pay bills. He said. Most of it probably went to Bang.

She finishes her coffee.

On impulse, she pulls off the sweatshirt and walks naked down to the pond. The snow falls on her shoulders and melts into beads.

She makes it to the end of the dock. It's too dark for her to see her reflection on the pond's thin skiff of ice. *Can you,* she wonders, *see your reflection in ice?*

She dives in.

Her body jerks, hard, as if the meat might shake loose from the bones. She screams underwater: a terribly silly thing to do. She's a strong swimmer. She once posted the sixth-fastest hundred-yard butterfly time in the college's history.

She whip-kicks to the surface and screams out into the morning darkness.

The scream echoes back from the pine woods, animal-sounding and hollow.

Caroline wades through the pond's icy muck to the snow on the grassy bank. She starts to laugh. *Beats the alternative. Look where I find myself,* she thinks. *Never in my wildest.*

SHE'S PREGNANT, of course. She hasn't even torn the shrink-wrap from the test kit. But she knows. This isn't the first time she's been pregnant, and she doubts it'll be the last. She and R. C. are careful—condoms always, sometimes in tandem with a diaphragm. Life has chosen Caroline to be spectacularly fertile.

The other pregnancy was with Pete Miller, her then fiancé, a guy you could look at and tell he'd spend his adult life with a good job, pattern baldness, a pampered lawn, and many Stanley tools. Pete accepted this, which was the best and the worst thing about him. The abortion was a mutual decision. Pete paid half and helped her elbow past the picketers outside the college health center. Not long after, Pete and Caroline went platonic, except for the occasional lonely night. For a year or so, Pete was a good fallback escort.

Caroline was in danger of graduating until the sight of R. C. rescued her. She met him at the Boar's Head, a townie bar. She'd gone with two girls and Pete. Pete had been there before. How cool, the women said. An actual boar's head. A bowling machine. Football jerseys from the townie high school. Pete bought them a pitcher of cold beer. "It's cool," he said, "only because we'll never wind up in a place like this. You know," he said, "really wind *up* here."

Caroline filled her own plastic cup and drank most of it in a single pull.

One of the other girls, Cat, said that Pete had a point, and weren't they all lucky. Cat and Pete were both going after M.B.A.s that fall. The other girl, Dawn, had taken a job that would force her to sell some esoteric industrial product that she kept trying to explain.

Caroline caught sight of a slim-hipped man playing blues songs on the jukebox, poking the buttons with the long slender fingers of a pianist. Baseball cap in his rear pocket. Caroline got up, brushed past the feet of her friends, and walked over to him. She and R. C. exchanged names. "What's 'R. C.' stand for?"

"Some people are named after their daddy," he said. "I was named after pop."

She regarded him.

"Soda pop."

"I'm serious," she said.

"Doesn't stand for anything," he said. "Just letters, is all."

She asked him to dance.

He looked her up and down. "No," he said. "Thanks."

She nodded. "Got the class thing going, huh?"

"Class ring?" He shook his head. "Don't wear one."

She was about to roll her eyes. She caught herself. "Class *thing*," she said.

"Joke," he said. "You think I'm this real person, right? You're sick of Mr. Polo Shirt." He jerked a thumb toward Pete. "You want someone dangerous." He smiled. "Of course, it's Mr. Polo Shirt who's *really* dangerous, right? Same old song." He drummed his fingers on the jukebox. "Thing is, I'm an old-song guy." He pressed a quarter into her palm. "Pick something you like."

She handed it back. "I like *your* taste."

"I bet you do," he said.

"It was just a dance," she said. "Don't flatter yourself."

"I used to be a civil rights lawyer. Does that surprise you?"

She said it didn't.

"It should." He turned his back on her, laughed, and ran one tapered finger along the face of the jukebox. "It's a lie."

He walked away from her and sat down at the bar.

She went back to Dawn, Cat, and Pete.

On their way out, R. C. stopped her. Caroline motioned for her friends to go ahead, and she and R. C. danced to slow Chicago blues until last call.

He walked her home. He worked at the plant, he told her. He screwed legs on to sofas. They kissed good night: kissed only.

Over the next few days, one thing led to another. Sex with R. C. was feral and glorious. Behind the sliding plywood door of his bedroom closet, he kept a milk crate filled with hand-cuffs, oils, lubricants, scarves, and condoms. R. C. took responsibility for birth control. He insisted; finally, someone. Caroline kept using her diaphragm, though not always. To document this era in her new life, she kept the condom wrappers in a bulging manila envelope under the bed.

She spent the rest of her time reading books she stole from the bookstore. She quit going to class. She learned more, faster, on her own. All those classes where you read more about the author than by the author: good-bye and good riddance.

A month before graduation, Caroline packed her things, drove her Saturn out to the woods, and waited for R. C. to come home. "Surprise," she said.

"Surprise yourself." He shook his head. "I was afraid of this. You want to move in, right?"

"How did you know?"

"They always want to move in."

Caroline hadn't counted on this. "Excuse me? 'They'?"

"So I've heard," he said.

"I'm not a 'they,'" she said. "If you can't see that—"

"That's what they all say," he said. But he was making a joke. That's how Caroline took it.

BANG PLOUCK OWNS a roadhouse outside town, filled with vending machines and jukeboxes; every coin-operated machine in town is Bang's. He also sells kegs of beer to underage frat boys and makes personal loans. Supposedly Bang once had a shot at the flyweight championship of the world but took a dive for the sure money. He is a local legend even to those, like Caroline, who've never laid eyes on him. And despite R. C.'s story about inheriting this land from his grandma and buying the trailer cheap at a police auction, Caroline's sure the money came from Bang. Before the phone company cut off service, they'd get weird threatening calls at all hours. "Don't be late," a booming voice would say. "Regrets, you'll have a few." A few calls like this, and you stop thinking it's a wrong number.

R. C. doesn't talk much, which suits them both fine. But Caroline had been a journalism major for a semester, and, when R. C.'s gone, she walks around the trailer, investigating. He subscribes to *Playboy, North Carolina,* and *National Geographic.* He has Jell-O molds nailed to the paneled walls. On the fake mantelpiece above the fake fireplace is a deflated basketball from a high school playoff game, played before he was born. He writes huge checks each month for cash. He keeps his pay stubs in his nightstand, in perfect order even though each is for precisely the same amount. The overtime doesn't show up on the checks, R. C. explained once, because they're paying him off the books. Right.

SHE GETS SUCKED deep into *Mrs. Dalloway,* loses track of time, hears a plane buzz overhead, and just like that it's noon.

She's interviewing at two for a job as a nanny. Of the jobs advertised in the town's weekly paper, this one seemed the least appalling. She's not a qualified machinist or associate admissions director. She's not about to sell insurance or clean toilets in a dorm. She'd called from the pay phone at the public library. A black woman answered. They hit it off. The woman gave Caroline directions. Take Rydell up Box Hill. It's the fourth driveway. Go past the stables. Excuse the columns; the painters can't come until spring. Don't be late.

She pulls back the curtains. The snow is really falling. She can barely see the edge of the pond. Travelers advisory is right. She doesn't have time to walk; she'll have to take her bicycle.

She puts on a pair of corduroys and a hand-knit sweater her brother's wife had picked out last Christmas. Then she finds R. C.'s snowmobile suit, wriggles into it, and rolls up the sleeves and legs. She yanks a ski mask over her head.

The utility shed had been cobbled together from corroded scrap aluminum that was once an awning. The shed houses a red lawn mower, a chain saw, the tires from R. C.'s wrecked car, a life jacket, and Caroline's bicycle: a heavy blue ancient retro-cool Schwinn with a white basket tied to the handlebars, and tires four fingers wide.

Caroline climbs onto the bike.

She guides it down the road, its tires popping along the snow-covered gravel. She stands up to get enough leverage on the pedals. Twice, she falls, but the snowmobile suit cushions her. Each time, she picks herself and the bicycle up, dusts off the snow, and heads toward town, bouncing off the stones, cheeks stinging as the wind cuts through her acrylic mask.

The steep, tortuous road up Box Hill is glazed with ice and snow, and Caroline has to walk it. Halfway up, she sets the bike down in some brush along the shoulder. She's lost the feeling in her fingers and toes, but she's not far now, and she keeps going. At the entrance to the fourth drive, she passes an enormous red pickup truck going the other way. The driver stops, unzips the window. "You nuts?" he shouts. He has on a cap with earflaps, a flannel shirt, and a down vest. His voice is deep and familiar.

"Yes," Caroline says. She's shaking. "Is the house far?"

"Far enough." The man shakes his head. He's about fifty, with sharp cheekbones and one hand in a cast. *A townie,* she thinks. Not soft-enough–looking to be a professor or busi nessman. "Get in," he says. His eyebrows arch. It seems to Caroline like a leer, until she remembers how she's dressed and decides it can't possibly be. "I'll drive you."

There's classical music on the radio. The heater is going full blast, and Caroline begins to feel her extremities throb with renewed feeling. She pulls off the ski mask and shakes her hair.

"You're late," he says. He throws the pickup into reverse and backs up the long, narrow drive. "That's a strike against you."

She nods. "They're into that? Being on time?"

"'They'?"

"These people."

He drives past the stables and up to the house. "I'm 'these people,'" the man says. "It's my girls you'll be watching, Crimson and Clover. Twins," he says, as if in apology. He starts to extend his hand. Then he seems to remember the cast. He holds the hand in the air, palm upward, and shrugs. "You from the college?"

"No. I'm from everywhere. Army brat." She introduces herself, and the man purses his lips. "What'd you do to the hand?" she says. The plaster is whiter than the falling snow.

"What can I say," he says. "Some guys have hard heads."

They sit in the truck, the engine idling.

"Better get in there," the man says. "Good luck." He puts

a hand on her shoulder. "Words to the wise: never get married. Never have kids."

Caroline stands with her back to the columns. The man noses the pickup around a bend in the driveway. For a moment, she feels as if she's been dropped off at school, late, alone, with a test in progress, armed only with an excuse she'd had to write for herself.

TWO LITTLE GIRLS, dressed identically in sweat suits that feature the college's logo, pull open the huge oak door. Their skin is the color of a chocolate milk-shake; they are the two most identical twins Caroline has ever seen.

"We're Crimson and Clover," one says.

"You'll never tell us apart," says the other. "We're seven years old, and we know how to mess with your mind."

"You're late," says the first one. "I'm Crimson. I told my mom you ought to get the job, anyway."

"Nuh-uh," says the other. "You said we should let her stand out there and freeze." The girl looked up at Caroline. "She's lying about her name, too. *I'm* Crimson."

The two break into laughter. They hold each other, shaking, hysterical, exaggerating. Caroline unzips the snowmobile suit. She looks for a mirror to comb her hair, but there's nothing. The place is like a warehouse. The rooms are huge, uncarpeted, unfurnished. She hears high heels coming down a stairway, wads up the suit, and sets it just inside the door, next to a radiator.

"Excuse the mess." This is the woman from the phone. She's dressed in a violet business suit with a gold scarf tied in a complicated knot at her throat. "We've just moved in. There's furniture upstairs. The downstairs things are on order."

She introduces herself as Emma Freed. She takes Caroline

to the living-room window. The house looks down on the school and the town. The snow makes the world below look like one of those shake-up paperweights, and Caroline realizes that's how college seems to her now: faraway, plastic, and toylike.

"I love watching people's faces when they see the view," says Emma Freed. "But I have no time to waste. Did you bring a résumé?"

"It's on disc," Caroline says. "Right now, I don't have a computer or a printer that works."

"Did you bring the disc?"

"No. I'm sorry." Of course there is no disc. She swallows, feels herself do this, feels the interview going south on her. "I'm good with kids. I practically raised my little brother."

"You've made me late," says Emma Freed. "I have a department meeting. You'll have to do until after I get back, which should be about six." She hands Caroline a twenty. "I'm paying you in advance for the rest of the day. I have no choice but to leave now. We'll resume the interview upon my return."

The woman sweeps out of the house, a blur of perfectly draped wool and new-smelling leather.

"She'll fire you when she gets back," says one of the girls. "That'll be a while, though. She's the chairwoman of the education department. They have the longest meetings in the whole world."

"Our mother says that people who are late are doomed to failure," says the other. "Can you guess my name?"

"I don't care," Caroline says. "Clover."

"Right!"

"Nuh-uh," says the other. "*I'm* Clover."

They fall together again in an embrace of laughter and conspiracy. Caroline goes to the kitchen, intending to eat the refrigerator bare, but the refrigerator is new and bare already.

She walks back to the picture window. On the floor is a white push-button phone. Caroline picks up the receiver. She looks at it. Why not? She dials her parents' number.

"You're not allowed to use the phone!" says one of the girls.

"We're telling."

Caroline flips them off, and they run upstairs, screaming. "You're in for it," one calls.

"Dead meat," says the other.

"Hasta la vista!" calls the first one, and, together, they shout: *"Baby!"*

Caroline gets the answering machine. It's her father's cigar-raspy voice, all business, telling her what number she's reached, promising to return her call as soon as he can. There's a television going in the background. He sounds tired.

"It's me," she says at the beep. "Caroline." Her father's voice has caught her off guard. She lets the tape run. For a second, she wants to tell him he's going to be a grandfather. Then she wishes she could somehow erase what message she's left. A lump rises in her throat. *What a sap I am.* "I'm coming home," she says. "I'll be a little late."

She hangs up and sits cross-legged on the floor, hugging herself. Then she picks up the phone and hits the redial button. He again promises to call her back. "Scratch that," she says at the beep. "Changed my mind. Have a nice life, everyone."

She wants to take a nap, and she considers finding the master bedroom and locking herself in there for forty winks. She doesn't want to be here, though, to give Emma Freed the pleasure of lowering the boom. So Caroline goes to the door, gets into the snowmobile suit, and starts to walk down the drive. She hears Crimson and Clover yelling at her, but their words get lost and distorted in the wind.

———

THE BICYCLE IS gone. All the way there, she fantasized about the downhill glide, the cold effortless journey. But the bike's gone. There are four sets of footprints near the bushes where she left it. Who'd steal an old Schwinn on a day like this, Caroline wonders. But she knows. College kids. In a college town, crime doesn't need to be motivated. Anything that happens might be someone's idea of a prank.

WHEN R. C. GETS home, she's waiting underneath a pile of every blanket they own. "You're late," she whispers.

"Sorry," he says. He's talking with a weird lisp. "Long day."

"Me, too." Caroline peeks out. R. C.'s left eye is blackened, and his jaw is badly swollen.

"A hydraulic line busted," he says. "I got hit in the head with a sofa. I sound funny on account of my jaw. Broke. Wired shut." He has a six-pack in one hand. He opens two cans and hands her one. "Looks worse than it is."

Caroline takes the beer. She remembers the man's fresh, white cast. "What's the other guy look like?" she says.

"The sofa's DOA at County General." He rolls the beer can back and forth over his jaw.

They make love, but it's strange. The only thing he gets from the milk crate in the closet is a condom. They skip foreplay. He's on top at first, but he's unequal even to that. They switch. Caroline moves quietly above him. Finally, he shakes his head.

She rolls off him and listens in the dark while R. C. drops the condom in the toilet. He runs water in the sink, gets back in bed, rustles the sheets, and falls into a cycle of even breaths. Caroline lies still, watching the advance of the red numbers on the clock radio. It's after midnight. Her father has been buried. What a strange idea, buried.

An hour later, Caroline eases out of bed, goes into the

bathroom, and locks the door. She unwraps the pregnancy test and unfolds the directions. She pees on the plastic stick. A line appears. No matter how many times she rereads the directions, they say the same awful thing.

She goes back into the bedroom. The lights are on, the bed's made, and R. C.'s awake, fully dressed, and lying atop the covers. "We got a problem," he says.

How could he know? The walls are thin, not transparent.

"But I have the solution," he says.

"You do?" she says.

"Fire," he says. "I got enough insurance. We just fry up an egg, let the flame catch the curtain, and *bang*." He smiles. It's not a happy smile. "No pun intended."

"None taken," she says. "I knew you were in deep to Bang."

He shrugs. "I knew you knew." He gets up. "Wait in the car."

She decides not to argue with him. This is a way out and, in a crazy way, a sign. "Let me pack my stuff." She heads for the shelves with her books and CDs.

"Leave it." He grabs her. "It's covered. If we take anything, even a suitcase, we're dead. Just the clothes on your back, baby."

"I'm taking a few books. We can say they were in the car."

But R. C.'s already in the kitchen, pulling out a frying pan. She sets his coat out, puts on her own, grabs an armload of books, and gets in the car, in the driver's seat. She knows now she won't ever tell R. C. she's pregnant.

By the time R. C. walks out, smoke is pouring from the kitchen window, obscuring the glow from the security light. He's in no hurry; it's as if he's done this before. He sweeps the snow from the windshield. "Let it really catch," he yells. "That'll look good." He sits on the hood and watches the trailer burn.

Eventually, he gets in, hands her the keys, and nods. She drives down the snowy gravel. There's a part of her that's terrified and angry, that wishes she could have left with all her things, even the manila envelope full of condom wrappers. But she keeps going down the snowy gravel, looking for traces of her bicycle tread, of her boot prints.

"We'll call nine-one-one from the Gas 'n' Go." R. C. stares straight ahead.

She gets to the main road and turns toward town. Would the thieves use the bike? Or would they throw it off the roof of a frat house just for a smile? Somehow it would be better if they used it.

Caroline parks her Saturn on the apron of the Gas 'n' Go. R. C. hops out. The arsonist-father of her temporary child. Or maybe not so temporary. She has no money for an abortion. But she has no money to raise a baby, either. And she can't see herself a person who gives a baby up for adoption. She can't imagine it. She can imagine adopting, someday, but she can't imagine giving a baby up so it can go to a good home, as if it were a puppy, as if she were herself unfit for a good home.

She pulls a map from the glove compartment and tries to calculate the distance to Woodbridge. She has about forty dollars in her purse. The tank's full—forty bucks may or may not be enough to get her there. She's not good with maps.

R. C. glances up, phone cradled against his shoulder. He winks at her and smiles. This time the smile's happy. That does it.

Caroline puts the car in drive and stomps on the gas.

She doesn't stop until she's been on I-95 for hours, hours spent punching the radio buttons like some kid with attention deficit disorder, hours spent thinking about nothing and everything, hours spent driving the speed limit. Still, every time she sees a cop, she feels like she did yesterday, diving into the ice. But no one stops her, until she stops herself. The needle is under a quarter tank. You don't wait until *E*. If there's one thing her father said, it's that.

It's dawn. After she pumps her gas and pays, she almost passes the pay phone on the wall. She lifts the receiver.

"I'd like to make a credit-card call," she says. She recites her father's calling-card number.

The call goes through and the machine clicks. Her father yet again tells her the number she's dialed, yet again promises he'll return her call as soon as he can. *Right. Sure you will.* The television's still going in the background. *Turn that crap off.* He still sounds tired. *Get some sleep.* But he'll always sound tired. The machine beeps. The tape begins to roll. It rolls for a long time. Finally, Caroline clears her throat. "Don't screw up," she whispers.

Obvious Questions

One night near midnight, late in the lost decade of my life between marriages number one and number two, my ex-brother-in-law Wes Papenhagen, just out of college, called me in Chicago and asked if I'd play drums on a demo his band was making. I said no. I hadn't been in a band since our first and only album stiffed. I was thirty-six, living with a woman named Holly and her two kids, and teaching English at a prep school in the burbs. Holly had made me a better, more responsible person. People like that tend to get theirs. I used to think it served them right. I used to think a lot of things.

"But this is a new band," Wes said. "A new direction. We have a girl singer. We need a human drummer." They were recording the demo in an abandoned church, land his dad had bought near Tullard, Ohio, the town where Wes and I grew up and where his sister—and my ex—still lived.

The idea of going home made something move inside me, like tumblers. On the morning after Christmas, without thinking about it too much, I packed a week's worth of clothes and a dozen drumsticks, kissed Holly good-bye, and, on my way out, dropped a trash bag full of torn wrapping paper on the curb.

I stepped off the train at the Tullard whistle-stop into a waist-high snowbank. Wes wasn't there. I waited in the Plexi-glas hut near the tracks, watching the snow fall in undimin-ished curtains. Then I walked the mile into town.

At the Citgo station, I stopped for coffee. The manager was Carl Gilson, a high school buddy, one of the few black guys in town. I asked if I could borrow a car. Tullard has no cabs, and I wanted to get to the church. Carl pointed to his motorcycle, stored in the back of bay two. He was joking, but I took him up. I knew Carl wouldn't renege, even on a joke. He said he didn't have a helmet here, and I said I didn't care. He opened the bay door, shaking his head and telling me I better have enough money to buy him a new bike.

I rode over ice-slick county roads, doing about twenty-five, which was as fast as my face could stand, fishtailing through curves and wondering what sort of a dumb ass I was. No, that's not true. I knew.

The church was a white cinder-block building. I parked the bike in back, next to a cemetery. The only open door led to the basement. I bumped around in the dark until I found the stairs, went up, and turned on some lamps and space heaters. In the pulpit was the drum set Wes had rented and a note: *Dan! Chick-a-boom. Wes.* The set had extra-deep toms and rock 'n' roll cymbals: A brilliants and K chinas. I pulled two sticks from my bag and played so long and so hard that I had to take off my sweater, then my shirt, then my T-shirt. I knew then I'd never go back to Holly. I packed it in for the night, curling up on the pulpit floor, covering myself with my clothes.

WHILE I SLEPT, one of the space heaters shorted out. The fire didn't even wake me up.

Wes showed up the next morning, bearing groceries, sleeping bags, a blind guy, and a violet-eyed young woman with auburn hair and a bomber jacket. By then, the flames had crossed the floor and were nibbling at the Sheetrock. Wes roused me, and we took the drums apart, filling each with snow and putting out the fire bucket-brigade style. I was no kid. This was work. We leaned against the pulpit rail, wheezing, laughing, drinking beer.

"Sorry I'm late," Wes said. "Though I *was* just in time."

"Will the drums be okay?" the woman said. "They got pretty wet. I used my dad's credit card for the deposit."

"They'll dry," I said. "It may change their tone, but that can be a plus. A distinct sound."

Wes introduced the other two. Luis Carrera played keyboards and had been a teaching assistant at Yale. Cait Killian met Wes at U Conn, and they'd once been engaged. Now it was platonic. Cait had never even sung in a choir.

"This band have a name?" I said.

Cait laughed. "Suggestions?"

"I'm just a hired gun," I said.

"Burnt Church," said Luis.

"Toasted Ghost," said Wes.

"Hired Gun," Cait said.

I was glad I hadn't quit my day job.

WES WAS EIGHT when Pam and I got married. On his eleventh birthday, we gave him a red Les Paul Junior that we picked out in a shop in Austin. This was before Pam quit the band. She sat on the floor, playing and humming, and we convinced the clerk the guitar was a wreck. He sold it to us cheap. Pam refinished it and replaced the frets. We gave it to Wes, who hadn't even asked for a guitar. He mumbled thanks and put it in a closet. Sometime later he picked it up again. That's how it is with gifts.

WE UNLOADED THE equipment from Wes's big ancient camper, and Wes and Luis set up. I went out and threw snowballs into the cemetery, aiming at a huge pink marble angel.

"Your bike?" said Cait.

I'd made about fifty throws and my arm was sore. "Borrowed."

"You drove it here from Chicago?"

"From town. I took the train from Chicago."

She peeled off her bomber jacket and hung it on the handlebars. Gloveless, she fired a snowball at the pink angel.

"Close," I said.

"Wes played us your album in the van."

I nodded. "That's nice."

"I didn't know there were alternative country bands back in the '70s. Except the Flying Burrito Brothers. Obviously."

I wasn't quite sure what she meant by *alternative country*, and I let it go. All I said was, "Yeah." And then, "Well, we weren't the Flying Burrito Brothers. Obviously."

Cait hit the angel with three straight throws: hard overhand strikes. "You're crazy," she said, "riding a bike in the snow. Yet you married Pam, who's as responsible as, like, God."

"Can you really sing?" I said.

"Like an angel." She said this as a challenge.

"Honky-tonk or otherwise?"

"Otherwise."

I handed her the jacket. "Want to ride into town?"

"Do you have an extra helmet?"

"Don't even have one for me."

"Fuck it. Sure. Let me just tell Wes and Luis."

"Just let's go."

She got on behind me. The road had dried, and I drove so fast, I went from cold to where the wind whipped past me and I couldn't feel a thing. Cait pulled her arms tight around my rib cage and didn't say a word. We rode past the fast-food joints, past the machine shops and small factories on the east end, into the wreath-dappled courthouse square. We watched shoppers traipse around getting haircuts and returning gifts, then we rode to the west side, where the houses are newer, the parks larger. Where Pam and I grew up. I drove by her house as slowly as I could without tipping over. Finally, Cait spoke. "Let's bring the guys some burgers," she said. "And beer." She was shivering, hard, which only then registered on me.

When we got back to the church, the burgers were as cold as the beer, but we ate them, anyway, and drank the beer, too, as Wes and Luis finished setting up. Near dusk, we began to play. Wes started us with "Johnny B. Goode," then on to early-'70s Stones (the Gram Parsons–influenced stuff, naturally), on which Luis, from his bank of electronics, coaxed forth a road-house piano. Wes had brought six guitars, but mostly he played a '64 Epiphone Riviera, which gives you that jangly blues-guitar sound. Cait played stand-up bass and sang. She had a warbly alto that was half spoken and a half-note flat, an ironic touch that reinterpreted anything. She was born to sing covers.

The problem was the originals. Not the music. The music was fine. Luis, who'd written it, had pieced together every type of American music he could think of—Tex-Mex, blue-grass, western swing, straight country, urban blues, delta blues, zydeco. The beats were varied; for me, it was a kick learning the songs, a musicology quiz. But I'd been in bands for twenty years. Your average CD buyer wouldn't catch the influences, or care. The problem was Wes's lyrics. Wes is my friend; I won't embarrass him by quoting his mopey-ass, gloom-doom-tomb lyrics. Maybe it was hip in his set to feign nihilism. But tell me this: why does a middle-class white boy from a happy family write about being a flyspeck on life's windscreen? (A Britishism he apparently used because it rhymes with *Abilene*. My point is bigger than that unfortunate couplet.)

We played all night. When morning light began to spill through the church's long unshuttered windows, I asked if anyone wanted to drive into town for breakfast. Actually, I wanted to go to sleep, but I needed to get out of there.

"Too tired," Cait said. "We have doughnuts and stuff here."

Wes, sweaty, set down the Fender and walked to one of the big windows. "That cemetery's so real," he said. "When the Northwest Territory was settled, surveyors carved up the square counties into square townships. In each township, before anybody moved in, they mapped out where the school and the cemetery would go. Squares, schools, and cemeteries. Makes you think."

"I'll go," Luis said. "I need something hot. Wes, give him the keys to the camper."

"The only time the dirt in that cemetery's ever been turned," Wes said, "was to dig and fill those graves. The soil between the graves hasn't been disturbed since the Ice Age."

"Give him the keys, man," said Luis, feeling his way around the edge of his electronic wonderland. "I'm not riding into town in the dead of winter on a damned motorcycle."

THE BUCKEYE STAR DINER, made of the requisite aluminum, was adjacent to the county's biggest trailer park. We used to go to the Star after the bars closed, making pyramids of ketchupy plates and picking fights with truckers, who'd leave us on the Star's parking lot, woozy and bleeding. After our honeymoon, Pam and I drove all night from Ocean City and pulled into the Star at about four. We drank coffee and laughed and ate fries, two twenty-year-olds waiting for daylight and pretending to grasp life. So I went there out of sentiment for the ambience—pretty dumb, given that my breakfast partner was a blind guy.

I read Luis the songs on our jukebox console. He pulled out a handful of coins, fishing through it for quarters. "Play 'I Fall to Pieces.'" He shoved the change toward me.

"You got enough for—let's see." I counted his quarters. "Thirty-two songs."

"Play it thirty-two times."

I looked around. Shop owners, schoolteachers, and professional idlers. The truckers and factory workers—guys who'd stomp you for a stunt like this—tended to be clientele of the night. "Why 'I Fall to Pieces'?" I said, pouring the quarters into the console and punching A-17. My hands were raw. I had to switch index fingers every few punches.

"Why *not* 'I Fall to Pieces'?" Luis, who didn't wear dark glasses, held the menu as if he were studying its catalog of eggs and yankee pot roast. It was a shtick, meant to unnerve, but Luis was the one who seemed bothered. He kept rubbing his temples, though when I asked if he had a headache, he said no.

Amazingly, no one in the Star seemed to notice that the same Patsy Cline song had been playing again and again for forever. Maybe that's what they had going at home, too.

We finished eating, waited for Patsy to sing it one last time, then drove to the Citgo to tell Carl his bike was okay. "You're not dead." Carl was fixing the radio in a Jeep. "Yet."

"I'll bring it back tomorrow."

"Keep it long as you need. It's bad luck to nag crazy people."

Carl finished with the radio, and we drank coffee in the lobby on a hard vinyl couch. Carl's grandma was blind, and he started telling Luis about her. Luis changed the subject to talk about the band. Carl stared out the window at the self-serve customers and blew on his coffee; over the years, he'd no doubt heard enough band talk from me. "You need a sax player?"

Luis grinned. "Great! I been handling the sax lines on my synth, but I got a song I'd love to use a real horn on."

"Too bad," Carl said, "'cause I don't play sax." He slapped me on the shoulder.

Carl had the afternoon off. At noon, we walked to a bar down the street. Luis wanted to get back, but he was tired, too, and he crashed in the bed above the cab of the camper.

After a few beers, Carl and I decided to take the camper up to Clear Lake, about a half hour away. Carl had a boat stored up there, and he said he'd heard the lake wasn't iced over.

He was right. We left Luis in the camper, still asleep, then rolled the boat onto the skids, laughing like schoolboys. We wrapped ourselves in blankets, and Carl tried to sing songs from our old album, though he couldn't remember the words. I closed my eyes and thought of Pam's even voice. We tossed our empties into the lake and started singing TV theme songs. And then came the appointed time for me to throw up and pass out. Carl fished while he waited for me to come to.

When we got back to shore, it was dark. Luis was sitting in the cab of the camper. He yelled at me all the way back.

"We left you a note," I said. That was a shitty thing to say, and I regretted it right off. "You want to fire me, fire me. Otherwise, Luis, let me be. I don't need another mother."

"Yes," he said. "You do. You need a battalion of mothers."

I let it go, this kid telling me what I needed.

I dropped off Carl back at the Citgo. I looked at the pay phone. I should have called Holly: knew it then, know it now.

Holly, if you ever read this, I'm the sorriest man alive. Some things happen for a reason; some things just happen. There's a difference between the two, yes, but it's not for us to know. Timing is everything.

I PARKED THE camper behind the church. I heard Wes playing his guitar, more bluesy than he'd played the night before. On our way in, I noticed the bike was gone.

"You slept with her." Wes sat on a window ledge, watching his fingers on the guitar. "I can't believe you slept with her."

"I didn't," I said. "When would I have slept with her?"

Wes played the guitar break from "Broken Elm," the only song of Pam's that had wound up on our album. He kept his head down. "I wasn't talking to you."

Luis made his way to his keyboards and began to play along. They swapped leads and improvised. It was the best I'd heard them play. I almost joined in, but they did not need a human drummer.

I asked Wes if he knew where she'd gone. He shrugged.

IN A WINTER drizzle, I drove into Tullard, following the route I'd taken when I drove Cait into town—when? Yesterday? It seemed like longer. I felt old, piloting a top-heavy camper down county roads and side streets, searching the shoulders and curbs for a wrecked bike and the mangled body of a pretty woman.

I finally went to Tullard Christian Hospital. I parked near the emergency room. A line had formed in front of the admitting desk. Holidays are hell on people. There were guys with bloody towels wrapped around their wrists, women in labor, drunks too beaten up to go home, and—in front of me, buoyed by a parent on each arm—a kid with horrible acne who'd dropped his Christmas gift, the engine block of a vintage Dodge Charger, square on his right foot.

The admitting nurse wouldn't talk to anyone who wasn't at the head of the line. I kept thinking that I should drop the name of Wes and Pam's father, a surgeon, who for all I knew was on duty now, trying to save Cait's life, but instead, I fixed my eyes on the wall clock, as if I were watching a sporting event. If I made eye contact with the acne kid, he'd no doubt tell me even more about his Dodge. At 11:38 P.M., the kid was wheeled down the hall, and the admitting nurse began leafing through her records, asking me, four times, to spell *Killian*. "We did have a motorcycle crash victim here. Died."

I tried to stand up straight and deal with this. "Was it—"

"In October. Guy named Foley Jackson." She never found anyone named Killian, and, not as relieved as I'd have expected to be, I walked out the sliding glass doors into the night.

The camper was gone.

The curb next to where I'd parked it was yellow. A sign warned about parking there. The fine was one hundred dollars. And so I did all there was to do: I walked to Pam's house, the house where she'd grown up. Her parents had given it to her after the divorce and built a new place out by the country club.

When I got there, the porch light was on. She answered the door, dressed in a business suit. She had her hair bobbed, and she wore a lapel pin that read Solidarnosc.

"What are you doing New Year's Eve?" I asked. "I was just in the neighborhood, and I was, y'know, wondering..."

Pam smiled and welcomed me inside. "I just got home from Dad's. Wes's woman crashed a motorcycle into Dad's neighbor's lamppost." She took my coat and motioned me to take a seat on the living-room couch. Her father once caught us making love on that very piece of furniture.

"Is she okay?"

"The lamppost is dead, and the motorcycle's going to need major reconstructive surgery, but the girl's unscathed."

It struck me odd that anyone would use the word *unscathed* aloud, but I hadn't talked to Pam since she finished law school. I almost told Pam that I'd been out looking for both girl and motorcycle, but my failure to drive by her and Wes's parents house seemed too ferociously stupid to advertise. "The motorcycle is Carl Gilson's."

"Really?" she said. "I haven't seen Carl in—"

"Jesus, he just works at the Citgo over there."

"I don't need that tone. I haven't seen him, is all." She took a breath, got up, and walked to the window. "Sorry. It's been a long day." She went to the kitchen. "Dad'll pay to have it fixed," she called. "The motorcycle."

"I managed to get Wes's camper impounded," I said.

"Good. That thing's a menace." She handed me some coffee and a saucerful of Christmas cookies. "Dad's neighbor—you remember Mr. Spangler?—he wanted to sue. No need for that. Dad'll pay for that, too. But he had me go over and placate Spangler." Another one: *placate.* She sat in a ladder-back rocker that had belonged to her great-grandmother and untied her scarf. She had Coltrane on the stereo: vinyl. An antique. "I might join a firm in Chicago. It's a political job. I'd be working for a long-shot mayoral candidate. He was my con-law prof at Northwestern." (Whether that *con* is short for *contracts* or *constitutional* I don't know. Go ask a lawyer. Hang on to your wallet.)

"I used to live in Chicago," I said. "Back on Wednesday." When Pam was in law school, we both lived in Chicago, and we both knew that, and we never once saw each other then. I had old-fashioned ideas about divorce and not looking pathetic. What a load of crap. How much more pathetic could I have looked than I looked then, in those bare-fork'd-beast days between marriages number one and two?

"You left?" she said. "You left to join Wes's band?"

"Maybe I haven't left. I'm not really in the band, either. I'm just here to do the session. It's hard to explain."

"With you," she said, "what isn't?" Even poured into that chair, she still had that fierceness in her eyes. "Is the band any good?"

"They're developing their sound. They're on to something."

Pam laughed. "You still suck at lying, Dan. The girl can't sing. She and Wes came to visit last Christmas at Dad's. She couldn't even sing 'Jingle Bells.'"

"The lyrics aren't much, either. Wes needs to read."

"I know. I got him a poetry anthology for Christmas."

The music stopped. Pam rose to change the record. "Requests?" she said.

Pam stood there, a vision from the best poem ever, lit by the glow of a streetlight. For a moment—breathing hard on that old couch, filled with regret, lust, and a soft-headed belief in my ability to mend fences, clutching an empty coffee cup in one hand, a headless Santa Claus sugar cookie in the other— I nearly made another sort of request entirely.

The funny thing is, for months after this moment with Pam, a moment that changed things forever, my life would hurtle forward as it had since Christmas. For example: late the next day, Cait and I took Mr. Papenhagen's other Cadillac out to the church. Cait flirted with me, but it was a front. She was scared. When we got there, Wes and Luis were singing harmony with tape loops of their own voices. When we tried to join in, they fired us. Wes said he and Luis had decided they meant more to each other professionally than Cait meant to either of them romantically. Luis further explained that two is the ideal number of people in a band. If you have more, one guy wants to go, say, to a strip joint, one guy wants to see *Star Wars,* and another wants to stay home and wait for a call from his lover. Did we get it, he said, and Cait and I said we did. We went out into the cemetery and threw more snowballs at the pink angel and finally one of us—I don't remember who— asked the obvious question, which was, "Now what?"

Strange, how obvious questions pretty much never have obvious answers.

We went into town, and Cait gave Carl Gilson two hundred dollars and the name of her insurance company. Carl gave me hell, but he's seen me pull dumber stunts than this, and we all wound up laughing about things: life.

Later that day, I called Holly. Before I had a chance to lie to her, she interrupted me and told me my things were boxed and ready and I could pick them up whenever. So, on what I thought was a whim, I asked Cait if she'd come with me to Chicago—strictly platonic—and on New Year's Day, in booth four of the Buckeye Star Diner, she said sure, why not.

That was what most people would see as the turning point.

Cait helped me find a place, and I helped her catch on with another band—a good one, with CDs that get played on college radio—and now I have tenure at the school, and she's pregnant with our second baby.

But here's what I've learned from life so far: turning points don't come at the point where things actually turn. And so I take you back to Tullard, to that night in Pam's house.

Pam kicked off her shoes and put on a popping, hissing Al Green forty-five.

Vinyl!

I came up behind her, sliding my arms around her waist and pulling her close. We knew the words—we'd sung the song at our wedding reception—and we murmured them in each other's ears as we swayed across the living-room floor, reaching out to click off lamps as we passed by. She'd set the turntable on repeat. We kept dancing until our legs gave out, and we collapsed on that old couch. She kissed me on the cheek. I kissed her on the lips. She got up and turned off the music, and we sat listening to the wind in the trees and the ghosts in the house. "Happy New Year," she whispered.

"You're a little early."

"You're a little late."

"I'm a lot late," I admitted. "Better late than never?"

She didn't say anything.

"We had fun," I said, "didn't we?"

"You're a lot of work, Dan. You're *such* work. You know? Plus, I'm tired. Very, very, very, very tired. Sleepy tired, weary tired. Tired. You know? Can you understand that, at least?"

We fell asleep, entwined and fully clothed. I woke up alone, covered with an afghan. I cooked breakfast, and we ate together, laughing and reminiscing, completing each other's sentences, refilling each other's coffee cup.

Then Pam drove me to her father's new house. It was huge, a two-story contemporary with rough-hewn siding and a security system that no one in a town like Tullard needed and a lot that stretched back through the snowy trees to the snow-covered golf course. I turned to Pam and begged her to sing one of our old songs, right there in the driveway. She refused. I asked her again, and of course she refused again. Her father watched from the window, scowling, and then the massive front door opened, and Cait came skipping out (skipping!), though not exactly unscathed: her bomber jacket was badly scuffed and she had a large bandage on her cheek. Her hair was ablaze with the hard miracle of winter sunshine.

Rain Itself

This is a story about what really happened last summer at
the five-mile bridge, from a guy who was there. My name
is Toby Houtz, and I mow lawns for a living. I started with ten
neighbors' lawns the summer I was eleven. At first, I used my
dad's rider and a greasy red push mower with three wobbly
wheels. The Tigers went to the Series that year; I had a blue
transistor radio with an earphone and I listened to games
while I mowed. Today, I have a college degree, six employees,
and an aluminum storage barn by the train tracks, near where
the handle factory used to be.

You need to know about Doug Parrish, too. His great-
grand somebody made a fortune during the Depression selling scrap iron. It's not a *fortune* fortune, but in this town, it is.
Even though most of the money's in shopping malls in Cleveland, the family stays here. Doug Parrish played halfback. I remember sitting in the stands at Trojan Stadium, wearing a
school jacket, holding on to a cup of hot chocolate and the
rolled-up program my dad always bought me, listening to
grown men compare Doug Parrish to the best they'd ever
seen. He wore number eight and was one of those herky-jerky
runners. I guess he hurt his knee in college out east. Since

then, his family's had its ups and downs, and Doug was the only one willing or able to take over the business when his grandpa died, so he did. He pretended to be part of the town, but his business is in the cities, and the only time you'd see him was at county commissioner meetings, and he only ran for that as a stepping-stone to something bigger.

Doug and Jan Parrish have a fancy house on Lake Erie, outside Cleveland, but their place here is a pretty average white frame deal on a quarter-acre lot—to give people the idea they're just folks. Jan is six feet tall and had been a beauty. She's from, like, Maryland or something. Horse money. Doug met her at college, and I heard from my dad that she made an effort at first. She played golf every ladies day, had a hobby-job at the hospital, held office in the PTA, those kinds of things. Now, no. I'd mowed their yard for years, even back when I was a one-man operation, and I can tell you: she likes her martinis. Et cetera.

They have three kids, two little girls and a teenaged boy named Jeffrey. He won't go by Jeff. I don't have a whole lot of respect for boys old enough to mow their own lawn who don't, but Jeffrey was on swim team, and he convinced his mom he needed to conserve his energy during the day, so I kept mowing their lawn. I don't have respect for kids like this, but I'm happy they exist. Bucks are bucks.

Get this: Jeffrey graduated from high school and applied for a job with me. A different kind of guy might have turned him away. Me, I found it funny. And it's not like you need much experience in my business. I had an opening, and I hired him and assigned him to trimming, raking, and bagging.

The kid shocked the hell out of us all. He was a giant, about six six, and he worked like a fiend. I'd teamed him up with a convicted felon named Gary, one of those small wiry guys you know can kick your ass. The summer before, I'd dated the assistant county prosecutor, a mousy little blond woman who, if I may say so, was a miraculous lay. As a favor to her, I got involved in the work-parole program and hired Gary, who'd been sent away briefly for dealing. Gary hadn't mended his ways. I got the special boss's price. He who is without sin can't first get stoned.

Gary hated Jeffrey. "He's killing me," Gary told me. "He *runs* from tree to tree, even with the trimmer strapped on." Gary was on break at my storage barn, sitting on the tailgate of one of my green trucks. He ate sandwiches one piece at a time: bread, tomato, lettuce, baloney, cheese, baloney, cheese, baloney, bread. "Says he wants to keep in shape."

Jeffrey spent his lunch breaks swimming laps at the pool in Van Gundy Park.

"No time for naps behind the garage, huh?" Gary wasn't the only guy who did that. I acted like it ticked me off, but, hey. We're paid by the hour. As long as the customers don't find out.

"It's my heart I'm thinking about. Seriously. My uncle had heart problems."

"Your uncle shot himself."

"Yeah, because he had heart problems."

"You don't expect me to tell the kid he's working too hard, do you? Get real."

"The big ape ought to just join a health club."

"This is the only real job the kid'll ever have," I said. "His path is golden. Abuse him however you want, but don't kill him, and don't expect me to tell him to be a fuck-off like you."

Gary stared at the mustard-covered piece of white bread in his palm. He squeezed it into a shit-yellow ball and lobbed it out into the gravel parking lot.

EVERY SUMMER, on the courthouse square, our town closes off High Street and Main Street and has this week-long carnival called the Jubilee. I must be coming up in the world, because that year, I was on the Jaycees' planning committee for the big parade and fireworks display that ends Jubilee Week. I was surprised to find Jan Parrish on the committee, too. Like I said, she'd cut back on the civic bullshit. I didn't mind it. I'm a businessman now. There comes a time when the things you used to make fun of are the things you spend your free time doing. It's painless. It just happens to you. Some of you have probably been there.

The meetings were run by the mayor, Art Tracker, who was also the best plumber in town. Art had read up on parliamentary procedure. Points of order were always being debated, but not a whole lot got done, even though most meetings lasted until after the bars were closed. I figured we'd eventually just take out the plans from last year's parade and fireworks and do pretty much the same thing, only with a new grand marshal and parade theme. In the meantime, I took notes on a legal pad and pretended to care. We had assigned seats, and Jan Parrish sat across from me. Most times, you could smell her breath. She wore black loose-fitting T-shirts. She never took notes. Generally, she made smart little proposals about stuff that no one was much interested in: for example, a plan to make Center Street one-way just after the fireworks so traffic wouldn't be backed up until midnight. Her skin seemed one size too big. There was something quick and reckless in her eyes.

Toward the end of our last meeting—on a five-to-four vote, we'd just approved the theme, "Way to Go, America!"— Jan recommended that we change the parade route. She'd been sitting with her hand raised for ten minutes, waiting to be recognized. Art Tracker was scared of her. "I move the parade turn right at Union Street," she said, "head east, and keep going. Once they get to a body of water, they can decide if they want to swim across, find a bridge, or just incorporate a little village right there, supplying the world with band members, bad clowns, Shriners, firemen, Cub Scouts, and beauty queens."

She sat back in her chair, folded her arms and smiled, first at just me, then at everyone. They all looked down at their notes, clearing their throats and tapping their pencils until Art Tracker got hold of himself and asked if he heard a second.

"Second," I said. It was self-defense. If I hadn't said that, I would have busted out laughing.

Art Tracker noted what it was that had been moved and seconded and asked if there was any discussion. Then came this terrific strained silence, what with the city's young leaders trying to roll their eyes without making eye contact, and Jan and me grinning at each other. I called for a vote, but then the band director moved we adjourn, and a dentist seconded that, and the meeting slipped into better anarchy than I would have hoped possible, centering around what Roberts Rules of Order says about the preeminence of a motion to adjourn. I excused myself to go to the bathroom, but, to be honest, I had to leave before I lost it.

When I got outside, Jan Parrish was leaning against the side of my truck, smoking a joint. "I found this in your glove compartment," she said. "Hope you don't mind."

I shrugged. She was playing her role, and I'm not the kind of guy to get in people's way. "You ever wonder," I said, "what it is that makes people wake up one day and want to be a Shriner?"

"What do you think?" she said.

"Probably it's the urge to wear a fez and whiz around in those little cars."

She nodded. "My theory is, it's loneliness."

I saw where this was going.

"You want a ride home?" I asked.

She took another toke and thought about that. "No." She turned and started walking down an alley. "Not home." I was going to let her go and, in fact, even got into my truck. But I was curious. So I caught up to her. She was sitting on a fire escape. She saw me, smiled, and headed up the iron steps.

The three-story buildings along the courthouse square went up in the 1840s, and this building was the tallest of them all. I followed her to the third floor and into a vast, mildewed room at least thirty feet tall. Three floor-to-ceiling windows facing the square bathed the room in the flat haze of streetlights. Flocked Walltex hung from the ceiling like paper stalactites, or stalagmites, whatever it is that hangs down.

"This was the Knights of Columbus dance hall," she said, pointing to the water-eaten gold crest on the warped floorboards. "The dances they used to have here would have made you think this town was really a place."

There was all sorts of crap on the floor: splintered baby furniture and broken display racks, furnace parts, drop cloths, and upended pinball machines.

She turned to me, grabbed my hands, and squeezed hard.

"We own this place," she said. "And just look at it."

She walked out of the room. I guess you could say she was giggling. A little bit later, she appeared on a small balcony.

"Hello, Toby." She'd stopped laughing and stood there without her T-shirt on. In that light, I couldn't tell what color the bra was, but it wasn't white.

"Hey."

"C'mon up."

"Okay." But I didn't move.

"I have a mattress here." I bent down, and I heard a poptop. "And beer. There's a refrigerator."

What I'd like to tell you is that I stayed frozen in that spot. Though with every fiber of my being I wanted to charge up there and have strange, adventurous sex involving silk ropes

and ice cubes, instead, something—morality? maturity? fear?—
held me back, and I found a gracious way to leave. That's what
I'd like to tell you. But you'd never believe it, and it's not what
happened.

AFTER THAT FIRST night, I began to mow her lawn myself.
Maybe that wasn't the most subtle thing in the world, but neither is sex. While her daughters were at swim team and her
son was out working for me, she and I would turn the AC off
and spend slippery, sad hours making love in their attic. She'd
bring up chilled cherry vodka and a stack of towels for after.
We never said a lot to each other; there wasn't a lot to say.
That night in the dance hall was beginning to seem less and
less real, which spontaneous, unlikely sex always will, with
time. The problem is, when you remove the spontaneous and
all you're left with is the unlikely, what you're dealing with becomes all *too* real.

Doug Parrish came home for the Jubilee Parade. Every
elected official rode in the parade, each with his own happy
family, each in a convertible supplied by the Top of Ohio Kar
Klub. I hadn't seen Jan for days.

A couple times, I was at the Jubilee, just to do a lap
around the square and buy an elephant ear, and I'd look up at
those three long windows. I must have driven by that building
a zillion times, and I'd never really noticed those windows. I'd
never once wondered what was behind them.

I thought, then, that I could become someone else, maybe.
I might have been in the process of it. Who could say?

You live your whole life here, and you're forever who you
were in the sixth grade. Or maybe it just seems that way when
you go to something like the Jubilee. For little kids, there's the
rides and stuff, and for geezers, there's the Kiwanis Club tent
to work in, but for most of us, things haven't changed much

from when we were standing around at lunch in the gym, trying to strike the right pose and get close to the cool kids.

I'll show you what I mean: the night before the parade, I
was hanging with Kenny Arbenauer, the public works director,
because Art Tracker told me the city might vote to contract
out its lawn maintenance. Of course, the subject never came
up. We just wandered around the square, shooting corks at
stuffed alley cats and paying to see the death car from some
redneck-sheriff movie.

When the carnies started to pack it in, I picked up a six
and headed to the bridge. The paper called for rain, and you
could hear real thunder now. But understand: in my business,
you become like a farmer. First of all, rain is money in your
pocket. Second of all, it's not the threat of rain but only rain
itself that makes you stop doing the task at hand.

When people here say just "the bridge," they mean the
one five miles west of the courthouse. The one-mile and the
three-mile are both concrete bridges on state routes, but
the five-mile is this creaking old wooden bridge with big tarry
gables and one long beam (known as the plank), which for no
structural reason I could ever figure juts out perpendicular on
the west side. The bridge connects two beanfields. You can
stand there for hours without a car coming by. It's more an el-
evated party deck than anything. You bring out some tunes
and a beer cooler and wait for a train so you can piss on it
while the bridge shakes.

I wasn't the only one not put off by all the thunder. In the
middle of the bridge were some college-kid lifeguards with a
tape player as big as a suitcase. On the far end, some guys my
age, mostly second-shifters from the candy factory, sat on the
hood of a station wagon, smoking dope and listening to a ball
game. On the near end was Gary. Every Friday and Saturday
night, he loaded this ratty orange love seat onto the bed of his
pickup and drove out to the bridge. He sat on that couch,

waiting for customers, holding on to both armrests like it was some kind of throne.

"Do any good tonight?" I said.

"I always do good." His eyes were fixed on the lifeguards. A train whistle sounded, off to the west, followed as it died by a thunderclap. Gary got to his feet. "Oh, Jeff-re-e-ey?"

The kid was with the lifeguards; I hadn't noticed. I knew, in a flash, what Gary was up to. The plank. Jeffrey smiled and waved, and I'm thinking, *Wow, his dad's a business whiz and his mom's*—well, you know about his mom—*but this kid's clueless.* Gary had been riding Jeffrey pretty hard: loosened spark plugs on the trimmer, dog shit in his work gloves. Basic stuff, but I knew Gary couldn't leave it at that.

Gary hopped down. "You said I could abuse him, boss."

I nodded. "Be careful."

The train was getting closer now, and I sat on the west rail to watch it. Some of the second-shift boys came over, too. They were already unzipped.

Now, like I said, most of the time you'd just piss on the train. But a lesser-known thrill was to climb out on the plank, hold on to this cable, and face the wind of the onrushing train with nothing beneath you. Perspective plays a trick on you; it looks like something's gone terribly wrong, and the train's too tall, and it's going to smash into the bridge, beginning with you.

Things happened pretty fast then. I bent to pick up another beer, and the next thing I know, there're these screams.

"It's not that *I'm* chicken," Jeffrey yelled.

Gary had pulled a gun.

I started across the bridge. I didn't know what I'd do, but when I saw that Jeffrey was smiling, I backed off.

"Put it away," Jeffrey said. "I'll do it. Be happy to."

"You're playing my song," Gary said. They walked toward us. Gary tucked the gun in his pants. I thought the second he did that, Jeffrey would punch him into the next county. I would have. Well, no, *I* wouldn't have. But if I was as big as the kid, I would have. Instead, they went straight to the guardrail—Jeffrey first, Gary following. They swung their legs over, grabbed the wire, and inched their way to the end of the plank.

I'd say the train was a mile away.

Jeffrey turned around, saw me, and waved. "Hi, boss. Somebody's gonna get hurt, huh?" He was grinning ear to ear.

"Nah," I yelled over the roar of the oncoming train. "I've done it a million times."

Jeffrey nodded. "You've just about done it all, haven't you, boss? You're quite a man."

At the time, I couldn't figure that. Or didn't want to.

Gary sat down, holding the wire with both hands. The bridge shook from the wind. A few of us yelled at Jeffrey to sit down. But the kid shook his head and turned to face the train, arms outstretched and hair flying back like he was Moses or somebody. The guys around me were cheering.

The train whistle sounded; you could feel the vibration from it, and, though I couldn't hear over the roar, I knew Gary well enough to know what he was yelling: *Look out kid, something's wrong, the train's gonna hit us, we're dead men, dead motherfuckers, dead, dead, dead, my god.*

And still, the kid just stood there, like he wanted to hug something. The hot wind whipped his shirt. I could feel a few more raindrops, and the one-eyed train bore down on us like a dentist's lamp from hell.

All around me, the second-shifters and the college guys began to pee, huddled shoulder to shoulder, aiming for the light.

Jeffrey spun around and grabbed the cable. He stumbled, but he held fast and looked right at me. Then he dipped down and grabbed Gary by the belt. He lifted him up. There was nothing between Gary and the tracks below, not even the beam. Gary lost hold of the cable, and his gun dropped down into the darkness.

The train engine shot by and blasted me with dust and rain and maybe urine.

And then it was quieter, just the clacking of the track, the patter of warm rain on wood. Gary twitched in the air like a swaying, dying bug, and Jeffrey's teeth were bared and shining. He was still looking at me. I heard the ball game coming from the truck radios. I heard men zipping up. Cleveland was winning.

"I believe I'll let him live," Jeffrey said.

"Good idea," I said.

Drop him, other people yelled out. *Let him go splat.*

"Or not," Jeffrey said.

"Bad idea," I said.

I heard Gary whimper.

"Beg me, Gary," Jeffrey said. "Boss, tell him to beg me."

"Beg him."

The rain picked up, but no one ran for cover.

Gary just kept whimpering.

I started to hook my leg over the railing, but Jeffrey shook his head. "You're not man enough," he said. "Trust me." He began to swing Gary back and forth, like a pendulum, until he was cutting these huge semicircle arcs through the summer rain.

The caboose passed underneath us.

"Catch," Jeffrey said.

Gary flew toward us and smacked against the side of the bridge. A few of the other guys caught fistfuls of cloth, or an arm or a leg or something, and they dragged him up and over.

"You didn't think I was going to kill him, did you boss?"

I shrugged.

"Well, you don't know everything." Jeffrey climbed back onto the bridge. "Do you?" Gary was a wet lump on the road now. "I need tomorrow off, boss," Jeffrey said. "My dad wants me to ride in the parade."

"I doubt if there's room in that convertible."

"We'll make room." Jeffrey shook his head. "You really are quite a man, boss." The rain fell in sheets. We watched Jeffrey walk across the bridge to his car. We just stood there, getting drenched and wondering what had just happened.

By then, Gary had gotten to his feet. I was one of the few who turned around in time to see him jump. He dropped over the edge like a scared kid going off the high dive for the first time—one hand over his eyes, the other grabbing at the air—except that there was no splash.

GARY WOULDN'T SAY why he jumped. He was more than a little wasted, and he claimed he couldn't remember doing it. I told the cop my theory: Gary felt too humiliated to live. "Just think," the cop said, "how much more humiliating it is to decide you're too humiliated to live and then wind up alive, broken-legged, and under arrest." The cops found the drug smorgasbord Gary had stashed under that wet, orange love seat.

I didn't get home from the police station until four. I never slept. The rain fell all night but stopped right as the sun rose. I made coffee, read the paper, then went out alone, the morning of the Fourth of July, and cut two of our biggest lawns, just to keep myself from thinking.

THE PARADE COMMITTEE members who weren't riding or marching in the parade were supposed to help the parks-and-recreation people line everybody up. The staging area was a church parking lot on the edge of town. By the time I got there, Doug Parrish was working the crowd, shaking hands and laughing too hard. He was, rumor had it, planning to declare his candidacy for state rep. In the back of a Mustang convertible the color of a legal pad, Jeffrey read a book to his little sisters. Jan sat in a lawn chair under a tree, smoking. The parks-and-rec people seemed to have things under control, so I sidled over to her; no one seemed to be looking.

"What do you think you're doing?" Jan whispered, though the only people within earshot were four Brownies playing freeze tag.

It was a good question, one I certainly couldn't answer except on the most literal level. "I'm talking to you," I said. "How are, you know, things? With, like, Jeffrey. And—"

She laughed. "Please." She did not remove her sunglasses. None of this was said with any eye contact. "Spare me."

"Spare you what?"

"Spare me everything," she said. "'Spare me that I may recover strength, before I go hence, and be no more.'" She laughed again. "Amen."

"Oh." Someone later told me that comes from the Bible.

"Toby," she said. "You think that you matter, don't you?"

I looked at her. "Jesus," I said. "I don't need this."

"Yes, you do," she said. "So do I," she said. "But we can't have it."

"Whatever," I said. As I walked away, I saw that Jeffrey had been watching us. *Well,* I thought, *so be it.* All we were doing was talking. For all he knew, for all anyone knew, I could have been saying, *Hey, Mrs. Parrish, let's go. The parade is about to begin.*

I WATCHED THE Jubilee Parade from the reviewing stand, with people from the radio station and a few other committee members. I hadn't slept. Kenny Arbenauer, that wit, said I looked like something the cat dragged in.

After the color guard, a fire truck, a marching band, the Optimists' float (realtors, car salesmen, and Wal-Mart managers, flouncing around in waistcoats and powdered wigs), and another marching band came the dignitaries. Jeffrey was driving, sitting up straight, looking straight ahead. Jan was slumped in the passenger seat, one hand over her eyes. The two little girls, ribbons in their chlorine-greened hair, flanked their father atop the backseat of the car. Doug Parrish was tanned, unshy, and large. His hair was as perfect as a TV weatherman's.

I looked at Jan and then at Jeffrey, for eye contact or approval or condemnation. Anything. But I couldn't connect.

When they drew even with the stand, a photographer stepped from the crowd. All five Parrishes swiveled their heads toward the camera, smiling on cue, the father's arms sweeping around his daughters so that he could rest his fingertips on the shoulders of his wife and son. Then Doug Parrish winked—kind of like at me, I thought—and I could picture him, number eight, breaking loose at Trojan Stadium on a cold and long-ago Friday night. For one idiotic second, I felt like I'd shaken hands with Superman.

Then they passed by, and I was just this enormous child, hiding inside a man's body, kidding myself that I'm fooling everyone, kidding myself that I'm fooling anyone, kidding myself that I'm fooling myself.

How We Came
to Indiana

*If I speak the truth it will be my wife and my children
who will pay in hardships for my outspokenness.*
—JOHN CHEEVER, "THE DEATH OF JUSTINA"

A t dusk one day in the late winter of our family's final year
in Westchester County, my sister (who was then eleven)
and I (almost fifteen) came home from swimming practice (a
long walk; what hair protruded from our stocking caps was
frozen) to find my father standing on the porch hatless, coat-
less, and smoking, his steamy breath smelling of gin, the
Windsor knot of his plain red necktie still intact at his throat.
He was not, as a rule, home so early. Paige reached for my
gloved hand, then squeezed. "Cousin Justina has died," my father reported. "She is on the green sofa in the living room."

She was an ancient, charming woman who, despite her
age, was somehow a cousin of Mother's. Paige and I hardly
knew her. Justina's death had been quick and agreeable, my
father said, coming a decorous ten minutes after the departure of the last guest at the lunch party my mother had given
for her. "It's nothing of which to be alarmed," my father stiffly
said. "Nathan, take Paige to her room. And go to yours." He
flicked his cigarette butt out into the dark, toward the small
lopsided snow fort Paige had made Sunday after Mother, she,
and I returned from church and where she had spent that

afternoon alone. "And stay there. Your mother and I have matters under control."

That seemed unlikely. This was three days after my father, then employed in what he called the ad game, had been told by his doctor to stop smoking and drinking and had come home and boldly announced he was doing so—which made it two days since I'd seen him slip into the downstairs coat closet with a jelly glass full of clear liquid and olives and emerge a minute later, chewing ice, the glass empty. But I did as I was told, placing a hand on Paige's shoulder and guiding her through the foyer, dining room, and kitchen, past the library to the stairs. Even by this route, however, we did not quite avoid the living room. As we climbed the stairs, Paige and I saw the huge, bedsheet-draped figure on the green velvet sofa (the sofa was a dear part of family history, having been a favorite, if theoretically forbidden, napping place for a big-hearted incontinent schnauzer named Fritz, who'd been run over the previous year by a school bus). Justina had been a stout, merry, oddly formed creature. Covered by a sheet, she appeared to have grown larger. The room smelled like lilac-scented aerosol. Sticking out from beneath the sheet was Justina's right hand, clutching a brandy snifter.

By the time Paige and I arrived in our rooms, the image of the dead Justina was implanted forever in our minds as a thing of nightmarish grandeur—worse, I now know, and also better, than the diminished reality of corporeal rot that is death up close and from which my well-meaning, death-haunted father hoped to protect us (Paige's take on this might be less generous).

The cook (our last one, Inga) brought our dinners up to us. While I sat on my bed and ate (squab, peas, baked potato, chocolate cake; death renders memorable the food eaten in its proximity), I heard my father yelling at people on the telephone about zoning regulations, death, advertising slogans, and burial. At one point, he threatened to bury Justina in our garden. He and Mother exchanged cross words in loud hissing whispers. I set my dirty dishes in the bathroom sink. As I did, the front door slammed, a pot smashed against the dining-room floor, and the car started (a new Buick—his first, having just arisen from Pontiacs). Briefly, it was quiet.

I threw myself on my bed and wished for the home lives of my friends, imagining each in turn, naïvely supposing them to be better and less strange than my own. Their parents—dull, sober (in both senses of that), and less handsome—would make sure I did not hear ugly fights or anxious discussions of money, would never hurl flatware at one another, never dispense those odd too-hard hugs, and would always take a game interest in the admittedly small problems of their children. This, my pet fantasy, was interrupted when, downstairs, Mother put on her Time-Life set of Sibelius records (her favorite of the earnest twenty-eight volume *Great Men of Music* collection I inherited and cannot bear to play). Softly, she sobbed. I hoped Paige could not hear this.

I had spent a desultory hour doing algebra when a knock came at my door. I opened it; it was Paige. She wore a robe and that ferocious Olympian scowl that her competitors, then and later, would look upon, and despair. Without invitation, she sat herself down in a hard chair in the corner, and, though it was a school night, we talked for hours about swimming: strategies and techniques, goals, complaints, nemeses, and dreams. She was a much better swimmer than I, and had, in fact, won a state age-group championship as a ten-year-old. She was the youngest person allowed to practice with the high school team (for which I was only a member of the *B* medley relay team, its backstroker).

Neither of us mentioned the dead woman in the living room.

Past midnight, my father returned home. My mother was

still playing Sibelius (it is a six-record set). "It's taken care of," he said, and I could not hear what she said.

"Quick," I whispered to Paige, motioning. She hurried to her room. I turned off her light for her, and then mine, too.

A car pulled into our drive, its tires crunching against snow, and did not kill its engine. Doors—heavy car doors—slammed. The voices of two men (one a Negro) and the sound of their hard-soled indelicate boots entered our house. Also a squeaky-wheeled contraption. My mother switched off the music. The front door closed and was locked, and the car drove off.

"Please, Moses, don't," I heard Mother say. She sounded more tired than the late hour could account for. Older. "You don't need it," she said to my father. "Just come to bed."

"I'm quitting," my father said.

"Fine," said Mother. "Just come to bed."

Later, I heard him call out in his sleep: "No sale!"

I spent the rest of the night awake, adding up one by one the days until I was old enough to leave this house and join the army. The sum (I remember as if I arrived at the figure this moment) was one thousand one hundred thirty-seven. By then, Paige could fend for herself.

JUSTINA'S FUNERAL WAS the next day. We Episcopalians have no doctrine requiring burial by sundown the next day, and I cannot explain the rush. Neither can I explain why Justina, who was making an infrequent visit from I'm not sure where (the vicinity of Boston?), was buried in the cemetery on the outskirts of Proxmire Manor, where we then lived. Much about a human life—especially the adolescent portion of one—involves accepted truths that later seem strikingly odd, impossible to explain.

The rain began at dawn. By the time we got to church, all

that remained of the snow was the filthy gray hillocks left by the plows. The minister—a vigorous, hairy man with whom my father sometimes golfed—greeted us in the narthex. He struck a balance of gravitas and candor, comforting Mother, briefly raising my father's low spirits. Inside the church was a clutch of what I thought were hired mourners, since I'd never seen any of them before. I hardly had known Justina but felt guilty for not being able to grieve on her behalf, and so I looked to the likeness of crucified Jesus behind the altar and prayed for tears. I was rebuffed.

The service was short. During it, my father scribbled the word *Elixircol* on the church bulletin and started making notes. Mother frowned, pretended not to notice, put an arm around Paige, pulled her close. Paige wept. Good, perfect Paige.

At the grave site, my father seemed preoccupied by the undertaker's hovering men, wheeling his head around like a sentry expecting snipers. He did not participate in the recitation of the Twenty-third Psalm. The minister, at the conclusion of the cermony, had to ask him twice to cast the shovel of earth down upon the casket. Mother elbowed him, my father fulfilled his duty, and she dropped a red rose into the grave. Touching a gloved hand to her lips, she blew Justina a kiss.

On our drive back home, where elderly ladies of our congregation were busy arranging casserole dishes and baked meats and generally irritating our cook Inga's proprietary Scandinavian nature, my father took a right where he should have taken a left.

"You missed our turn," Mother said, confused. My father prided himself on his sense of direction. Missing a turn, especially near home, was fiercely unlike him.

"I did not," he insisted. "I am dropping myself off at the train station." He checked his watch. "I'll just make it." He patted Mother on the knee. "You and the children will be fine. I'm sorry, darling, I'm tired, and I'd like nothing more than to be at your side now. But if I don't finish the Elixircol commercial, MacPherson will cook my goose."

"Moses," Mother said, with no inflection I could hear. Just his name, Moses.

Paige fixed her scowl on the hill to our house. The sky was dark from the storm; every house glowed with electric light.

My father got out, kissed Mother's cheek, waved to us, his children, in the backseat, and disappeared into the rain.

The car sat idling. The radio crackled with static: a baseball game, the Brooklyn Dodgers, somewhere in Florida.

"Shall I drive?" I said.

Mother turned around. Her makeup was quite destroyed. She smiled. "Yes," she said. "Why not?"

"Why not!" said Paige, ever the scorekeeper in the unhappy game of what was fair and what was foul. "*He* gets to *drive?*"

"I've done it before," I said, which, though Paige protested and Mother raised her eyes, was true. My father had taken me to the large new parking lot of a church (not ours) and let me. He was a good teacher: succinct in his instruction, and patient.

I took my place behind the wheel of our new Buick. "Start slowly," said Mother. She gave no other instruction whatsoever.

I pulled out—slowly—onto the boulevard, and a speeding, honking tow truck had to swerve to miss me. Paige screamed. Mother told her to hush. It had been, she said, more the truck driver's fault than mine, and the rest of the ride home up the hill went without incident.

I pulled the car expertly into the drive. Proud of myself, I had a lapse of concentration, veering onto the wet grass and crushing what was left of one wall of Paige's snow fort. I jerked the wheel, righted the car, then oversteered the littlest bit and, just barely, struck the side of the garage, leaving a long white stripe of a dent the length of the front quarter panel.

Then, because I panicked, the length of the entire passenger side. If I close my eyes, I can still hear the groan of metal against wet wood.

No one spoke. Finally, Mother said, "I suppose we should see to our guests." We got out on the driver's side. Only Paige, our staunch realist, glanced over her shoulder to see the damage. She loved us enough, and was eager enough to please, that she withheld the satisfaction of saying she'd told us so. She is an old soul. I love her. Her marriages have turned out as unhappily as you might have already guessed.

OUR PORCH WAS a thicket of drying umbrellas. Neighbors must have heard the news via the tribal drums of suburbia and showed up at our house to be of glib comfort and for pie. As for the mourners, they turned out to be distant relations, connected through routes I would need pen and pad to explain. Ours was a family cut off from its past. On Mother's side, this had to do with her having married my father, son of Irish immigrants. On my father's, it had to do with most of them being back in Ireland or killed off in shipwrecks or in other colorful ways. Of those who came to America (this being six: father, mother, and four sons), all but my father were dead. Rarely were they mentioned.

Mother's entrance elicited a low expectant sigh, not for her beauty (which, as I said, had that day been tested) and not out of empathy, but rather that, first, they'd heard my encounter with the garage and had to turn quickly away from the windows to pretend they had not, and, second, they'd left it to a member of the immediate family to okay the liquor. The neighbors—women, plus a few husbands with jobs nearby—stared at the lowboy, willing my father's decanters to break into song. Ever one to know what was expected, Mother went straight to it. "Justina," she said, "would not have countenanced such a sea of long faces." She poured herself a whiskey, neat. "That's a joke, people," she said. "Countenance, faces. A pun. Well," she said. "Okay, fine." She held up her glass. "Here's to Justina."

"To Justina!" echoed our full house, though many of them had never met her, or had met her only once. One of the relations, a bald man from Shady Hill named Trace Bearden, drafted himself as bartender. The line was long, and I found myself in it. Paige, in a corner by the dormant hi-fi, glowered at me. I grinned. I knew I could get away with a lot on a day like this. How much worse could this be than strafing the side of the Buick?

When I got to the front of the line, Mr. Bearden stopped, looked for my mother, who was out of his line of sight. "Right, then," he said, icing a glass. "It's been rough, I imagine, losing dear Aunt Justina."

"Yes," I said. "Very."

"Scotch?" he said.

"Yes," I said, because it sounded like *butterscotch*. "Please."

"Soda, too?"

"Is it good that way?" I asked.

Mr. Bearden laughed. "Sure, kid." He handed me the drink and patted me on the back. "Don't tell your mom."

"She doesn't care," I said, presuming the opposite.

Mr. Bearden nodded. "Tough break," he said, "with the old man's car."

"You saw that?"

"Nope." He shook his head. "Didn't see a thing, sport."

I slipped out onto the porch with my drink, holding it low so as not to attract attention. I saw this as a sacramental moment, one untempered by anything outside my vast adolescent world of self. I took a drink, as if it *were* a glass of soda, and it burned and choked me as it went down. I was certain that Mr. Bearden had played a party trick on me, had, instead of my father's scotch, given me hair tonic to teach me a lesson. I stood, coughing, breathing heavily, spitting out the taste of it, off the porch and into the mud. I set down the glass.

"You're supposed to be in training," Paige said.

"Don't sneak up on me like that."

"The coach would kick you off the team if he knew."

"Well, he doesn't know," I said. "And besides, these are special circumstances."

She considered this. She held her arms out, into the rain, watching the sleeves of her dress turn dark with water. "Does it taste good?"

"Yes, very," I said, hoping to trick her as I had done once with chocolate-covered bees my father had received in an office Secret Santa exchange. "Have a sip."

"No," she said. "I'm in training. Moses is going to kill you when he gets home." She called our father Moses and would soon begin doing so to his face.

"Training for what, the Olympics? You're eleven years old."

"Think about it," she said. "You're offering your eleven-year-old sister a drink. You're as bad as they are."

She has always terrified me: before that moment, then, thereafter, and now. But especially then.

"It's just a sip," I said, hopelessly, watching her sidestep umbrellas and go back inside. I studied the glass, took a smaller gulp this time, poured the rest onto a rosebush, and went back inside to begin the long wait for my father's ire.

As the reception was winding down—scarcely enough time for the ride into the city and back—my father returned home. He had, extravagantly, taken a taxicab from the station. He strode in, bouyant: the bearer, one might have guessed, of good news.

"I've done it," he announced. "I'm free. Inga!" he called.

Most of the guests had gone, but there were enough left over, finishing drinks and talking about stocks and athletics, for my father to have an audience.

"What did he do?" someone asked. "What is he free from?"

The cook pushed open the kitchen door. Behind her were two old ladies from the church, washing dishes and speaking in hushed voices. "Yes?" Inga said.

"Dear, I'm sorry," said my father, "but you're fired."

Inga nodded, as if he'd only said he would prefer his meat broiled rather than grilled, then let the door close.

"It's nothing you've done, Inga," my father called. "It's me. It's all me. We will provide you with the best of references! If any of you are looking for an excellent cook...," he said.

It was clear to the remaining guests that he was not free from drinking. They might, under different circumstances, have stayed late and tried to keep up with him, but this was a postfuneral reception for a woman whom no one but Mother knew well. As they filed out, my father shouted things about death, our denial of it, the castles we build in the clouds, the measures we take for our health and the evils of ignoring that likely as not we'll go like Justina, alone in a strange house where no one's supposed to die, our funeral conducted with great piety and solicitude by a bunch of drunken frauds we could not give a goddamn care about.

My father rarely swore. I imagined I was now a goner.

With the room drained of guests, it fell to Mother to say something about the Buick, but, enraged, she locked herself in their bedroom. Paige, had she been the driver, would have confessed and taken whatever punishment fate decreed. But Paige was in league with me, not them, and so she, too, went upstairs, and my father and I found ourselves seated on the same malodorous green sofa upon which Justina had died, talking about, of all things, zoning. He claimed that our village was zoned so that no one was allowed to die here, and wasn't that a crock of shit?

"Yes," I said. My heart felt too small for my rib cage. "A real crock."

He got up, turned on the radio, let it warm up, then dialed through the stations, looking for who knows what. He switched it off, switched on the television set. "Requests?" he said.

"*Life with Father?*"

It was a joke, and he got it, and grinned. "Not on," he said. The tube glowed to life. It was a Western. "This okay?"

"Sure," I said.

He had another drink: of all things, a scotch and soda. With a drink in my father's hand, you could picture him sailing, his face ruddy from the setting sun. Or telling jokes in the bar of the Saint Regis Hotel, to men and women with tailored wool clothing and big white teeth. I had, of course, never been sailing or set foot in the bar of the Saint Regis Hotel, but that *is* what I saw. He took a sip. My stomach lurched. He, however, closed his eyes in bliss.

On television, a beautiful woman fell in love with the hero. "Watch," my father said. "She'll die. In about—" He checked his watch. "Ten minutes."

"How do you know? Have you seen this one?"

"No," he said. "Just watch."

I did, and he was right. A bullet from the pistol of the bad guy, meant for the hero, ricocheted off a saloon door and, as the poor woman exited the millinery, pierced her heart. Our melancholy hero, eyes narrow and cheeks dry, got quick revenge.

"How did you know?" I said.

"I'll tell you when you're older," he said. "Do you think this sofa smells?"

"Smells like what?" I said, though I knew what he meant. Actually, it smelled like a can of disinfectant had been exhausted on it. "It always smelled kind of funny," I said. "You know. Fritz."

"Fritz?"

I was shocked. "Our dog, Fritz? You don't remember Fritz?"

He squinted. "Ye-e-es," he said. "Fritz. Huh."

Neither of us moved, neither of us spoke. I was thinking of Fritz, and my father, I'm certain, was thinking of something else.

"Hey, listen," he said, getting up to pour himself another. "Do you know what we need to do?"

"Go to bed?" I offered.

"No," he said. "Here. Help me." He picked up one end of the green velvet sofa. "C'mon." We dragged it to the front door. "First," he said, "we burn this sofa." He propped open the storm door. "Then we need to move. Westward ho! Make ourselves explorers. New immigrants."

"Where were you thinking?" I said, imagining, in a panic, moving to a new school where even the tenuous friendships I had here would look good.

"Nowhere in particular," he said. It was still raining. We carried the sofa out to the front lawn, about where the snow fort had been. If you knew where to look, you could see the tire track I'd made there.

I took a deep breath. "I wrecked the car," I said.

"Good," he said. "Who needs it? Do you have a match?"

"No."

He patted himself all over. "This is what happens when you quit smoking," he said. He went inside and returned with an oil lamp Mother had been given as a gift and never lit. He doused the sofa with lamp oil, then produced a matchbox: OHIO BLUE TIP MATCHES. "Maybe Ohio," he said, cupping his hand, striking a match, tossing. The sofa whooshed into flame.

"There," he said.

But the rain picked up, and, moments later, before any of the neighbors had a chance to wake up and call the Proxmire Manor VFD, the sofa was extinguished. Ashen, sodden, ruined, clotting our front yard like something truly shameful.

"Oh well," my father said. He poked at the smoldering

sofa with the toe of his wing-tip shoe. With my brown Hush Puppy, I did precisely the same. When you and your father set a sofa aflame on the front lawn of a house in Westchester County, you will find that there isn't much to say. We stood there in the rain, and he kept looking at the sofa and then at the darkened windows of the neighbors' houses, and I looked wherever he looked. "Look, son," he finally said, "if you'll excuse me, I'm going to go pick the lock to my own bedroom door."

"Okay," I said. "Good night."

We went inside together. He went upstairs, and I took off my wet clothes and lay down on our family's remaining sofa. I did not want to go upstairs. I could hear the scratching of a penknife in the lock, and I could hear Mother ask to be left alone. Be rational, my father said. He kept fiddling with the door. Please, Mother said, can we talk about this in the morning, please. I went to the window and looked at the sofa. Still there: large, wet, black, and green.

There was a long silence, a terrifying silence, and my father said, certainly, tomorrow would be fine, and then there was a longer silence yet.

Suddenly my father began to pound on the door, calling her vile names, words I knew but had never heard from his lips.

"Moses," Mother said. "The children."

"They're asleep," he said.

"No, we're not!" shouted Paige, from her room. "We can hear everything!"

"Go to sleep," my father said. "This doesn't concern you."

I switched on the television. But it was hard to hear over all the shouting, and I did not want to turn it loud enough for anyone to be aware of me. I prayed to be overlooked, undetected.

Upstairs, my father had lowered his voice, was speaking in consoling tones. This went on for some time, broken by

Mother's angry voice: "No one *forced* you. Dig *ditches* for all I care."

"Here we go again," said my father.

"Do you want to fight?" said Mother. "Let's."

The night erupted with the sound of splintering wood and then my mother's screams. I sprang from the sofa and ran upstairs. In my parents' bedroom, Mother stood in the corner, her nightstand lamp absurdly held above her head, like a sword. Across the room, Paige rained slaps and blows upon my father—glancing his abdomen, glancing his flanks—as he held her back from him with a straightarm, like the halfback he'd once been. Heartbreakingly puzzled, he stared blankly at his wife, splinters in his hair and a cut above one ear, his jaw-bone covered with blood, dripping onto a new yellow rug.

"I hate you, I hate you, I hate you," said Paige.

I stood in the hall, stock-still. Suddenly everyone looked at me. Mother lowered the lamp. Paige lowered her arms. My father cocked his bloody ear. "Is the television set still on?"

"Yes," I said. "I was watching it."

"Isn't it your bedtime?" he said. "Isn't it a school night?"

"Yes," Mother answered for me, and for Paige, too. "Children, please, it's a school night. This is nothing for you to worry about. Nathan, go turn off the television set."

Paige's eyes grew wide, her jaw fell open. Betrayed, she could summon only one word. "Mother."

"This is no concern of yours," said Mother. "Please, let's all just get some sleep."

My father, ludicrously, tried to go tuck Paige into bed. She slammed her door in his face. He stopped, turned around, and faced me. We looked in each other's eyes, and I could imagine him at my age: skinny, confused, desiring too deeply the acceptance of others, a creature whose life might go any which way. I saw him swallow hard. He reached a shaking, bloodied hand toward me. It hung there in the darkness of the hallway, unaccepted. He seemed to want to shake my hand, as if I had just swum a fine backstroke race and he had risen from the bleachers to offer manly approval. I didn't move. He exended his other hand. Neither of us moved. Finally, he cleared his throat, smoothed his hair, and said, "The television set."

"Right," I said. "The television set."

In the morning, everyone was embarrassed for everything. Mother swept the floor and attempted to clean the rug. My father carried the remains of the door to the woodpile. Paige and I vacuumed the downstairs floors and dragged the charred green sofa to the treelawn. Before noon, Mother said, it was gone (the sofa, not the treelawn). My father again vowed to stop drinking. Mother even convinced him that he had been the one who'd dented the car, and that was the end of that. Whether my father quit his job or was fired remains unclear. I believe it was equally unclear to him.

THAT SUMMER, WE moved to Deerlick, Indiana, where my father had taken a job as a sales manager for a bakery that made English muffins, fried pies, and packaged cake doughnuts. He moved there before us. The family's move was forestalled until Paige and I finished school, which gave Mother time to cast off many of our lendings. We would be living a more frugal life, less given to appearances' sake. As a symbol of this, my father chose not to repair the gash on the side of the Buick.

Several boys from the swim team helped us pack the van: juniors and seniors, who I hoped, with colossal illogic, would like me because I had made them some quick money. Yet, in a way, this happened. Throughout the house—behind books in the library, paint cans in the basement, stuffed in a wicker bassinet stored above the garage—was liquor. Gin, whiskey, vodka. Most half full. I said it was mine, dispensed it equitably among them, and they loved me. With the van fully loaded, we snuck into a neighbor's bomb shelter and together shared five warm cans of beer.

Paige and I now call our move to Indiana the Death Quest, named for my father's many detours to cemeteries and grave sites, beginning with Justina's. Only from the date on the stone could you tell how fresh her grave was. I could not picture where the stakes of the canopy tent had been, what route we'd taken from the hearse to the grave. My father stood at her grave and softly wept. His hair was graying. His back was rounded. The two months he'd been in Indiana seemed to have aged him ten years.

Next came what I thought was a wrong turn. We had been heading west—my father and Paige in the van, Mother and I in the Buick—when, without signaling, he turned onto a northeasternly road. Mother followed. "I'm humoring him," is all she would say. "It really isn't far." We drove to a small town in Rockland County and stopped in front of a frame house, white and unremarkable. It was the house where my father had grown up. The new, wary owners refused to let him tour it. We then drove to the edge of town and up a steep hill. In the corner of a tiny cemetery were five small tombstones, identical but for the names and dates. I had thought his three brothers all died in the war; judging from the dates, only one could have. I did not mention this, then or ever, but I imagine the other two died the way you've already imagined. At these graves, my father did not cry. He knelt and kissed each stone in turn.

At Scranton, we picked up the road that would take us to Deerlick. On the way, we stopped at Civil War battlefields, French-and-Indian War fort sites, and monuments where slave rebellions failed. We roamed through sunny, fragrant meadows and paid small prices to see large dioramas. Mother and my father held hands. It was more a vacation than a move. Paige, now, can't believe we were subjected to this, but, truly, it was a happy time.

The move to Deerlick would place hardships upon Paige's ambitions (the nearest indoor pool was an hour away), yet she still became a varsity swimmer at a university with a fine tradition of women's swimming and where she now coaches. I mentioned her marital woes. She has made several therapists rich. Though our parents have been dead for years (*Mother*, it turned out, was the one killed by drink; my father died from years of smoking in those poorly ventilated church basements where AA meetings are held), Paige has of late become involved in this adult children of alcoholics movement. She dragged me once to a meeting (church basement, no smoking). Everyone had the same story. My parents made me grow up too fast. They made me feel that if I didn't get too close to anyone, no one could hurt me. They made me feel I had to be good and make everyone happy. Et cetera. I could see Paige wince at the most self-pitying of these people, which gave me hope for her. But, riding home in the car, when I started making fun of them, she whacked me in the chest with the back of her hand. "These groups," she said, "really do help people."

Fine. But, dear Paige, everyone's parents have ruined them, which is another way of saying they have prepared us to live bravely in our imperfect world. I would not have become a writer without the terrifically picaresque circumstances of my upbringing. Paige would not have become such a single-mindedly competitive athlete and coach. See it as a gift: perverse, lovely, lively, and enduring.

Who can say what it is to be an alcoholic? People want hard, fast definitions, but about every important matter in life you will get mixed signals, conflicting advice. Love. Art. God. If denial means you have a problem, then what do you make of the teetotaler? (Paige is a teetotaler.) Hard, fast definitions won't suffice. Ever. I see alcoholism as a pit in the middle of a road: always there, waiting for the next lost wayfarer. I fear it may be only a matter of time before drink becomes a problem for me. I like to drink. I like its taste. I am rarely, if ever, drunk. But if I am honest, I must also say that I drink more now, and enjoy it more, than I ever have.

Halftime

The day my wife leaves, I fall asleep en route to the station—the first time in twenty-seven months, since I
began taking Provigil and Effexor together. I'd had plenty of
sleep; I'd gotten a workout helping her load the truck, but,
bam: four in the afternoon, and I drive maybe ten miles of the
Florida-Georgia Parkway without remembering a thing. At
the I-10 on-ramp, I jerk awake, and it's only then that I go off
the road. The ditch is flooded. I barely avoid the water, kicking up this big plume of mud. My heart's beating so hard it
hurts. I get out. Above me are these massive power lines, humming and crackling. A semi roars by. For no reason, I wave.
It's December but hot. I'm shivering. The trucker honks. He
could just as easily have been calling 911 for someone to come
fish my fat corpse out of the ditch; people would have their
simple way with cause/effect and blame it on the Stephanie
situation. I slap my face. I have a game. I get back in. The rest
of the drive, I'm so rattled, I turn on my own radio station and
try not to think about what people will say about Stephanie.
But I get there, and instead, everyone's talking about some
kid Duke McKibbon hired.

His name is Jason Truax, and he's a senior in *high school,* no experience whatsoever. Marsha Marsh, our receptionist, who despite her name is Cuban, says Duke showed the kid around, then bugged out and didn't tell anyone, Jason included, what the kid's responsibilities were. People are afraid he's there to take their job. It's Marsha's cousin that Stephanie's leaving me for, so I know Marsha knows. She doesn't let on. She hands me my paycheck and keeps yammering. Jason, Jason, Jason.

He's still there, a big blonde yutz, hunched over a console in the editing room, marking up press releases and wire copy. I stick my head in. He jumps up like I caught him jacking off. "You need to use this?" He points at a cart machine, but must mean the room. "I can move."

"Later," I say, which is a pointless lie. "So long as you're done in ten minutes."

Dietz sees me, hangs up the phone, and rushes over. The kid's father owns Truax Mobile World, Inc., Dietz says, and his grandfather is Billy Ray Truax, who played football at FSU not long after they stopped being a women's college. "The trailer sales is a smallish account," Dietz says. "This is about Billy Ray."

"They don't make 'em like that anymore," I say, though I'm unfamiliar with Billy Ray Truax. I started out twenty years ago doing news, spent time as a deejay, and drifted into sports. Dietz breathes sports. He used to produce my call-in show and do color. More than once, he shook me awake on the air. Then he got married, had kids, and got promoted to sales director. My meds started working better, and I got by fine solo.

Lassiter, the program director, is finishing up his show: *Today's Country.* This involves flavorless pop music that arbitrarily qualifies as country. His Arbitron ratings are double anyone else's.

"That Jason's a swimmer," he says. "Duke's been talking about him for months, remember?"

I make a who-can-make-sense-of-what-Duke-says face.

"This summer," says Lassiter, "the kid won some race by a zillionth of a second. Duke got so excited, he spoke in tongues." Lassiter tries speaking in tongues. "*That's* why he hired him."

Lassiter's lying. No one, not even him, listens to us when we do swimming. Duke's grandkids swim. Duke does play-by-play (I begged off, pleading ignorance), snagging older kids from the team, weak swimmers with only an event or two, to do color. I'd guess that's where he found Jason.

"Are we sure," I say, "that he's not just an intern?"

"Marsha did the paperwork. He's getting eleven smacks an hour, dude."

Dude. Lassiter is in his forties. The other day I heard him say *word* to indicate accord.

I go out the back door. No one's around. On my cell, I call my shrink. She's not there. It's the service. "Tell her Bob Deldermuth needs new meds—stat."

"'Stat'?" the operator says.

"Don't you watch TV?"

"Religiously," she says.

"I don't even have a TV," I blurt. "Yesterday I had three, but my wife took 'em. I have DishNetwork and nothing to watch it on."

"How does that make you feel?"

I'm sweating like it's August. "Why don't you just give her the message, okay?"

"I'm telling you, anyone could do that job. Talk into a tape recorder, play it back, listen to yourself, really *listen*. You'll save tons of money. You'll have yourself some new TVs in no time."

I'm not rich, but money isn't my most pressing problem. "I have an HMO," I say. "It only costs me the ten-buck co-pay."

"Even that," she says, "adds up."

The door opens and, of course, it's Jason. He mouths the

word *sorry.* I frown. *I'm done,* he mouths. I wave him off. His shoulders sag, and he goes back inside. I feel a blast of AC. "Are you new?" I ask the woman. "Do you have a name?"

"Everyone has a name," she says. "You have my number. Call any time, hon."

She hangs up, and I hold my cell in front of my face and look at it. I slap my face. I'm awake. I've been awake. This all happened.

THE NEW NIGHT guy comes in as I'm loading up the van and Marsha Marsh is leaving. He's a pale young man, anyway, but when she stops to tell him about Jason Truax, he takes off his gigantic sunglasses—the kind old people wear—and goes practically translucent. He mutters something: *I'm toast* or maybe *I'm a ghost.* Whatever he says, Marsha doesn't refute it.

"I knew it," he says, loud enough that I'm sure that's what he says. He puts the shades back on. Marsha pats him on the arm, calls the world a crazy place, makes eye contact with me but gets in her car without mentioning Stephanie. The night guy slams the front door behind him.

All the office people leave. No one says anything to me but good night. By now, everything's loaded and I'm sitting on the bumper of the van, waiting for Dietz. I consider going to get him.

Jason Truax walks out like someone who's spent the day breaking rocks. He apologizes for inconveniencing me. I tell him to forget it.

"Hey, are there manuals?" he says. "For all that equipment?"

"I'm sure there are," I say. "Somewhere."

"Right," he says. "Thanks." He sounds sincere. I don't introduce myself, and he drives away, rap music blaring, in a battered pickup with TRUAX MOBILE WORLD painted on the side.

When Dietz finally comes out, I ask him if he'd like to do color tonight. For old times' sake. "It'd be a nice change of pace from the solo act."

He raised an eyebrow when I said *solo act.* "I wouldn't get paid any extra for it."

I grin. "That's what it's about, is it? What it all comes down to? Money?"

"Yep." He's studying me like he's afraid I'm going to cry.

"Fine," I say. Whatever else I do, crying's not in the cards. Various shrinks have tried to pinpoint when this started (I'm not sure). Of all Stephanie's grievances—my weight, my lack of ambition, the porn (her idea, originally)—my not being able to cry seems like the one that should have provoked mercy.

"I should go," Dietz says. "My turn to cook. Some meal-in-a-bag thing, but still."

Though we are friends, I've been to his house once since he got married. He's had to do games for me on days I called in sick, for which his wife I'm sure dislikes me. He starts to go. Then he sees all the red mud on my car. "Word of advice," he calls, pointing. "Get a Jeep."

I drive a six-year-old Toyota Camry. "I had a, you know," I say. "A thing."

"A sleep thing?" Dietz says. He comes over to me. "The game's in Tallahassee, right? Oh, man." Meaning that I have an hour's drive on my hands. "Have you been..."

"No," I say. "It's been twenty-seven months. It's probably a fluke. I'm fine."

Dietz snaps into action. He calls his wife, and before I know it, he's driving me to the game.

We talk about sports—in other words, nothing at all—all the way there.

The game is so lopsided I can't imagine who wouldn't have tuned out after the first quarter. Dietz and I still work well together, though. I pause, and he's just *there*: a quick stat, a comment, something I'm talking too much and caring too little to think to say. One of the schools has a world-class cheerleading squad, and all game we're pestered by their parents, who want us to broadcast the halftime routine. I lack the strength to fend them off. Dietz points out that we're *radio*. More than one parent brings up swimming. They're relentless. Dietz breaks down and agrees to watch the routine and, afterward, interview the squad's captain and the coach.

I watch some of it myself—these girls and the boys who throw them. Am I cheered? No. I'm old enough to be their father. I look upon these flying, newly muscled bodies, the hoisting, hands on hands, feet, shoulders, asses, and imagine cheap beer, fogged car windows, college rejections, disappointing jobs, doomed marriages. If I were any of their fathers, I'd handle it badly, that my kids—good kids!—are no longer children.

I walk the perimeter of the grounds of the school, stirring up endorphins. A precaution. It's dark but still absurdly hot. Marriages end. Fact of life. The night's full of revving cars and muffled pep bands. I stop on the empty bleachers behind the baseball field. I dial Stephanie's cell. It's call-forwarded; on the voice mail, Vic Santiago promises to attend to all my insurance and investment needs if I will just leave my name and number. I do.

Then I fall asleep. I may not even have gotten the whole number out. Happily, in one of the dugouts is a couple, presumably doing what teenagers in dark dugouts do. They see me keel over. They tell me they thought I had a heart attack or something. "Or something," I say. "My heart's black with poison and remorse," I say, tapping my chest, "but it's fine." They're spooked. Youth. They'll eventually see enough to join the unsurprised. The girl hands me my phone, which is still going. I hand her a dollar and Lassiter's business card. She accepts. I hang up. I was asleep for six minutes. I can't say why I gave her those things, why she took them, or why I even had Lassiter's card. Me, I've put away childish things. Bob Deldermuth sees through a glass, darkly.

I make it behind the mike in time. No one's the wiser. I ask Dietz how the thing with the cheerleaders went. "Just what you'd think," he says.

THE NEXT MORNING, I pack up what's left: what's mine. Our house is a rental, and our lease is up Tuesday. When we moved in, the house was on a lake. The lake has a sinkhole in it that every seventy years or so sucks all the water out. This happened a few days after we moved in, and now the lake is a marshy prairie. Experts swear it will fill up again. Even lakeless, it's been nice, way out in the country. When the bugs weren't too bad, we'd take a boom box and some CDs out to the end of the dock—Lucinda Williams, Wilco, Emmylou Harris, that sort of thing—and have nonalcoholic cocktails. Yes, we fought, but no worse than most couples. Stephanie fell in love with someone else. To listen to her, it was more or less an accident. Vic Santiago is her AA sponsor, and so probably helped save her life, then things no one planned on happening happened. Maybe she's right. The heart wants what it wants. She and I were happier here than a lot of other places we lived. I can't even *say* Shreveport without getting a little sick.

I'm thirty-nine years old. I have a job, a paid-for car, and, yesterday aside, good control over my condition. My family, most of whom are still in Cleveland or its exurbs (a brother in Chagrin Falls, a sister in Oberlin, cousins in Akron), loves me. I had a happy childhood. I can start over, lose weight, get a dog, find someone else, build a deck, have kids. In this part of

Florida, unless you get too close to Tallahassee or the beach, land is cheap. I can get a lot, put a trailer on it, and build later.

One moment I'm sitting down to tape a box full of stadium cups and melamine dishes, thinking about all this. The next, I'm packing up the rest of the kitchen, still mulling, but deploying a care I'd never use and bubblewrap I never bothered to purchase, because it's all a dream. What wakes me up is the phone, though I somehow think that *that's* the dream, and don't pick up as Stephanie says she appreciates how adult I've been and is just calling to make sure I'm doing okay.

When I realize I'm awake now and that I've *been* sleeping, I'd been asleep for hours. The phone had even rung before— Dietz, saying his wife would be happy to come take me to work. He'd followed me home from the station last night, without incident. I check my watch. No game today, and my show doesn't start until seven, but I have a phoner with a NASCAR flack in an hour. I don't have enough time for Dietz's wife to come get me. I pop an expired Dexedrine spansule, wash it down with a Red Bull Energy Drink, shave, shower, and hope for the best.

On the way in, I call my shrink. It's the service again. My shrink's out of the office today, and the receptionist is sick. "Are you the same woman as yesterday?"

"I am," she says. "It was an uneventful night."

I'm in radio; I *know* that sexy voices are inevitably disappointing. Case in point: me. If it was all about voice, Stephanie would have driven away down a road flanked with eager supermodels. "Yesterday, I drove ten miles sound asleep."

"Hypnagogic hallucination," she says. "Ten *miles*? C'mon. You'd be dead."

"Are you a doctor?" I'm running the AC full tilt, but it's nowhere near as hot as yesterday.

"Just a student."

"Premed?"

"Prelaw," she says.

"Same difference," I say.

"*Animal House,*" she says, catching the reference.

"I think I love you," I say.

"So what are you so afraid of?"

"David Cassidy," I say, catching her reference. "Nice. No, really."

"You don't love me." It's a voice three degrees shy of husky, a voice too womanly to giggle. It's a voice you can crawl inside of and order out for the best pizza you ever had.

"How do you know?" I ask. "You've never met me."

"That," she says, "is what they all say."

"There's a *they?*"

"There's a world of they."

"My wife just left me."

"Women," she says. "You're driving *now,* aren't you?"

"I'm on my mobile, but no. I'm not." For you, it might be dangerous, talking and driving. For me, it's a lifesaver. I'm right where I ran off the road yesterday. My ruts are full of water and look like they were made by Truckasaurus. "It definitely wasn't a hypnagogic hallucination," I say, merging onto I-10. "It was sleep. I didn't remember a thing."

"Ten miles is a lot."

"It's not my record," I say. "Listen, isn't there another doctor on-call? For emergencies?"

"If it was really an emergency," she says, "you wouldn't be driving."

"I'm not driving," I say, relieved she didn't ask about my record.

"You're making me hot," she says. "Ooh, baby, ooh."

"Mockery will get you everywhere," I say. "I really may love you."

"I know," she says, and hangs up. I know it's crazy, but she sounded like she meant it.

———

EVERYONE'S PRETENDING to be too busy to show Jason
Truax how to use anything. Several of us give him the evil eye
so he won't even ask. He busies himself circling stories in the
Atlanta and Jacksonville papers. He asks Lassiter if he can use
the production-room PC to add a news-headline scroll to our
Web page. When Jason gets it set up and asks for the pass-
word, Lassiter says only Duke has it. Duke, who can barely
turn a computer on, hasn't shown his face all day.

I boot Jason out of production to tape my interview. It's
December, but my demographic can't get enough NASCAR.
I'll say this: no sport gives the speciously credentialed more
free food and gear. Back in the day, Stephanie and I made lost
weekends of it. Daytona, Atlanta, Darlington, et cetera. Suddenly I feel a presence. Paranoia, I think, from that Effexor-
Provigil-Dexedrine–Red Bull cocktail. Then, out of the corner
of my eye, I see something move. I shout the Lord's name in
vain. The flack keeps right on debunking Dale Earnhardt Jr.
conspiracy theories. From behind the computer table, Jason
Truax rises. He makes a *yikes* grimace. Paranoia, hell. Deldermuth's Razor: the simplest explanation is just the simplest
explanation.

The flack asks if I'm okay. Never better, I say. We wrap
it up.

"I'm *so* sorry," Jason says. "I just wanted to . . ."

"Forget it." My heart won't slow down. "Next time, ask if
you can watch, okay?"

He nods. "You're Bob Deldermuth, right? I've been listening to you all my life."

"I've only been here four years."

"Really? It seems a lot longer."

"That's a compliment?"

He frowns. "Yeah," he says. "Hey, I'm sorry to hear about,
you know. Mrs. Deldermuth. My mom left once. She came
back. It was rough."

If this kid knows, everyone knows. "I'm sure it was," I say.

"I want to be a journalist," he says. "News. But maybe sports."

"I want to be a dentist," I say, in the manner of that elf from *Rudolph the Red-Nosed Reindeer,* which Stephanie and I watched together last week in an otherwise dark and silent room. Then she went to bed and I watched a porno. I pop the cart. I say it again: "I want to be a dentist."

Jason stands there, blank. My heart begins to slow down. "It's not you," I say, mopping my face with a paper napkin. "It's me."

He cocks his head the way a big blond dog would.

What the hell. I show him how to work the board.

Marsha is the first to peek through the little square window and notice. Moments later, everyone in the station is filing by. Dietz shoots me a palms-up what-gives look. The night guy flips me off. "You want to learn radio, Jason?" Lassiter says, clamping a hand on my shoulder, "my man Bob's the one to teach you."

I'm feeling better. It's nearly time for me to get ready for my show when I hear Duke's booming voice, calling Jason's name. Duke spent the day scouring memorabilia stores. He's holding a plastic bag with a program in it. On the cover, Billy Ray Truax strikes a vintage 1950s knee-up stiff-arm pose. Duke is an excitable man, but I've rarely seen him more excited.

"Granddad's in Key West," Jason says. "We'll be there for Christmas. If you want, I'll get him to sign it for you."

"Could you?" Duke says. "My god, it'd mean a lot." He thumps the program. "I was at this game, you know."

He launches into a blow-by-blow version of it. I escape. A half hour later, Jason stops in the studio to thank me for the lesson.

"Is that why a big kid like you doesn't play football?"

"Is what why?"

"Getting compared to your granddad. Not wanting to be."

"Ten seconds," the night guy says.

"No," Jason says. "It's because I suck at football."

That cracks me up. He looks grateful. "Maybe I can teach you to be my color guy." I say this on a whim, but, realistically, Dietz can't keep doing it. He's already working twelve-hour days on the sales side. "You drive, right?"

"What's driving have to do with it?"

"Everything and nothing," I say. "You want to do it or not?"

"Five," says the night guy. "Four. Three."

Jason gives me a thumbs-up and leaves.

It's a long night. The night guy—who, as my producer (his *Legends of Country* show follows), is supposed to be screening calls—lets everything through. I get people speculating about who in pro football might be gay, people who think we should do winter swimming, too, and countless conspiracy theorists who want to talk about Dale Earnhardt Jr.

After the first hour, I ask the night guy what his problem is.

"If someone's getting fired," he says, "it's not going to be me."

If taking calls from cretins was going to get me fired, it would have happened years ago. "C'mon. He's a kid. It's just an after-school job."

"Watch your back. Word to the wise."

"My back? You're all talking about Stephanie *behind* my back, every one of you jerks, and Jason, who's been here two days, is the only person who's said anything to my face."

"Who's Stephanie?" he says.

He has those sunglasses on. It's hard to tell if he's serious. I give him a look.

The next caller, according to my screen, is "Brian." His topic: "FSU kicking game."

"Brian, in Monroeville, you're on the air."

"Hey, Bob. You okay to drive home?"

It's Dietz, patched through from the private line.

"We're on the air," I say. "*Brian.*" On the other side of the glass, the night guy laughs like hell.

Dietz is flawless. Wide right this, hang time that. At the next break, I call him back and tell him I'm fine. What am I going to do, ask him to come follow me home? Then I screw up my courage and tell him about Jason. Not only isn't Dietz mad, he's thrilled. His wife is teaching yoga classes. He'll be a hero when he tells her he can watch the kids.

I HAVE THE next day off. I get through to Dr. Jacoby's office first thing in the morning. The receptionist says she got the message from the service and was about to call to see if I could make it at one. "*Today?*" I say. "You're kidding. Don't you people have a Christmas rush?"

All she says is, yes, today, in a North Florida accent so thick and bovine I have to play a Dusty Springfield CD all the way through just to regain the will to live.

I hose the mud off the car. I finish packing. I call the realtor who sold Dietz his house and make an appointment to look at lots.

On the way to Tallahassee, I call Vic Santiago's office. He's not in. I ask for his voice mail. I tell it I'm serious about getting my insurance needs squared away.

DR. JACOBY ASKS if I think it's ironic, the condition flaring up the same day Stephanie left.

"That's one of my pet peeves," I say. Her office is freezing. I'm in Dockers and a Hawaiian shirt. She's wearing a wool suit covered with cat hair. "Misusing *ironic.* You mean coincidental."

She doesn't apologize. "Do you think it's coincidental?"

"You mean the opposite, I think," I say. "You mean, do I think there's a connection?"

She sighs, exasperated. The woman at the service was right; I make a mental note to run tape on tomorrow's game. Which I should do, anyway, so Jason can learn from his mistakes.

I tell Dr. Jacoby I have a theory. When I was repainting the nursery, I didn't have a mask. The hydrocarbons from the paint affected my hydrocretin-sensitive cells. Yesterday, the effects of that faded. After the thing in the morning, I was fine.

"The nursery." She might have at least said *I see someone's been on the Internet.* She just sits there. We've covered this territory. To sum up: my record is thirty-some miles of I-75, coming back from the Firecracker 400, I totaled Stephanie's Mazda. She, too, was asleep. She was eight months pregnant. We weren't otherwise hurt. Afterward, we avoided that room. Careful with the cause/effect assumptions. This was a while ago. Other things happened.

"We'd painted it really bright colors. It needed to be redone. To get our deposit back."

"You could have hired it done. Or forfeited the deposit."

"That's what Stephanie said. She had a girlfriend pack the room." Marsha Marsh, in fact, who's expecting, again, and took everything. "Look, this is no time for me to throw away money."

"That's not what I meant. You took the initiative. Why do you think you were motivated to paint that room," she says, "and unmotivated to do other things?"

I just shake my head. If I tell Dr. Jacoby that I haven't called in sick for weeks, that I'm reracking my life just fine, I'm afraid she'll dial down my meds. I avoid eye contact and stammer. She prescribes Ritalin and ups the dosage on the Provigil. She tells me to exercise daily. I tell her I am. She looks at me over the top of her chunky glasses.

A relationship is simply what two people choose to believe.

"By the way," I say as I'm leaving, "the new woman at your service is terrific." Because I'm sure there have been complaints.

"I never meet those people," she says. "But I'll be sure to convey the compliment."

Those people, for a moment, sounds like a racial slur. "Other patients have said things, right? About this new woman. I can tell." Probably it's not, of course.

Dr. Jacoby says no, no one's said anything. "What's terrific about her?"

This stops me short. "Her phone manner," I finally say. "It's amazing."

I wait for a moment for her to say *Amazing how?* She doesn't.

Across from the drugstore where I get my prescription filled is a Play It Again Sports. On a whim, I buy a used treadmill. They don't deliver, and I tell them that's okay, I don't have any place for them to deliver it to yet. On another whim, I stop and buy a TV—huge thing, picture-in-picture, the works. Two scrawny kids lash it to the roof. I'm out of there before I realize I have no way of getting it down alone.

Truax Mobile World is on the way home.

The man who waits on me is an older, more rabbity version of Jason. I don't want any favors. I don't mention Jason. I ask Jason's father how business is. He curses both the month of December and the American president. I tell him I voted for the other guy. He frowns and looks at me as if he's trying to place me. I get this all the time. It's my voice. I keep waiting for him to say something—he advertises at my station, his son works there—but he doesn't. I get what seems like a good deal on a used trailer that smells like tar. I write a check for the whole thing. He's got connections, he says, both for lots and in a mobile-home park. I tell him I'm set. Even as we're finishing up the paperwork, with my name right in front of him, he acts like he's never heard of me. We just talk about my TV and what all it does.

The store takes the TV back, no questions asked. I buy something I can handle myself. After that, I swing by the Don Pablo's on Capital Circle that Stephanie used to manage, before they refused to pay for rehab stay number two and fired her. The store's vacant. Out of business. I pull around back and, despite being in full view of the Office Max a hundred yards away, piss on the wall. Feels great. A cop even sees me pissing but just shakes his head. I wave. The heat has broken, and it looks like rain. By now, it's after business hours, so I call my shrink's office. It's not her. I ask the woman if she's the only one there. She says she knows what I want. I say I have no idea about that. She snorts and says that Kelly will be back tomorrow.

I call my bank's Anytime Line and punch in the numbers I need to stop payment on the checks for the treadmill and the trailer. It keeps me focused all the way home. I lug the TV in but don't unpack it. I should. This is my last day with satellite. Instead, even though Stephanie left the bed, I go into the empty nursery, now blister-white, open all the windows, spread out on the floor, and listen to the rain. In no time, I'm out. All night, I sleep, and while I have no memory of tossing and turning, when I wake up it's like I've just run a marathon.

STEPHANIE'S MASCARA IS smeared, and so is Marsha Marsh's. Could be the rain. Lassiter has a hand on each of their backs, and they're all hunched over the reception desk. They see me and stop whatever they've been saying. Lassiter smiles insipidly. "Alrighty then," he says, and rushes off.

Stephanie stands. She's wearing a sundress. This is the Vic Santiago influence. With me, it was big shirts, the kind of thing a woman with large breasts wears when she thinks large breasts are ugly. The heat has broken. It's seasonably cold. I took a Dexedrine along with double the Ritalin and am starting to feel it. We exchange pleasantries. Marsha pretends to be writing something.

"Your boss says he got a call from some high school girl's mother," Stephanie says, "who told him her daughter saw him have a heart attack or something, only he recovered and gave the girl his business card. The mother thought it might be serious."

"Lassiter has no heart," I say. "He's also not my boss. Just the p.d."

Stephanie never met Duke. This isn't the kind of workplace that has a lot of dinner parties. Stephanie and I haven't invited a lot of people over. Dietz and his wife were there once. "Obviously, it was you," she says. "And it wasn't a heart attack, was it, Bobby?"

Marsha has dropped the pretense and is watching us. I'd move, but a private conversation could go on and on. Here is best.

"It's under control," I say.

Everyone at the station is finding an excuse to walk down the corridor behind Marsha's desk, slowly. Even Jason and Duke, who walk by abreast, theoretically immersed in conversation.

"You've got to stop harassing Vic," she says.

"What are you talking about?"

"Vic has lawyers, okay?"

"Lawyers plural?" I say. "This Vic is some catch."

"Don't be this way. You had a girlfriend all along. She *called* me, Bobby. Okay? She called me. Don't give me that look. She told me you drove ten miles sound asleep and claimed it was a hypnotic hallucination. The bitch blamed it on me."

"Hypnagogic," I say. "When did she call?"

Stephanie shakes her head. "Does it matter? Here." She lifts a Xerox box from the floor and thrusts it into my solar plexus. I hold on. "I took these for what I told myself was your own good. It was mean. I'm sorry, okay?"

I don't have to look inside. A percentage of male users of Effexor experience abnormal ejaculation (I'll spare you the specifics). One day, Stephanie came home from work with two tapes—bought, not rented. For a while, we incorporated porn into what we did. It helped. She's an addictive personality, and might well have empathized when my interest took on a life of its own.

"Thanks," I say. "Is that all you need?" I am so, so tired. "I have a game, right, Dietz?"

Dietz is standing in the corridor, trying to look transfixed by a plaque the Seminole Boosters gave Duke McKibbon. "Excuse me," he says. "What?"

Stephanie walks into the downpour, no umbrella and not bothering to hurry. Her wet sundress adheres to her shoulders and wondrous hips, like shrink-wrap. She's not wearing panties. She doesn't look back or hurry. She's technically still my wife. For now, I know this woman better than anyone on earth. Someday, I may not even know where she lives.

"Careful working up such a sweat, dude," says Lassiter. "With your heart problem and all."

ALL OF WHICH brings me to the tape. In real time, the game was throttle and blur. But I ran tape on the clean feed, so this next part is reconstructed from that.

At first, I'm talking at auctioneer velocity. Jason—who'd gotten a broadcasting textbook from the library and on the drive there peppered me with questions—keeps score and keeps quiet. How I answered those questions I have no clue.

We go to commercial. There's a pause, and then the night guy asks what I'm on. At the time, I thought the jig was up. Listening to it, I'd say he was kidding. I don't answer. Then Jason, in a whisper, asks if he's doing okay.

"*Chimeindon'tbeafraidsaywhat'sonyourmindit'sjustagame, talk! say! do! be!*"

I remember Jason looking like the guy in that commercial, listening to Wagner, his hair blown back from the death-angel force of it. Probably I'm exaggerating. The night guy mimics me.

Jason loosens up and, despite me, gets heard. He's watched several million hours of ESPN. He actually, with conviction, says both "this guy must be buttah, because he's on a *roll*" and "boo-yeah!" He also calls me Bobby D. I let this go on until the end of the first quarter. "You're doing high school basketball in Monroeville, Florida," I finally say. "No boo-yeah. No more Bobby D."

"I didn't know I said that. Did I say that?"

I announce that I need to pee. You hear me taking off my headset. Moments later, the night guy says, "Primo performance by the Bobster. Damn."

"He's on something, I think," Jason says. "My mom was on a lot of stuff at one point. Prescription stuff. That's why Mr. Dietz called in last night, right? About Bob driving home?"

The night guy just laughs. "Keep saying boo-yeah," he says. Jason takes his headset off, too. Then some fumbling as we put our headsets back on. Jason's explaining that a job gets you out of school in the afternoons. I ask why he doesn't work for his dad.

"You ever work for your dad?"

"I did. He was a foreman at a steel mill. I worked there Christmas breaks. Loved it."

"I'm not cut out to sell trailers," Jason says.

"I actually bought one today," I say. "From your dad."

"My dad? My dad's in Key West with my granddad."

"It looked like your dad."

Jason doesn't answer. I mumble stuff about the first-quarter stats. I'm talking a little slower. Right before we go back on, you can hear me tell someone I'll think about it. Cheerleading parents. They heard the thing two days ago and want equal coverage for *their* kids. I've played this part of the tape a lot. I can't believe I left the door open. I can't believe I didn't give them a polite no.

Jason starts making comments about different players' weaknesses that would be more appropriate if we were talking about NBA millionaires rather than teenagers from North Florida. I just let it go. I don't even remember him doing this.

"Why do you drive the truck," I say during the next break, "if you don't work there?"

"It's the old truck. It's for sale."

At the next break, you can hear a Britney Spears song. Cheerleaders are doing something. Different parents come up and tell me this is nothing compared to what their kids will do at halftime. Again, I say I'll think about it.

"So why aren't you swimming?" I ask Jason. "You know, I didn't know until last night that there *was* winter swimming."

"What happened last night?" he says.

"Someone called and said we should broadcast it."

"God," he says. "That's even worse than cheerleading."

I shush him, apparently because I'm afraid the parents are within earshot. "What's wrong with cheerleading?" I say, in a venomous near-whisper. "Your first time on the air and you think you know what makes good radio and what doesn't?"

The night guy tells me to let the kid have it.

"You know why everyone at the station's so cold to you, right? They think you're going to take their jobs."

Jason laughs.

"Why *did* Duke hire you?"

I remember Jason shrugging. The night guy asks what Jason said. "To take your job," I say. Jason starts to say something, and I talk over him. Basketball stuff. The night guy cusses us out.

And so, we come to halftime.

Again I say I have to go pee. For the next few minutes, I'm in a stall in the Monrocville High boys room, fighting hyperventilation. There's nothing on the tape but ambient whatnot. A school band plays a medley from *The Lion King*. A contest is conducted; someone fails, and the crowd groans. Jason tells the night guy that I'm really going to broadcast the cheerleading exhibition.

"Perfect," he says. "Look, don't bullshit me. Seriously, why did Duke hire you?"

I get back right then. "What are you going to say?" Jason says.

"The secret's not having something to say—" I say.

"It's saying something," says the night guy. "You fucking blowhard."

I don't say anything. You can hear Jason take off his headset. Moments later, the night guy throws it back to us. And so I do it. I don't know how I did it, but I do: describing their every vault, their every sad, wobbly pyramid, with terminology I didn't know I had. For maybe thirty seconds, it's dull but fine. Then I hold out a microphone to capture the clapping and the boy-band music. "It's a truly gorgeous display, ladies and gentlemen," I say, "and I wish you were here to see it. These girls are beyond the shadow of a doubt the most stunning and wonderful and lively and lovely cheerleaders this reporter has yet seen. Bob Deldermuth would not pull your leg. These are girls you'd be proud to have as daughters, nieces, neighbors, lovers, or friends. These are girls that make you proud to be drawing breath. Their skin is perfect. Their skin is perfect, and you could see that if you were here. Jason Truax, did you notice that their skin was perfect?"

I don't know at what point in all that I fell asleep. Oh, hell. That line is so blurred for me, I'm not even sure it's right to call it sleep.

There's some dead air, then Jason, out of breath, puts on his headphones. "What do you think it will take," he says, "for Monroeville to get back in the game?"

"You're the color man," I say. "What's your precious book say?" By now I must be awake.

Jason starts to talk about certain players and their defensive shortcomings.

"My lord, but those girls were wonderful," I say. "Do you know what?"

"Um, no." Jason says. "What?" The fear in his voice is just awful.

"It made me want to cry," I say.

Jason pulls the plug on me, which I didn't know he knew how to do.

There's seventy-four seconds of dead air, then the night guy is swearing like a hothead in a mob movie. When I come back on, I'm furious, at first. Then I try to reconstruct what happened and can't, then I beg Jason and the night guy to let me do the second half as if nothing happened. I'll be fine. Given my ratings, I say, it's possible no one was listening, or listening all that closely.

We do the second half as if nothing happened. During commercial breaks, no one says more than the bare minimum.

JASON DRIVES THE van back to the station. The rain is ridiculous, and he has to pull over several times. Still, we don't say a word to each other. There are three cars in the lot, mine, the night guy's, Jason's truck, and Duke McKibbon's Cadillac. "Whatever you do," I say as Jason pulls in, "don't apologize. Don't accept any blame for anything. And I know you're about to say something about the time your mom left, but here." I hand him ten bucks. "Don't."

He shoves the money in my mouth. For whatever reason I accept this. I chew it. I swallow.

I am the only one fired, of course.

It's Dietz who talks to me most of the way home. But right near my ruts, I tell him I've arrived. I mean to call the service, but it takes me the rest of the way home to summon the nerve. When I do, hosanna, it's her. Kelly. "It's me," I say. "Bob Deldermuth."

"I've been thinking about you," she says.

"Same here."

"I think you need a creative outlet. There are studies that show that's a help."

"I'm a man of few skills," I say. "Though I did just eat ten dollars."

"You know how to sweep a girl off her feet," she says. "You're in your car, aren't you?"

What she hears is the rain as I get out and run from the car to my empty house. I get in and stamp my feet and apologize. "I can't sing," I say. "Can't dance, can't draw. I hate gardening. Anything handy: no."

"Cooking?"

"Don't ask. I did take acting lessons once."

"You're kidding," she says. "I have an agent."

"I thought you said you were a law student."

"I was on one of those reality TV shows." She says which one. I never heard of it. "I thought it might lead to other things. It led to this. Hah."

"My teacher described himself, in his own brochure, as 'a Suncoast dinner-theater legend.' The lessons were pricey to work with a guy like that. Also I was self-conscious about how I moved."

"How *do* you move?"

"I'm in the process." I am sitting on a stack of boxes by my back door. I know, now, that I'm not going to ask her about calling Stephanie.

"Me, too. When did you live in Tampa?"

"Bradenton. My wife got transferred there to open a restaurant." Which made me think of Stephanie, which made me think about being alone for Christmas, and I flashed on the Christmas she was first in rehab, when I went home and saw my brother do a birthday party for our sister's twin daughters. "I could be a clown," I say. "My brother is a clown. He lives in Chagrin Falls and his clown name is Cousin Blammo."

"C'mon. Chagrin Falls?"

"It's true," I say. Swear to God. "He's good: juggling, magic, jokes, pratfalls, the works. He's a math teacher, but he makes a lot of money on the side, clowning."

"I've always wanted to, you know," she says. "*Be* with a clown."

"That's common," I say.

"*Never* call me common," she says, and hangs up.

I walk to the back door. It's dark as hell, but then lightning flashes. The lake is filling up. Cleveland, here I come.